PRAISE FOR SUIN(

"Stephanie Mack's books are the ⌐
with your best friend—they're fresh and transporting, y⌐⌐ ⌐⌐⌐
comforting and authentic. *Suing Cinderella* more than delivers on its intriguing premise, bringing together themes of love, loss, and hope through endearing characters you can't help but root for. Chapter after chapter, this book will keep surprising you in the best way, ultimately leaving you feeling full of fairy-tale magic."

NATASHA BURTON
AUTHOR OF *101 QUIZZES FOR COUPLES* AND *WHAT'S MY TYPE? 100+ QUIZZES TO HELP YOU FIND YOURSELF—AND YOUR MATCH!*

"Most of us fall somewhere between Realist and Dreamer. Mack deftly forces readers to hold court in their own hearts, to debate if whimsical notions offer hopeful solace or inevitable discontent in a pragmatic and unpredictable world. This book will permeate your thoughts—I simply couldn't put it down!"

SHANNON LEYKO
AUTHOR OF *YOU'RE COMPLETELY NORMAL: TRADING WHERE YOU THINK YOU SHOULD BE FOR WHERE YOU WANT TO GO*

"Knowing every story—and many lawsuits!—have two sides, Mack brilliantly weaves two ambitions, two childhoods, and two redemptions in her second character-driven novel. Readers will delight in nostalgic flashbacks and witty banter, and may just find that discovering the truth, the whole truth, and nothing but the truth about love is more enchanting than magic itself."

ERIN CLARK
FORMER PRACTICING ATTORNEY LIVING HER HAPPILY EVER AFTER AS A STAY-AT-HOME-MOM

SUING
Cinderella

A NOVEL

STEPHANIE MACK

sm.
STEPHANIE MACK

Suing Cinderella is a work of fiction. While some elements are inspired by true observations and experiences, names, characters, scenes, and incidents are written products of the author's invention or are used fictitiously. Certain real locations and public figures are mentioned, but the story is wholly imaginary.

Copyright © 2023 by Stephanie Mack

All rights reserved. No part of this publication may be reproduced, distributed, or transmitted in any form or by any means, including photocopying, recording, or other electronic or mechanical methods, without the prior written permission of the publisher, except in the case of brief quotations embodied in critical reviews and certain other noncommercial uses permitted by copyright law.

ISBN: 979-8-218-28183-0

Library of Congress Control Number: 2023917874

Book cover and interior design: Natalie Lauren Design

Author photo: Kimberly Hope Photography

Editor: Jessica Snell

Scripture quotations marked (NIV) are taken from the Holy Bible, New International Version®, NIV®. Copyright © 1973, 1978, 1984, 2011 by Biblica, Inc.™ Used by permission of Zondervan. All rights reserved worldwide. www.zondervan.com
The "NIV" and "New International Version" are trademarks registered in the United States Patent and Trademark Office by Biblica, Inc.™

Printed in the United States of America

www.stephaniemack.com

*For everyone who
has ever believed in
fairy tales.*

TABLE of CONTENTS

PART ONE

PRELUDE: Once Upon a Time 13
CHAPTER ONE 15
CHAPTER TWO 28
CHAPTER THREE 44
CHAPTER FOUR 58
CHAPTER FIVE 68
CHAPTER SIX 80
CHAPTER SEVEN 95
CHAPTER EIGHT 110
CHAPTER NINE 129
CHAPTER TEN 139

PART TWO

CHAPTER ELEVEN 155
CHAPTER TWELVE 169
CHAPTER THIRTEEN 192
CHAPTER FOURTEEN 207
CHAPTER FIFTEEN 220
CHAPTER SIXTEEN 229
CHAPTER SEVENTEEN 244

CHAPTER EIGHTEEN 256

CHAPTER NINETEEN 266

CHAPTER TWENTY 283

PART THREE

CHAPTER TWENTY-ONE 293

CHAPTER TWENTY-TWO 303

CHAPTER TWENTY-THREE 314

CHAPTER TWENTY-FOUR 327

CHAPTER TWENTY-FIVE 344

CHAPTER TWENTY-SIX 351

EPILOGUE 361

AUTHOR'S NOTE

ACKNOWLEDGEMENTS

Part One

Prelude

ONCE UPON A TIME

SCOTTIE

I believed in fairy tales until one gorgeous summer solstice.

The time was 5:14 p.m., if we are going to be specific. Which we are. We are going to be *very* specific. The law demands it, I've learned.

Plus, if curiosity killed the cat, then specificity saved the princess. You see, it was never the *prince* who rescued the girl, not really—but rather the *precision* with which a multibillion-dollar media empire chose to popularize ancient fables and persuade young females everywhere that happily ever after was not only attainable, but inevitable.

The prince does not bear the blame for this. Nope, he does not. Fault is held by the strategist, the puppeteer—the one caught blood-red-handed holding the strings.

But I digress.

More on that later.

For now, I'm going to tell you my entire story from the beginning. Isn't that why you're here? Everyone wants the salacious details, and I don't blame them.

Truthfully, I never thought anyone—save some friends and my dad—would hear about my endeavor to take down the Kingston Company. I wanted to stand up for myself. I wanted to recoup some (rather expensive) personal damages. I wanted justice served, privately but universally, through the reverberating *bang* of that gavel, felt from inside my ribcage to Shanghai, newest site for Kingston's world-famous theme parks.

This is a problem, right? This prolific insistence that perfect endings are real?

Yes, it's a sin, and I'd prove it, with shards of both my heart and my wedding dress submitted as evidence. I'd slip into my valiant role of invisible heroine...*of the law*! Like a masked maven from Kingston's comic-book studios, but with a great attorney and heels.

I'd be the guardian angel I never had.

Unfortunately, my pages didn't quite turn that way, as you know. I've been publicly slapped with every name in the storybook. Witch! Soulless villain! Snake!

Damsel, fairy godmother, queen.

Which is it, you want to know? Am I evil? Am I good? Can you stand on my side—and which side is that today? What do I believe now, after what I have been through?

As for Kingston's handsome defender, I know you want to hear from him, too. So I will give him the microphone intermittently.

But the only way we can tell you everything—objectively and comprehensively—is to take you all the way back, to the only spot we can start.

The place where all stories begin.

Once upon a darn time.

...

Chapter One

SCOTTIE

Dusky and low, the summer sun glowed onto the chair-lined lawn before me and silhouetted the vineyard beyond.

It's here.

The day of my dreams, right down to the last tied bow. And down to the date, of course. I'd picked summer solstice, naturally: the longest day of the year. This fairy tale would last, and last, sparkling well past the midnight chimes when I *wouldn't* turn into a pumpkin.

Our story would sparkle forever.

I squeezed the crook of his arm, flexed firmly, the arm that had led me and held me, pulled me always toward the promise that, yes, we could do this, together. Someday, we'd end up here. Us against everyone else, until I was ready to jump, my bar of great love set high.

Today, this day.

I'm here.

I heard a soft sob choked back, then a jagged breath blown, released to the Napa wind. I gripped his suited arm tighter. "Don't cry," I whispered. "I'm not going anywhere, Dad."

One last time, I reached up with my other hand, the one

also clutching my flowers—white lilies, fresh greens—to brush a strand of hair from my lips.

"But you are." I heard his sad smile as he patted the top of my grip. "It feels like you were just six. You know that?"

Six.

The year Mom left, of course.

The string quartet paused, and I watched the audience rise. A gargantuan crowd, for me. I would've preferred, say, 75, to the 250 in front of us now.

But they're all here; everyone's here.

My own storybook in living Technicolor.

Our wedding party stood up front proudly, in their coral gowns and navy suits. The band tuned their instruments to "Souls of the Sun," my favorite Kingston theme song since I could speak. Trey called me his sunshine girl.

"Are you ready?" My own breath wavered now.

"I'm ready," Dad said. "Let's go."

Don't forget to look at the groom. Whatever you do, don't miss the face of the groom! You need to witness the priceless expression of a man finally seeing his bride!

Everyone said it, but the people were right. I'd been no stranger to weddings in the last decade, a bridesmaid seven times over. I'd witnessed every kind of groom imaginable more than once: the crier, the laugher, the wide-eyed admirer, all of them squeezing my heart.

For some reason, I couldn't imagine what Trey's expression might be, what his boyish face might reveal beneath his sandy scruff and thick hair. Honestly, I couldn't picture it—and wondered, sometimes, why this was. *Could it be a bad omen?* Maybe, or maybe not. He was playful most often and rarely emotive but would shock you by crying at *Bambi.*

"Did the mom really have to die?" he'd weep.

"Better than leaving," I'd mutter.

First-look photo shoots were trending hard, but I knew they weren't for me. I could not fathom forgoing the traditional moment. No matter how fleeting—or public—I wanted the grand reveal.

Time slowed then.

I remember it slowing, like the flashing frames of a vintage cartoon back when animation was new. I know I beamed; I could *feel* myself shimmering. With bronzer, but mostly, with joy. I'd never felt more luminous than when my dad and I took that first step.

My gaze swept over the stunning scene before landing and locking on Trey. He was smiling so hugely, that crooked grin, the one that had pulled me into his arms and tucked me into his life.

His eyes fixed into mine, and butterflies flapped in my stomach. I began the walk down my runway, white rose petals everywhere, toward Trey and our magnificent arch. The square, rustic structure was swirled in vines, framing him and our minister. Trey looked so peaceful. Content.

Until—

Almost imperceptibly, I saw something stiffen upon his face, then quickly disappear.

Subtle and swift, a blink.

A doubt?

My imagination, surely.

But then, his jaw tightened, released.

Tighten, release. Again, and again.

One more pulse, and another.

His gaze darted sideways, his smile dropped, and—*weird*—then, so did his eyes.

Looking down, down, *down*—

No longer at me.

My stomach flipped inside my corset. He looked sick.

Did he look ... panicked?

Something else floated across his face. I wasn't sure what, but I saw it there.

No.

God, no—

Please, no.

He hadn't spoken of cold feet in months, insisting his soles were on fire now. But he was slipping, in front of my eyes, rocking his weight back and forth, raking his hair like a criminal caught in the act.

I needed to pull him back.

He lifted his eyes up and behind me, as if seeking escape.

This was not happening.

Look at me, Trey.

I wiggled my bouquet like a magic wand.

Look at your bride!

But he did not look at me. Instead, his stare found the bridesmaids over my shoulder, in their satin dresses, golden tans, and Instagram-flawless hairstyles.

So, I looked to them, too. And they must've sensed my worry because every one of them mirrored it now. I hadn't dressed them in different gowns—as was also a trend—but their faces each shined now with distinct forms of shock as Trey stared their direction.

I clawed my nails deeper into Dad's arm.

My maid of honor, Peyton, shot me her *don't-do-anything-stupid* stare, aware I might just start screaming. She pulled on the ends of her flaxen hair, a nervous tic I'd known for twenty years.

I slowed my steps as uncertainty bloomed in my chest.

Trey's little sister, my youngest bridesmaid, looked terrified. Barely sixteen, she was timid and pretty, red hair pulled into a neat chignon not masking her youth nor her horror.

Christina, Rachel, and Colby had similar shades of *WHAT'S HAPPENING?!* sentiments plastered on their gorgeous faces.

My eyes flicked at last to Jade.

Wait. Were those … *tears* in her eyes?

And were those blue eyes fastened on …

Trey?

I halted, holding my dad back, sensing suddenly that to proceed would be to interrupt a moment between—

Trey and Jade?

Jade and Trey?

I realized then you could feel the heat coursing between my almost-husband and bridesmaid.

But on went the music, our song.

And love is the sun…

Or a blackening sky.

I looked at last to my dad, and I'll never forget his handsome face when he knew my world had just stopped. Worry aging his skin by a decade, apology filling his eyes.

I'm sorry, I'm sorry, I'm sorry, they said.

My groom's "look" had turned to a mask of horrors, but my dad—again—was right here, affirming one of the only truths I had known for most of my life. I was loved, and would always be loved, if only and always by him. His smile lines crinkled with empathy. I knew his heart crinkled now, too.

The music stopped as the band seemed to realize I'd halted. That I had no intention of taking *one more step* until I knew exactly why Trey and Jade were currently penetrating each other's souls.

I had a sick feeling, suddenly, that he'd penetrated more than just that.

I squinted between my false eyelashes, which felt suddenly absurd and too heavy.

I took in the scene, dissecting.

Denying with all that I had.

Trey and Jade both appeared to be *really very sorry* about something, communicating a cavern of secrets with their silent and guilty expressions.

They would never be sorry enough, as far as I was concerned.

Hot shame bubbled beneath my skin, under my fluffy white dress. It was a *fairy-tale* gown, all right. Dainty straps and a long train flowing like cake frosting. The full tulle skirt was overlaid with lace flowers and capped with a sweetheart-necked bodice. Every detail of this dress—*this day*—exuded royalty.

Hadn't my princess day come?

Now I felt like the jester.

A caricature in my own story.

Trey snapped from his trance, and I saw remorse in his features. "*I'm so sorry,*" they said, as his full lips formed the words silently and sweat pooled across his hairline. "I can't do this, Scottie," he then declared, loud enough for all to hear. "You don't deserve this. *I'm sorry.*"

With one last gaze at Jade, my best friend from college—*how did she know Trey well enough for that kind of eye contact, let alone ... God knew what?*—he bolted.

Trey sprinted away.

Past his groomsmen, toward the white modern farmhouse where all the boys had been staying.

The boys.

How had I not yet looked to the groomsmen for answers? A quick, thorough sweep told me everything. The guys had no clue what just happened.

Except for Dillon.

He couldn't hide anything.

Dillon was the best man, my favorite of Trey's buddies. He was good to me and tended to *know things.* I bore my stare into his guilty face as he flattened his shiny red hair. "What," I breathed, "is going on, Dillon? *Tell me.*"

Cheeks twitching, he shifted anxiously. I had to applaud him for keeping eye contact with me—because I knew then that he knew.

"I think you should hear it from him," he said, with the saddest shrug I'd ever seen. His answer pummeled me like a giant wave of nausea, and the truth.

There was something to hear.

Next, I did the only thing I'd ever known how to do when my body couldn't process my pain.

In front of our pastor, my closest friends, and the 250 guests gathered to serve as our witnesses, I collapsed into my dad. I heaved and cried until my hot tears soaked his shirt.

"Shhh, shhh." He held my bare back, my gentle dad, my wall from the whispers and gasps. "*Shhh, shhh. I love you. Shhh.*"

I couldn't help but think of *The Little Mermaid*, when she finally comes face-to-face with her prince after he almost married the sea witch—who had stolen her voice to lure him. Just as the mermaid embraces her prince, with her ultimate dream *this close*—and her prince shouts: "It's you!"—her human feet turn back into a fin, and she cannot even stand. The sun sets low and the lightning strikes, the fantasy shattered and done.

My story seemed to be ending here.

My ankles ached in their golden heels as I watched the sun drop, drop, drop. I felt my heart plummeting with it. Dad's, too. I hated that he didn't know how not to feel my pain.

My dad was the best. Ever since I could remember, he'd been the one to carry me through the vast expanse left by my mom. That time he went to a hair-braiding class, or when I got my first C on a test. My first small heartbreak—and my first real one. My realization as a teen that I had no woman to model womanhood for me.

In each case, my dad had buoyed me. He conquered the fishtail. He hired a math tutor. He told me how dumb those boys were. And he called his sister, my favorite aunt, to stay with us when I was fourteen. With the buffer of sushi and manicures, she stepped in as a mom. We covered every key topic. Kissing and periods, lipstick, good bras. When to say yes, and no.

My dad was a wonderful dad. He provided for me. He poured into me. He did everything possible to connect me with every resource imaginable. He was my hero forever. I knew he could do anything.

But no dad should need to be quite this good, to have to save his daughter from her own wedding.

...

Loungewear donned and knees hugged close, I sat across from Trey in the farmhouse, five hours later. Our wedding coordinator had stepped in to call a "brief intermission," right after Trey left the altar.

Intermission was one way to put it.

Fifteen minutes later, class act that he was, my dad had taken the microphone and confirmed that the wedding was off.

Thank you for coming, this is so unexpected, please know we'll return your gifts.

I, too, had run away by that point, to cry in the bridal suite inside the vineyard's main building—which was more of a castle. Of course, it was. *Stupid fairy tale.* Only Peyton and Colby had followed me. I hoped the rest of my girls were skewering Jade.

What happened next?

What did you do when you had a runaway groom? The food, the cake, the DJ, the guests? Would it have been the worst to continue the party? Once drained of my tears, I wondered. Why *not* eat the food? Why *not* cut the cake? Why *not* dance with people who loved me? Turns out this doesn't exactly feel right in the moment, but I considered it.

Instead, here I was, full face of makeup and barefoot on a tufted beige couch. Silent, seething, and stunned.

I couldn't even blink.

"So—you love both of us," I repeated eventually. "That's your story." It wasn't a question.

Trey blanched. I could see he was considering his confession from my side of the room, the insanity and the jolt. *Six months. It went on for six months. Met at our engagement party. She said she could work on my knee, you know I have knee problems, Scot. She's a healer; you know she is.*

Insert antagonized eye roll.

Why did that term sound so lame now—*healer*—and was he really stealing my words? Jade was undoubtedly gifted, the most sought-after physical therapist most people knew. She'd worked on everyone from pop stars to professional athletes. Jade—*my Jade*—was a star. And yes, a true fixer.

But she wasn't supposed to fix *him*.

"Why didn't you tell me you were going to her for treatment?" I rubbed my temples still frozen with hairspray. "She works on everyone. I wouldn't have cared, but you kept it a secret. Secrets erode relationships. You know that. You *taught* me that."

He knit his brow into a show of remorse for the seventeenth time that hour. "I ... was attracted to her," he admitted. "When I first met her, in that red dress—"

"Stop," I snapped, palm up. "I don't need to hear your meet-cute. What was I wearing at our engagement party? Do you even remember?"

He had the nerve to look wounded. "Of course. You were wearing white."

"Ha!" I held my chest and batted my lashes. "How *observant*, Trey! Your fiancée wore white to your engagement party. Great memory. Take a trophy on your way out."

He lowered his eyes and picked at some lint on his jeans. Thirty seconds of silence passed. "You were really tan because you'd just come back from your dental conference in Hawaii," he said finally. "Your dress was silk, and I remember thinking that I couldn't believe I got to spend forever with *you*, and that body, and your perfect face, exceeded only by your huge heart, and that incredible brain. Your eyes were so sexy and green that night."

My eyes burned now, with the bludgeon of betrayal and surprise at the ache in his voice.

"I didn't want to notice another woman, Scottie. I know people say this, but—it really did just kind of happen."

No, no, no.

I shook my head violently. "That's the thing, though, babe—Trey." I wiped at my eyes. He was not my babe anymore. "Cheating never *just happens*. You make a string of small, invisible choices. One after the other. You saw Jade, and she's beautiful. Of course, she is. But you let yourself go there. And then you *actually, physically* went to her. And then—you let her *get* to you."

And she'd better prepare for the moment when I got to her.

"Then one day," I continued, "You're *here*." I gestured around the cozy room, littered with wedding bits. Flowers, programs, tiny boxes of chocolate.

Chocolate.

I reached to the coffee table for one of the champagne-colored truffle boxes. Godiva. No more Maldives honeymoon diet for me.

We were both running out of words.

My mouth was full of chocolate instead.

"Where do we go from here?" Trey sighed. "Don't I get any credit for not going through with the wedding? Jade wanted to pretend it never happened, you know. For you and I to get married, move on, leave it in the past. She insisted it wasn't that big of a deal, that I'd forget about her—that really good people do really bad things sometimes."

I bristled with relief at the thought of him and me dancing right now—me, the idiot—surrounded by throngs of our friends, to "Love is Never Lost," the other Kingston ballad we'd picked together, probably the royal juggernaut's most famous song. A wedding day flanked by Kingston. *Barf.*

I'd learned within a few brutal hours that love could be lost in a blink.

And there was no sun shining here.

What was love, really, anyway? Trey certainly didn't know. Maybe I didn't, either.

But I knew it wasn't this.

You needed commitment, transparency, trust. Yes, I was relieved to my bones that I was not presently headed off in naïve bliss to our wedding night. But Trey was not getting any *free points* for owning this shipwreck.

And right now, love—love for myself—meant ignoring the pull I still felt toward Trey's misty eyes and movie-star face and clearly conflicted heart. It was collecting myself—and the rest of this chocolate—and getting back to my hotel.

"From here?" I stood. "We part ways, Trey. You take the apartment. I'll stay with Colby. Don't contact me. I won't answer."

With as much dignity as I could muster, and knowing I wouldn't be back, I raided the room for whatever other goodies might possibly bring me comfort from this matrimonial graveyard.

I grabbed one slice of cake, a bountiful centerpiece—and a framed photo of me as a little girl, long dark hair in a side ponytail and a huge bow bedazzled in crystals. Pink chiffon dress. The most innocent eyes.

As I walked out, I apologized to her for letting us down on this day.

...

Chapter Two

SCOTTIE

Several Months Later

I swore I'd never return to suburbia in any remotely permanent way. But here I was, winding through boxy tan retail centers and immaculate neighborhoods. So many buildings the color of sand, streets tidy as tic-tac-toe.

Irvine, California, was more predictable than a clock, but also, I had to admit, exceedingly comforting in its uniformity. Now more than ever, I was grateful some things never changed.

In a whirl of nostalgia, I even stopped for my favorite frozen yogurt on the way home. One personal size to devour immediately, plus four quarts for my weeks ahead. Heath Bar, Caramel, Vanilla Malt, Peanut Butter Cup. I'd never been more thankful for Dad's countless streaming subscriptions, nor his insane cooking skills.

I was ready to Netflix and chill, all by my very own self.

Suitcase rolling behind me, I pushed open the double front doors to my two-story childhood home. The moving truck, with my old life's remains, would arrive in a couple of days.

"Dad?" I sang into the entryway.

I'm home.

Each day right after the wedding had felt like a century. The things to do when a wedding was cancelled! It was all-bridesmaids-on-deck—except for Jade—while I hid in my Napa hotel room for as long as I could. I'd extended my stay by a week, soothing my wounds with robe life and room service. Trey's credit card, after all, was still footing the tab.

I hadn't been comatose like that in decades, wishing away the cloying reminders of why they called it a heartbreak. Hearts could crack and malfunction within you; it was simple as that. The sickness could find your stomach and head, stealing your function and appetite. The physicality was so brutal. Inhumane, really. I was only, finally, *sort-of* standing up on my two feet, more than three months later.

Breakup didn't seem like a strong enough word to describe this. Was there a term between that and *divorce*? Annulment, I guessed. At least we didn't need legal action.

Still, this whole ordeal had revealed just how entwined Trey and I had become, and we hadn't even lived together. For four years, I'd been living with Colby—my bridesmaid and roommate—while Trey settled into the Marina apartment where we'd planned to live as a married couple.

Oh, that *Architectural Digest*–worthy apartment, fully designed and furnished by Colby. Rustic industrial chic, she called it. Caramel leather couches, gray fur pillows, metal-framed black-and-white photographs of the city. Perfect touches of feminine to balance the masculine. Colby was an interior designer I'd met in yoga class during dental school, who became a forever best friend. We bonded over an abiding love for child's pose, acai bowls, and deep conversations.

Our newlywed apartment-never-to-be was just blocks from

the Palace of Fine Arts, my favorite landmark in San Francisco. The grounds always made me think of the movie *So I Married an Axe Murderer*, when Charlie and Harriet frolic and dance through the fountains.

Thankfully, I hadn't married him.

That axe-wielding dream-killer, Trey, and his annoyingly perfect scruff.

In the blur of summer turning to fall, I made decisions faster than fire, all without consulting my ex. I didn't know very much—but I knew I had to flee San Francisco. Around every corner lurked a new memory. Our early date at the Fairmont, our later love for its wacky Tonga Room, our Sunday walks through the Presidio. My running club, hairdresser, patients. Trey's Coit Tower proposal. Any one of our wedding guests, scattered through every district.

When I'd finally needed practical help, I called Dillon, the trusty groomsman. I needed some things from the apartment, and I couldn't move them alone. Thankfully he was happy to help.

I only asked him once, in a weak moment, clutching my Vitamix in the kitchen: "How's Trey doing?"

Dillon exhaled. "He's awful, Scottie. He's terrible. Keeping to himself. Really quiet. Working out obsessively and pouring himself into work."

"So … getting hotter and richer!" I joked, hating the sound of my laugh, pitched a little too high. "That's cool."

"Stop," Dillon chastised. "He's broken. He blew up his life and he knows it. Also, Jade told me he won't call her back. If it makes you feel any better."

It did.

A little.

Trey *did* murder his life, in front of everyone that he knew, but even that wasn't sufficient punishment.

For all I cared, he could wallow in isolation and regret for eternity.

One of the most painful things about all of this—almost as bad as the breakup itself—had been leaving the job I loved. I'd been at Dreams Pediatric Dentistry—ironic, the name—since dental school graduation. Now *Dr.* Scotland "Scottie" Holiday, I'd started to build a patient roster in my two-year residency at the practice. And I loved my kids; I adored them. Little George with too many cavities, Holly always in a Rapunzel dress. Every time I cleaned their teeth or sent them to my coveted treasure chest, I smiled and thought:

"What a dream."

And I get to live it.

Grief niggled in my chest when I talked to the mothers, though, as I observed their concern over the tiniest oral health detail. I watched their hand squeezes and generous hugs, which said without words to their babies: "I love you."

Meanwhile, my mom had just ... *left*. All of that, to my dad. The squeezes and hugs. The sack lunches, appointments. Soccer practice and SAT prep.

How had my mom known my dad could even handle it?

Of course, she didn't know.

She didn't even know how to care.

I dismissed the familiar thoughts.

I had new baggage to sort.

The heady, sweet smell of my dad's banana bread filled the kitchen, a space still untouched since the eighties. Tile counters, warm woods, cream walls. I smiled at my earliest memory of us two baking together. I was probably nine. Smashing bananas, snitching the batter, learning the gooey tops of the loaf were the best.

I'd offered many times for Colby to update the house—and by update, I mean give it an extreme home makeover, long overdue. But Dad never wanted to spend the money. He insisted on paying for my college at Berkeley, as well as for the wedding, on his modest but solid accountant's salary. He was always a shrewd investor and diligent saver. And today, I savored his penchant for sameness. The walnut kitchen cupboards even flirted now with the edge of a home fashion comeback.

I spotted a note on the counter, next to the treats.

Welcome home, Sweetie. I love you. Fridge is full. I'll be home at 7.

How did I get so lucky with him?

I found the slice of banana bread with the mushiest edge and grabbed myself a LaCroix, grinning to see that Dad had filled half the fridge with it. He would nourish me back to life. We both knew LaCroix was medicine.

Once I'd dragged my things to my room—also unchanged in its yellow French countryside splendor—I plopped onto my bed, eyes fixed on the ceiling.

Where *did* I go from here?

My gaze danced absently across the room to my vanity,

bordered in a collage of old photographs. Peyton, my maid of honor, was in nearly all of them. As my oldest friend, she was the closest thing I knew to a sister. We met in kindergarten, at recess, during a particularly competitive game of red rover. She'd grabbed my hand, sealing our friendship forever. We'd been a team ever since. Her parents still lived down the street.

I peeled myself off my floral comforter and trolled over to the pictures. I took a seat on the vanity stool, fingers outstretched. I brushed my own face in the photos I remembered most clearly.

Peyton and I at eighth-grade graduation. Peyton and I dressed as *Grease*'s Pink Ladies for Halloween. Peyton and I at prom, together, because we didn't have dates. Peyton and I in the now-hysterical glamour shots my dad had gifted to us for high school graduation. The oh-so-serious portraits were cheesy to the max, I could see now, but at the time, no one could tell us we weren't poised to change the world.

Future dentist.

Future lawyer.

Unstoppable.

Nothing had rattled our closeness over the years. No boys, no fights, no natural drifting that often comes with adulthood. Not undergrad in two different states, not law school (her in SoCal) and dental school (me in NorCal).

Peyton lived back in Irvine now, which would be my life raft. I knew it. I might not have returned otherwise. She was now a big law commercial litigator in Orange County. Despite her rigorous work life, she also managed to serve as my 9-1-1 breakup hotline.

I exhaled with fresh relief at the thought of us here, reunited, finally in the same city again.

My heart fell, though, as my eyes flitted from photo to photo, and I saw the look on my young face.

The hope. The trust. The naïvety.

Through all the trends over all the years—preppy headbands, baby doll tops, the widest high-waist belts possible— you couldn't miss my optimism.

I'd always been a dreamer.

And I'd dreamed of having it all. Fulfillment in a vibrant career. Enviable romantic love. Someone besides my dad would adore me. Maybe the whole world would. I would find my happily ever after—if it didn't find me first.

I had another quiet dream, too, that I'd never spoken to anyone.

I couldn't bring myself to admit it out loud, but I often imagined my mother. Where she was, who she became. I imagined her thinking of me, looking me up, seeing what I had achieved. I pictured her coming to find me, sometimes, in my most vulnerable moments. Lord knew I'd tried to find her.

Look at me, Mom! Look what I did.

Do you ever wish you had stayed?

I yanked open the vanity drawer. Expecting it to be empty, I lifted my brows at the sight of a diary, pleather pink with a latch. I thought all my keepsakes were up in the attic.

I smiled when the small book opened without a key. Returning to my bed, I flipped it over to see the back slathered in Lisa Frank stickers.

Sinking into my decorative pillows, I settled in for a read.

Dear Diary,   December 14
Tonight, Dad and I watched four movies while we decorated the Christmas tree. Four!!!!!!! He called it a Movie Marathon. Sometimes I get sad I don't have a mom, but Dad is so cool. He doesn't have many rules. I bet moms have lots of rules. We watched Rudolph the Red-Nosed Reindeer and the elf wanted to be a dentist. I think I want to be a dentist. I like that he was a misfit and found his best friend. See ya tomorrow!
Love,
Scottie

Dear Diary,   December 16
In Sunday School today, we learned about Noah and the ark. He built a really big boat, and everyone made fun of him. I heard the story when I was five, but today it was like new. I bet Noah had to really believe God, to do that. You have to be really brave to do something when people think you are crazy. That's what the teacher said.
I want to be brave!!!!
Love,
Scottie

Dear Diary,   December 18
I want to go to Kingston Court for Christmas. It's all I want!!! I wonder if it will happen. I told Dad and Santa that I don't need any gifts. I just want to go to Kingston Court. I love Kingston movies, even more than Christmas ones. I like that the princesses don't have moms. Like me.
Love,
Scottie

Dear Diary, *December 25*
YOU ARE NOT GOING TO BELIEVE THIS!!!!!! I AM GOING TO KINGSTON COURT!!!!! Peyton said Santa isn't real but when I tell her this, she is going to know he is. I told him at the mall that I wanted to go to Kingston Court, and he put a ticket in my stocking with a Cinderella Barbie. Then Dad got us a night at the Kingston Hotel and said I could have all the treats I wanted and get a new princess dress. I felt like I was going to cry even though I was smiling. "Love is Never Lost!!!!!"
Love,
Princess Scottie

    In the bottom corner was a smudgy sketch of a castle, and two figures, me and my dad. I held cotton candy in one hand and a swirly lollipop as big as my face in the other. Dad held up both hands in ecstasy. The drawing was touching—and impressive for an eight-year-old, I thought. I'd always loved to create. Dentistry was art, after all. You needed technique and precision.

    My throat tightened then. I couldn't stand the thought of that sweet little girl living my wedding day.

    I flipped for more entries, but none followed.

    I fished around in the musty drawer, wanting more.

    This was strangely therapeutic, reading messages from the past. Maybe it could help to recenter me—remind me who I really was. My therapist in the city would think so, I was sure of it. I'd never been one for therapy, but her name was slipped to me after yoga class by a girl Colby knew.

    "She changed *everything* for me," the girl said. "I don't even *think* about my ex-husband anymore." She couldn't have been older than thirty, and I felt a kinship that she had an ex-husband already. Her clear skin, sparkling eyes, and elegant dancer's gait made me give her "healer" a call.

Ugh.

I was very much still thinking about my "healer" friend and ex-fiancé.

Fixing each other.

Dr. Perrish didn't take insurance, but I'd pay anyone $250 an hour to make me forget about Trey.

I slammed the drawer, empty-handed, and reached up in a catlike stretch. I knew I'd find more in the attic.

Come to think of it, what else might I find up there? Dusty dolls and plastic toys. Boxes and boxes of books. Every one of my Kingston costumes, for no less than ten Halloweens. All my dad's, too. The giant genie, the beast, Prince Charming.

I shrugged.

What could it hurt?

...

Cross-legged on the musty wood floor, I took in the scene before me. The ache in my chest had surprisingly lessened with this dig through my millennial childhood.

I sat, transfixed by small piles of big nostalgia. Princess figurines by the dozen and their little prince counterparts. The ornate, doll-sized Cinderella carriage: a masterpiece, an investment. The equally intricate, human-sized mermaid castle that I used to fit inside.

Plus, a mountain range of Kingston stuffed animals.

Towers of ornate storybooks brimming with fairy tales.

Some of this had to be worth something.

Then, there was the collection of Kingston costumes *indeed*. At one time or another, I had dressed up as every princess on the royal roster. Sparkly gowns puffy as cupcakes, plastic heels to imitate glass. I remembered the twirling, the *dreaming*—just like the books and movies had told me to.

Finally, my eyes panned to the VHS tapes now stacked to my eye level, up from the ground, next to a box of DVDs and home videos. I wondered how many of those old tapes featured me, spinning, smiling, singing, so convinced I was the queen.

Crown on my head in the clouds.

I sighed, suddenly pensive—a thought percolating through me like coffee grounds.

Huh.

The notion dripped from my head to my heart.

Was I groomed to believe in … *magic?*

Or at the very least—in a fantasy?

Was I raised clinging to fairy tales?

I considered this.

Me, the unbridled dreamer who had held princesses on the ultimate pedestal. Me, the girl who had twirled, dreamed, and believed until she was dizzy. Me, the woman who had allowed love to drop-kick her heart, but only because she'd benched the defense.

I wondered.

Was I raised holding onto a false sense of reality and relationships?

Had I been cheerfully oblivious and painfully blind to the

hardships, and yes, *the bad endings*, that came with simply being a human?

Hadn't I assumed that the guy who'd asked me to marry him, well, wanted to *marry me,* and only me?

Hadn't I bought the lie—hook, line, and engagement rock—that true love really fixed everything?

Hadn't I thought Trey would rapture me into the sunset on his white horse, which, yes, was technically more of a pearly white Range Rover?

Clearly this was my ending.

And it was *happy.*

The proof suddenly seemed to surround me.

The costumes, the movies, the fantasy, *everywhere*, illuminated now by the light bulb dangling above me on a thin wire.

As thin as my theories on love.

As breakable.

Snap!

I imagined the glass exploding and raining around me.

The magic slipper finally shattering.

I shifted under the light, reflecting on my pieces of girlhood. The glorious, glittery costumes. Toy after toy. My one and only Christmas wish.

Kingston had built my whole worldview.

Oh my gosh, hadn't they?

I gulped.

Because of Kingston princesses, I'd believed from my earliest memory that a prince stood nobly, somewhere, as my missing puzzle piece—my prize at the end of the road, however bumpy.

He would sweep me up, rescue me. Come Pharoah's famine or Noah's flood, we would live happily ever after!

Or not.

I shuddered in visceral memory, again, of my wedding march to hell.

I touched the thick plastic of the Kingston movie cases, the titles familiar and intimate as my own pulse.

Sleeping Beauty. Snow White. Cinderella.

Was I a woman with my own ideas and realistic expectations for love—or was I a product of storybook soup, spiked with poison and lies? Of tales laced with empty half-truths that shaped the world's norms and kids' dreams?

The room swirled.

I noted then, also, that every Kingston princess was both gorgeous and pin-thin, with perky curves and lengthy locks that most girls could only pay for. I recalled some illustrations on Instagram a few years ago, of Kingston princesses redrawn in realistic human proportions. Their figures were drastically different from the originals, soft and supple instead of stick skinny, and they were depicted as less mainstream-sexy. The images presented an uncomfortable and eye-opening truth.

I wondered.

Were Kingston princesses also partially responsible—or at the very least a contributor—to unrealistic standards of beauty?

I found myself nodding and drummed my nails on the top movie case.

Bambi, go figure.

Trey's favorite.

My gaze shifted then to the box of DVDs overflowing with my favorite rom-coms, a shift into the early 2000s. I smiled and pulled it closer, hoisting them out one by one. *How to Lose a Guy in 10 Days. When Harry Met Sally.... Hitch.*

And there it was:

Legally Blonde.

Sassy, gorgeous, and very much blonde, Peyton had been spared no *Legally Blonde* jokes during law school, even less so after graduating number one in her class. We had most of the movie memorized.

One of my first smiles after the wedding came at a meme from Peyton, reminding me: *Live every day like you are Elle Woods after Warner said she wasn't smart enough for law school.*

With a text:

> What, like it's hard? You've got this. I love you!

My heart thudded as I glanced from the *Legally Blonde* DVD in my hand to the tower of Kingston movies—and back again.

Tick-tock, back and forth, like a lurking crocodile.

TikTok.

Wait.

I snapped up my phone and tapped to the TikTok app, which I used only for stalking, without any shame. Your dentist did not have time for content creation. But I did love the dances, the books, and sometimes the big viral trends.

I remembered one now that had had me howling. I dumped the words into the search engine:

Mad at Kingston.

I found the original video and let the anthem wash over me, title flashing in blood red to open the sequence. This girl was angry with Kingston—and she was telling the world, with her pop-art aesthetic, clever lyrics, and Billie Eilish balm of a voice. The catchy tune had gone nuclear, inspiring more than one million copycat TikToks and 25 million YouTube views:

I'm mad at Kingston, Kingston,
They tricked me, tricked me,
Had me wishing on a shooting star...

The rest of the lyrics summed up my feelings with glaring and humorous accuracy.

I was mad, all right. I was furious.

I was *here*, in my childhood home, jobless and single and *just exactly* this broken because I was fooled.

By powers much bigger and stronger and richer than I would ever be.

It wasn't fair.

And it wasn't okay.

My eyes burned at the injustice; I sucked in a breath.

Little Scottie hadn't needed a fairy tale. She had needed the truth. But you know what else? I had my own "healer" on speed dial, *Trey*.

She'd been fixing me since I was five.

I couldn't flick to Peyton's number fast enough. She was in court right now, but I'd leave a message.

Maybe a song.

Because we were doing this.

We were going to sue the Kingston Company for casually wrecking my life. For making me believe in a story that never existed.

For conning, for spinning, for deceiving us all.

For popularizing a lie.

Kingston had built a whole kingdom on a false fantasy, hadn't they? They'd built up my trust—and broken my heart.

Maybe the company couldn't repair me, but they could *repay* me.

Right?

Kingston had to be held responsible. How many other innocent children, around the world, were wishing this very instant on a star that would one day brand them with indelible burns? Maybe in righting my own injustice, I could prevent their pain.

I felt something tangible simmering.

Justice and truth could prevail!

Peyton and I were going to fight.

And we were going to win.

What?

Like it's hard?

...

Chapter Three

HARRISON

My name is Harrison Hayes, and the rest of my life began at the gym, with a girl who wasn't the one.

I flashed her a scripted smile, with the most enthusiastic fake interest I could conjure at 6:02 a.m. on a treadmill.

Which truthfully wasn't much.

This was women for you. Or at least: this type of woman. Hearing what she wanted to hear, instead of what I was saying. She was sweet, cute enough, and nothing if not persistent.

But I didn't date, and this wasn't negotiable.

I'd told her so outright, six weeks ago, when I first joined this place, ready for a *real gym*, an *expensive* gym, where nobody would bother me.

Or so I thought, and so everyone said.

This was no neighborhood 24 Hour Fitness, cluttered with half-committed, decades-long members who held onto the Costco deal they'd struck back in '98. The ones who especially loved the gym every January. I didn't have anything against those people. I just didn't like it when they crowded the pool lanes or made me wait for a treadmill. This was my sanctuary, my Hustler's Repair Shop, in the words of Robin Arzón. This was Cardiox, so they had Pelotons.

It's elite, they said. It's quiet, they said.

But here she was again.

Bothering me.

Maybe I should be *less* enthusiastic in our interactions? Not as polite? I could straight-up tell her I didn't want any new friends, in addition to not presently seeking romantic companionship.

Or I could turn my music up louder so I genuinely couldn't hear her.

Yes. *Brilliant.* I nodded to myself.

Or at least—I thought it was to myself.

"Really?!" I heard the girl squeal above the bass in my ears, even at its freshly ratcheted volume. Her blonde hair was scraped into a skintight ponytail, now swaying excitedly. "I knew it. I *knew* you'd come around. I was just telling my roommate last night—"

Wait, what?

"Ah—" I started. This was what I got for tuning her out.

Women. You could not be too careful.

I thumbed down the treadmill speed button; I needed deep breaths for this. "Look. Um … ?" I took out my earbuds, walking.

What is her name again?

"Ashley." She smiled broadly and rocked to her tiptoes, seeming undaunted by my lazy memory. She folded her arms across her tight torso, tan skin exposed between her neon pink cropped top and leggings.

What was wrong with me?

This girl was nice-looking, athletic, a teacher. No: a career nanny. No: a nurse. *Gah,* I was a jerk, but I remembered it was something specific and altruistic you used to see a lot on *The Bachelor*, before "social media influencer" became the norm.

"Ashley," I repeated, increasing my incline while I trotted this out. "I would love to"—*what exactly, I wasn't sure*—"but I'm just really busy right now. I think I told you, I'm a lawyer."

Wow, again, what a jerk.

"Yes, I know." She nodded hopefully, blue eyes widening, rope of hair swinging some more. "For Kingston. Which I think is just, like, *so* cool. Remember, I used to be a princess at the park? I was Cinderella *and* Rapunzel. What are the odds that we'd have this ... *connection?*" She batted her eyes, and I saw it, the princess thing.

I swigged my water. I had played college baseball, plus one year in the pros, passed the California bar, and now worked to protect the world's biggest entertainment media company, who owned basically one-third of the globe. They probably owned this treadmill. They definitely owned me.

Yes, I had achieved every one of these things, but could not seem to let this girl down.

There had to be something wrong with me.

I exhaled, releasing my will to keep fighting off her advances—and to keep believing this workout would happen. "Yes, what a coincidence." My voice was flat, but sufficiently kind. I toweled my face in surrender. Maybe one date would officially get her off my back and away from my treadmill for good. "What time and where?"

I still didn't know what I'd agreed to, but it seemed a safe guess that we would be *hanging out* soon—and thankfully, finally, somewhere besides my new gym.

"I'll text you!" She clasped her hands victoriously. "What's your number?"

I rattled it off as she tapped it into her sparkly pink-covered, huge iPhone. We said our stilted goodbyes.

I supposed I could run outside for a few weeks, instead of here, until she forgot about me and found a new Cardiox victim.

Or you could be a man and tell her directly—eh, more directly—that you just aren't interested, man.

Whatever.

My day was insane. Two meetings with corporate, three memos to finish, and my semi-annual review.

I lumbered my way to the showers.

It wasn't the worst thing to be wanted. This girl seemed to see something in me, despite my repeated insistence that *no, ma'am,* nope. *There is nothing to see here.*

I could thank her for that.

If only my boss had half a morsel of this belief in me.

...

Smoothing my tie, I took a seat in the white leather chair in front of Abel Iverson's desk. It was bold, smooth, and intimidating, like him. The light wood shined now in the afternoon sun slanting in through the massive windows.

The walls?

The window-walls. The walls were windows in here, as they were in every corner office occupied by Kingston executives.

My legal team reported to Abel Iverson, general counsel of the Kingston Company. I respected him greatly and appreciated his aversion to clutter. His desk was not just clean, but completely bare, almost alarmingly so.

Serial-killer-so?

Did the man have a family, a partner? Anything outside of these window-walls? Nobody knew. Not a single personal photo and certainly no art by children. Not even a Kingston tchotchke or paperweight like so many corporate employees.

My desk was bare, but so was my life. Surely an EVP at Kingston led a life full of wonder and meaning? Some exotic travel or breathtaking risks, some wonder-of-the-world hopping, maybe?

Then again, maybe not.

He always seemed to be here.

I gulped, though I was typically not this nervous for my performance reviews. But it was the first time since joining the company three years ago that I had something to say. These meetings were usually status quo.

You're doing great! Here's a modest raise! We're so thankful for you on our team. Please keep up the good work! Please, though. Don't leave us. Ever. Or we might have to kill you.

As general counsel, Abel Iverson was technically head of legal, so he conducted our reviews, but we didn't interact enough for me to gather any clues about his personal life. That kind of daily supervisory *pleasure* was reserved for Cooper Hollister, whom I liked less, to say the least.

Cooper dropped personal facts like grenades.

He was the most senior attorney on our team, but only because he'd been here the longest, which he made sure we remembered. Along with the fact that he loved the Lakers, younger women, and bragging about his golf game. Our team of five included Cooper, me, two other junior attorneys, and our legal assistant, Erin.

Most of the time, I felt like Cooper saw right through me. And not in the sense that he saw my soul or anything so complicated or interesting as that. He saw through me like I wasn't there. Like I might as well be air.

I liked to think that I saw through Cooper, too. In the interesting way, of course. At forty-five, Cooper was exactly thirteen years older than me—and exactly what I never wanted to be. Married fifteen years, four beautiful kids, completely and utterly miserable. Humming through midlife on cruise control, a perpetual mask of boredom on his vaguely good-looking face, like a prom king that peaked too young. Tons of golden hair and a leathery tan. He had great potential and little ambition, from where I sat, anyway. No drive to make his marriage happier, his paycheck higher, his rise through the Kingston ranks faster.

And if someone so fringy in his life as me knew he wasn't nice to his wife, I couldn't help but wonder about the reality behind closed doors. "Allie," he'd bark when she called. "*What now?*" I'd never heard him say a kind word to her.

So, you can imagine how much *positive reinforcement* I got at work. Did Cooper hate me, or was I the best young attorney he'd ever seen? It was anyone's guess, leaving me most days to wonder, wander, and work, head down, like the invisible man.

On the upside, Cooper was a huge Kingston fan, like all of us. Except for Erin, who was not so much a fan, but a true *fanatic*. Some might say: a freak. She'd told me once that, when the time comes, she'd like her ashes sprinkled over the Kingston Court theme park. The castle, specifically.

"Do you think that's *legal?*" she had whispered, eyes wide. Her platinum hair was chopped to her chin, framing her fair, elfin features. She could easily be cast as a fairy, one who loved blood-red lipstick and '90s punk rock.

I had told her kindly that scattering human remains on private property was most definitely not legal in California, but rather, a misdemeanor violation of our state Health and Safety Code. It was strictly prohibited—and frankly disgusting—but still done more than you'd think, I informed her.

There was one woman who'd been caught leaving a trail of something (*someone*) behind her boat on the Pirate Adventure Cruise.

There was a family who'd decided a memorial service for their young son would be most special and appropriate if held in the park's Haunted House—with some remnants of him left behind with the ghouls and ghosts.

In each case, the ride was shut down momentarily, and those "die" hard guests were escorted promptly out of the park.

Turns out plenty of people wanted their ashes scattered throughout Kingston Court.

Guard your slushies, kids.

Whenever people wondered what I did as an attorney for Kingston, I told them stories like this. They were my favorite.

The random laws I had to research; the enthusiasts that made our brand go round the world.

Because Kingston was so much more than a brand. We were a multibillion-dollar media and entertainment giant, yes—but also a seismic force of power, influence, and human imagination.

Wade Elliot Kingston had discovered, harnessed, and pioneered what no man ever had before, and no man would ever again. He founded a passion, a lifestyle, something that bordered on a religion for some.

Like Erin, for instance.

I, on the other hand, was a *normal* fan who knew how to keep his cool. I'd been a tough-luck kid raised with Kingston tales and characters as his shining hope. There had to be millions like me. I considered it a privilege to work for the company; unbelievable, really. My eight-year-old self was doing cartwheels in his Aladdin costume.

But still.

A classy wood coffin would do just fine when I croaked, thanks.

Speaking of classy wood coffins likely resembling this massive desk, where in the world was Iverson?

I texted Erin.

> My review is at 4, right?

It was already 4:04, and Kingston executives took pride in punctuality.

Weird death wishes aside, Erin was awesome and impressed

me often. She'd even secured quarterly costume days for the whole office, which was located directly across the street from Kingston Court in Anaheim, California.

"How is it possible that we work for *Kingston* and there isn't more *spirit* here?" she'd complained. It became her side hustle to inject more Kingston magic into our mundane workspace, to add some interest beyond the stark walls and cold floors.

I thought the costume days were hilarious. I always took the chance to dress up as a new Kingston sidekick. The other lawyers never—and I do mean never—veered outside our black suits and white shirts, even with the official encouragement, so I'd be the only blue genie or giant bear at a staff meeting. I was six five and 230 pounds, so you could say I stood out. How could I pass up this magical opportunity?

My phone buzzed.

> Yes! Just walked by. On his way to you. GL!!!!

I straightened, crossing my ankles, and tugged at the edge of my suit jacket. I turned around just as Abel Iverson tapped his knuckles on the glass door.

"Forgive me, Harrison!" he bellowed. "Scarlett Jackson. We finally reached a settlement. Brave new world. We need tighter contracts."

I knew everything about the high-profile lawsuit with Scarlett Jackson. We all did. The A-list actress was fuming that Kingston had released her latest film to our streaming service while the title was still in theaters. We knew it was sticky—but also that it would be fine. Kingston suits almost never went to court. We did anything to avoid the costs and the bad publicity.

"No problem whatsoever." I stood. By any other measure, Abel was tall, but I still towered above him. He smiled, shaking my outstretched hand, showing white teeth and grandfatherly dimples.

Seriously, any grandkids?

No wedding ring.

Who was this guy?

He was around sixty-five, I'd guess, but had the strength and build of a hyper-fit forty-something.

"Sit, sit." He gestured while taking a seat on his throne of expensive-looking black suede. He settled into the massive wood desk that now made me think of my funeral.

After opening his top drawer, he pulled out a stack of papers, which I could see were my HR review papers: position (senior attorney), salary (generous), responsibilities (grunt work), years at the company (three), infractions or performance issues (none, obviously), and finally, my employee semi-annual survey, in which I was viciously honest.

He flipped through them earnestly, as if scraping the edges of his scattered mind, determined to take this seriously. I knew he had more important tasks and felt grateful he took the time.

"As usual, you have glowing feedback from everyone on the floor," he noted, gray eyes skimming the pages. "You're very well liked here, Harrison. We appreciate you."

He looked up.

"Thank you, sir." I *was* thankful. I really was. I had to be sure he knew that before I voiced what I needed to say. "I'm so happy here. Working here is a dream come true, really."

After law school, I'd spent four years at a huge corporate law firm in LA—and hated every single minute of it. The ungodly hours, the barking attorneys, the tedium of daily work at the associate level. I didn't miss it, not ever. I loved the luxury of having time to hit the gym in the morning and leave the office sometime before midnight. I left before 7 p.m. most days, and no longer had to bill my waking existence in six-minute increments. Working in-house was incredible.

If I was frank, however—and I was in those papers he held—I had hardly assumed any new responsibilities at Kingston in the last three years. I valued the steady pay increases, and I knew the road to the next title bump—here or elsewhere—was long. I was young, with a lot to learn.

But I wasn't getting the opportunities I needed to grow. Holed up in my office, conducting research, writing memos and briefs all day—it was fine, good work, for a company I believed in.

And yet.

Like a mermaid trapped underwater, I wanted more.

Abel continued. "I'm glad you're happy here." He pushed his glasses up the bridge of his nose and kept flipping through the pages. I prayed to have a shock of silver hair that fantastic one day.

"Mr. Iverson—"

He waved his hand. "Call me Abel, please."

I cleared my throat. "Can I express something to you about

my work here at Kingston?"

He tossed his glasses onto the keyboard. "Of course." He relaxed, looking relieved by my initiative.

I nodded. "Well," I started. "Cooper's a great leader—"

"Cooper's a great *lawyer*," Abel interrupted, leaning back toward the bookcase that matched his desk. "I'm well aware that he isn't the best manager."

I sat back, surprised. "Well ... I don't want to complain."

"You're not complaining. You're telling the truth. As attorneys do. As *good* attorneys do, anyway."

I thought of Jim Carrey in *Liar, Liar* and swallowed a cackle.

"Well, sir—Abel," I continued. "As long as he's leading our team, I'm not sure I'll be able to—" I paused. "Reach my ... full potential. Cooper holds onto a lot that he could easily pass off to me, or to the other attorneys, even to Erin. I understand him being protective—"

Abel held up a hand. "Say no more."

What?

This couldn't be so easy.

I didn't have to feign speechlessness.

"I see big things for you here," Abel continued, pulling a pen from his desk and squiggling something onto my papers. "I see your drive, your ambition."

"Really?" I *did* work hard. I *did* love this company. I *didn't* think anyone noticed.

"Yes, Harrison. I see you leading one of our legal divisions someday, easily by the time you're forty." He leaned forward, stroking his chin.

"Wow, I—really appreciate that." I perked up like a dog at the pound who'd just been told he was getting adopted. It was hard not to glow in the praise of someone like Abel. "I want you to know that I'll do anything here. The hardest cases, the neediest clients—whatever the team needs. The other teams, too. I'm here to help, and I want to get better."

"You're already very good."

Was this the best review of my life?

Was it possible these years of skull-numbing busywork *had* been leading somewhere?

"Then let me prove what I'm capable of," I said, squaring my posture, emboldened. "Next time there's an opportunity, or a bigger case, I'd love to be considered."

"Consider yourself considered. But, you must know." Abel tapped his pen on the desk. "The next step is … *more*. More of everything. More on the line, more hours, more pressure."

I nodded. "Of course. I just—I want to stay at Kingston and grow my career here. But I don't think I can do that if I don't get the opportunity."

He nodded. "I'm hearing you," he went on. "But also know that if we put you on bigger projects, or a real case, you'll have to work with outside counsel. I know that's your background, so you know how it is. Aggressive. Demanding. Merciless. They're not going to rub your shoulders and tell you good job."

I dismissed the impulse to feel insulted. I didn't want to be pampered; I just wanted real work. "I know, sir." I also knew about Brent Callahan of Callahan & Lucas, our top outside firm. Brent was a legend. Alpha personified. You wanted to learn his moves, where he bought his suits, and what the man ate for breakfast. He might as well bring a sword to court. I knew for a fact he could make me a better lawyer.

"Well, then," Abel said, slapping my papers down. "That's settled out of court." He chuckled to himself.

Lawyer jokes.

Dad jokes?

Is he a dad or not?

I decided he probably wasn't a serial killer.

"By the way, did I see you at the new gym in Newport this morning?" It was a random question, as if he was breaking character.

I appreciated it, but I gulped. "Cardiox? Yes ... I was there."

"Running is good for you." He gave a two-fisted drum on his stomach, tight for his age, for any age. "It'll keep you young. And so will a little fun." He winked, and I knew he must've witnessed my rendezvous with Gym Ashley. You never knew who was watching.

"Don't forget to enjoy yourself, Hayes." He lifted his charcoal brows. "The magic. It's why we're here."

As I stood to leave, I spotted it.

Tiny, but there.

A delicate glass swan perched on the bookcase behind him, next to his dozen volumes of *Harvard Law Review*. The bird's downwardly tipped beak was shiny gold, feathers flung back as if to the wind. It was the only decoration in the room.

So graceful. Winsome. Enchanting, even.

It's why we're here.

...

Chapter Four

SCOTTIE

With bloodshot eyes and caffeine-addled veins, I stared, satisfied, at the twelve-page document on my laptop. Midmorning sunshine glared on the smudged-up screen. Peyton hadn't answered her phone last night, and *still* hadn't called me back.

I thumbed my phone screen to check for the millionth time.

Nothing, blank, save the background photo of me and Trey last Halloween, dressed as Tarzan and Jane.

Ugh.

Trey was so hunky in his faux-fur man skirt, and my abs looked good in that cheetah costume.

I was allowed to mourn.

It's Saturday, Peyton! Stop working!

It's possible I freaked her out with my three-minute, squealy, detailed voicemail—punctuated *maybe* at the end with my crooning the TikTok song lyrics.

But couldn't she feel it through best friend telepathy?

We had a Fortune 500 to frame!

What could be more important?

I knew everything about the human mouth and nothing about the law. This was the truth. But that didn't stop me from staying up nearly all night in my attempt to build, well, a case.

There has to be something here.

My biggest surprise of all, so far, was that no one had ever attempted this. For all the historical complaints against the Kingston Company—and there were many—no one else had filed a similar lawsuit against them. No other official complaints of giving false hope, of selling a lie, of packing poisonous lemons behind a saccharine facade.

The more I considered my claims, the more my frustration mounted. Peyton would need to help with the details, but I felt sure I had something solid against the company. For making me believe, with all my heart, in the promise of a sparkly fairy tale that turned out to be a big lie.

Talk about negligent infliction of emotional distress!

Google seemed to suggest this was a claim I could make.

I was trying it on for size.

Speaking of size—*supersize*—my new mission sparked the foggy recollection of those silly McDonald's lawsuits that once made the news. The public thought they were silly, anyway—surely the plaintiff did not, and I was the plaintiff now. My lawsuit would never make the news; at least I hoped not. But it might behoove me to see how those cases fared.

It didn't take long to find the two stories most familiar to me: the woman who infamously spilled hot coffee on her lap and blamed the franchise, and the man who sued McDonald's for making him fat.

My eyebrows arched in satisfaction at the results.

In 1992, the seventy-nine-year-old woman all *hot-and-bothered* about the coffee spill sued McDonald's and won nearly $3 million in damages for her suffering. Her burns were apparently horrible. Serious.

Probably almost as painful as being left at the altar.

The other headline said it all: *Man Wins Lawsuit Against McDonald's for Making Him Fat.* The thirty-two-year-old franchise owner claimed the free lunches and required sampling caused him to gain sixty-five pounds over the course of twelve years. He won $17,500. It wasn't a fortune. He probably didn't celebrate by buying a yacht.

But you're telling me there's a chance.

I'd been watching my old DVDs.

A chance for Lloyd Christmas, and me—but mostly for that innocent eight-year-old girl with a diary and a dream. Who believed she'd be rescued by the sword of true love instead of wounded by its cruel blade.

I would fight for that girl.

For every little girl who believed that Cinderella was real and that wishing worked.

Plus, $17,500 was $17,500 dollars.

Add a zero and you basically had the cost of my wedding.

I gulped. The thought coiled knots in my belly.

In my document, I had begun to list the extra costs I'd incurred so far in my Quarter-Life Catastrophe, i.e., Altargate.

Surely Wade Kingston—founder of the Kingston Company himself—could afford to help cover some of them:

The Wedding: $200,000

The Nonrefundable Maldives Honeymoon: $12,000

Post-Wedding Therapy with Dr. Perrish: $2,000

SUING CINDERELLA 61

Appointment with Naturopath to Make Sure I Wasn't Dying: $300

Overpriced Supplements from Said Naturopath to Help Avoid My Sure and Impending Death: $300

Travel and Moving Costs: $2,000

Shipping Costs for Returned Wedding Gifts: $2,000

I included these costs in my Kingston Case File—yes, I had named it that—along with the information about the McDonald's suits. Something about *precedence*; I wasn't exactly sure. At the very least, this homework might help woo Peyton if necessary.

I'd throw in some gourmet donuts, too, *if she would call me back*.

In the meantime, I kept digging, and eventually found a Kingston lawsuit that might matter. Several years ago, a woman had sued the company for $300 million, claiming they ripped off her life story to create the now $15 billion *Ice Queen* empire.

I couldn't help but giggle at this one, even if it also felt sad. The woman seemed to truly believe Kingston stole pieces of her autobiography for the most lucrative animated film in entertainment history. There were sisters, some mountains, a sky.

Come on.

Case dismissed.

Let it go.

I didn't include this case in my file; it made me too uncomfortable. My reasoning was *much more* sophisticated than this. I was nothing like that woman, I told myself. I had *doctor* next to my name, even if it came with piles of debt that Trey had insisted on helping me pay.

I added dental school debt to my list.

Cha-ching.

I'd done well as a dentist—great, even—and was certainly paid in dividends far beyond money. But my preset earning potential couldn't touch the fringe of Trey's private equity salary. I'd always considered myself an ambitious, independent woman. So how had I ended up *so very* dependent on such a sack of male money and lies?

Stupid Kingston.

Bzzz, bzzz.

Finally, my phone lit up with the time and Peyton's beautiful face.

10:42 a.m.

I'd saved Peyton's professional headshot in my contacts, so it's what stared at me now. I'd chosen the picture because it was funny and kept it because I was proud. Her mid-length blanket of butter-blonde hair framed her heart-shaped face, centered by blue eyes that shined with both strength and mischief. She wore a black suit, and bright pink lipstick, always, to work. Stilettos, too.

Peyton McKenzie would be your best friend. Take a bullet for you. Unless you dared think of crossing her. Then she would annihilate you in court and/or life.

I snatched up the vibrating phone like a hungry toddler needing a snack. "P., hi!!!! Where've you been?"

"Sorry, Scot, I'm so slammed." I heard chewing on the other end of the line. I tried not to feel disappointed at the obvious fact that she was squeezing me in. "I need a saddle for the weight of this caseload. Wait—that could be kind of chic, don't you think?"

"Are you eating ... salad? In the morning?" For such a poised girl, Peyton ate like a caveman, but it never stopped men from loving her. They were constantly begging for dates, if she could make room in her iCal stacked like a Tetris game. "And working on a Saturday—again?"

"Is it morning?" I heard her shrugging, pictured her stabbing at the garbanzo beans in that precise way she did. "I've been up since five. And I almost always work Saturdays."

I didn't envy that. Neat, orderly hours, lined up like teeth, were a huge perk of being a dentist. "So did you get my message?" I felt sheepish suddenly, my unbridled ambition faltering just so.

I forced myself to perk up in the swivel chair slightly too small for me. I reminded myself of the impressive case document I had started.

It was good.

Really good.

"I'm serious, P. Like totally, completely serious."

She blew out a longwinded breath. "Listen, Scot," she started. "You know I'd do anything for you. Even as busy as I am, and trying to make partner by thirty-three, you know I would basically die for you."

"Why thirty-three, again?"

"My Jesus year, Scot. Look it up. It's the year of enlightenment. When we reach our *mountaintop*."

"Or our crucifixion," I pointed out. "Plus, you're not even thirty yet."

"I will be next year," she said through another mouthful. "And this place is cutthroat. If you don't make partner in five-to-seven years, like, *yikes*. Bye."

"You know you have it clinched." We both knew it. The current partners loved her, and she'd never lost a case.

"Maybe." She paused. "But I can't let up. And let me get this straight. You want to *sue* Kingston? Like, *the* actual Kingston Company. Movie producer, theme park founder, who-runs-the-world Wade Kingston. His company. Legend at large. For ruining you. As a kid."

I swallowed.

When you put it that way.

"Yes, but—hear me out." I gushed it all out: the prior cases, my brilliant reasoning, my many noble points.

"Well." Peyton sighed. Impressed or exhausted, I couldn't tell. "It's bold. But there's no way this will ever get anywhere. There are so many crazy people out there—and sleazy people just looking to make a buck from corporations like Kingston. This woman hurt her neck on Star Galaxy, that lady swears they plagiarized her life for the *Ice Queen*—"

I blushed.

"It'll be a waste of my time and yours," she went on. "You're so smart, Scot. You're amazing. And this will also keep you … hung up on the past. And on Trey." She paused, voice softening. "I want to see you move on."

"This isn't about Trey," I insisted defensively. "This is about me. And my childhood. And who I became because of my upbringing without a mom. And the role Kingston played in ... shaping my hopes for the future. My very *false* hopes, in case you haven't noticed." I gestured sadly around my childhood room to no one but me. "Kingston—well, Kingston raised me, P. You were there."

My memory flickered back to my seventh birthday party, my first one without Mom. Her hole left in my small life had been cavernous, her exit hitting me like a meteor. I'd reverted to wetting the bed, and most nights, ended up on the floor of my dad's room, wrapped tightly in my pink sleeping bag.

I was struggling, and Dad knew it. So, he pulled out every stop to make it the best birthday party I could imagine. He invited every girl from my class, but only five of them came, as if the other moms were scared of us. As if you could catch abandonment like a cold.

But the modest size of the party couldn't ruin my day. Dad had found Cinderella—*the real-life, living, breathing, singing Cinderella*—to do our princess makeup, paint our nails, and regale us with tales of royalty.

I didn't have two parents, but I had the world's best dad and the vivid fantasy world he created—which was made possible greatly, I realized now, through Kingston's influence.

And look where it had left me.

I suddenly couldn't wait to talk to my dad about this. I knew he would support me. He'd even hire me a lawyer, probably—if he hadn't sunk his life savings into my wedding.

My stomach tightened again.

"Come on, P.," I pleaded. "What do you think Kingston has done to the American consciousness by erasing the pain of reality and sprinkling our problems with fairy dust? Princess culture, little girls—just think about it. You're a feminist, aren't you?"

"Of course, I am," she shot back. "And I'll always fight for you. If you kill someone, Scot? I'll literally bury the body with my two hands. Need help out of a ticket? *What ticket?*

"But sue *Wade Elliot Kingston's* empire? I can't, Scot. I just … no." A few beats passed. "My whole reputation would be on the line."

"I'll pay you!" I cried, feeling desperate.

"You don't have any income right now," she said quietly. "And I'm not taking your savings." Her honest words hung over the line between us. "Plus—you couldn't afford me anyway." Her sass lifted the mood. I could practically hear her flipping her hair, crunching her pricey arugula.

I gritted my teeth. "Well, I don't like it, but—I guess I can find another lawyer," I quipped. We both knew I could not.

"Good luck with that!"

I sighed, swiveling around to the pictures I'd been admiring yesterday. Scottie and Peyton, Peyton and Scottie. Forever knit at their invisible seams, but apparently, officially not suing Cinderella together.

Shame.

My eyes locked on the picture of us from senior prom, both in floor-length black satin dresses, smoky makeup, and the identical side-swept updos that were all the rage at the time. We were both a little heartsore that night, recently dumped by our boyfriends, but it was the best dance of our lives.

I had picked Peyton, and she had picked me. And I wouldn't know it till well beyond high school, but sometimes one good friend was really the best you could hope for—and often, all you would need.

Even if said friend would not sue a global empire with you.

"Fine, P.," I relented, ready to change the subject. "Want to get dinner tonight? Your treat, moneybags?"

She huffed, but I could tell she was smiling. "Shoot, I can't tonight, but tomorrow—yes. What about pedicures instead? Afternoon?"

I glanced at my gnarly toenails. "That would be great, actually. Just text me. I'll be, you know, here."

"Great! Talk tomorrow. Love you, Scot. Everything really is going to be okay."

Click.

Was it, though?

Pivoting, cracking my back, I supposed it was time to face this sprawling day on the home front.

But first.

I opened my email, tapped in Peyton's name, and ignored the dozens of unopened messages piling up from Trey Kelley. My ex was as bold as the font on his email subjects—and bold was how they would remain.

I tapped in a subject for Peyton: *LOVE YOU!!!!!!!!!!!!!!!!!!!*

I clicked the mini paperclip icon, hit send, and off my case file *whooshed.*

...

Chapter Five

SCOTTIE

The smell of pumpkin French toast filled the kitchen, syrupy and nostalgic.

"Are you trying to plump me up?" I asked Dad the next morning, my thoughts flitting to the devious witch in *Hansel and Gretel*.

I had fairy tales on the brain, clearly.

Hoisting myself onto a barstool, I could still taste Friday's banana bread. My dad was a saint—he really was—as far from antihero as one could be.

"It's Sunday." Dad tilted the pan with practiced ease, evening out the mixture he'd been perfecting from my earliest memory. I had to admit, it somehow was better each time. *Challah bread, vanilla, pumpkin pie spice,* most recently. Those were the keys to fall bliss in breakfast form. "Plus, you're looking a little too skinny," he added.

We always had French toast on Sundays. So had Trey and I, a tradition I'd happily shared with him. Trey's was never nearly as good as my dad's, though. It was a thought I hadn't let myself think until this moment, I realized—like others I had only recently permitted.

Trey was always so late.

Trey was rude to waitresses and baristas, a telltale red flag.

Trey showed off his money like a sixteen-year-old with a new Mustang.

Other thoughts, sweet thoughts, complimentary thoughts, on the other hand—those were now (mostly) forbidden.

Trey smelled so good, like clean soap and wood.

Trey worked so hard.

The sky today is the exact color of Trey's eyes. It's uncanny, really. Should I send him a pic of the clouds?

No, absolutely not.

Neither should I even consider reading one of his two thousand emails.

He deserved nothing from me.

My heart ballooned with affection for my father. Attention to detail was his specialty, but never took away from his warmth. Deep laugh lines despite so much hardship; social ease despite isolation.

He never said it, but I knew he had to be lonely. He worked, he hiked, he went hunting with his brothers a few times a year. Faith in God centered him; peace seemed to follow him. His coarse brown hair was shaggy, his stubble a fixture on weekends. He'd never remarried and had only dated three women I remembered by name. Never anything serious.

He reached across the island to pour a hefty slice of his masterpiece onto my plate, which was surrounded by toppings, not that you needed them. I picked up the syrup anyway. I was *feeling* a little too skinny—that carved-out, heartbroken hollowness I hadn't felt in years, but now remembered was every bit as painful as bad strep throat or the chicken pox.

"Thanks, Dad. For this. For everything."

"Thank you for coming back. It's been so quiet without you."

"For a decade?" I smiled, but the thought stung. I'd left for college and never moved back.

He shrugged and nodded. "For a decade."

He piled his own plate high and joined me at the granite countertop. He sprinkled powdered sugar, pecans. We sat in the solace of a father and daughter who'd raised each other.

He finally spoke between bites. "How are you feeling?" he asked. "Today? I know heartbreak is a fickle little beast. But—how are you feeling, right now?"

I propped up an elbow, resting my chin on the base of my hand.

How *was* I feeling, right now?

Not bad, was my first thought. *Not bad … today.*

"Well—" I dabbed my lips with a napkin. "Today, I feel like your pumpkin French toast might be the answer to every world problem. Should we start *selling* it? Maybe I should open a bakery. Forget the whole dentist thing."

He snapped two fingers and gunned them at me. "It's the nutmeg. New ingredient. And no, we should not. The overhead for bakeries is wild, and so is the failure rate."

"Well—okay." I shot a little finger gun back at him. "No bakery. But nutmeg: approved."

We sat in the cozy quiet, munching our mouthfuls, French toast healing me to my bone marrow.

My eyes combed around the kitchen. Yellow-beige wallpaper, timeworn appliances, the only new item: a white porcelain farmhouse sink, installed last year after a catastrophic garbage disposal malfunction.

Then I couldn't hold it in anymore.

My big new idea.

I needed to get my dad's feedback.

I breathed.

Truthfully, I'd been feeling better—overall—since Friday night, when the notion first struck me. I'd spent yesterday binging old Kingston movies, typing notes faster than I could think. Peyton's resistance presented a roadblock as to how, exactly, I would proceed without my own Elle Woods.

But I had hope.

And so, I told my dad everything. Poured it out like maple syrup.

As expected, he didn't respond right away. He was such a *processor*, a *muller-over*, a *ruminator*, no matter the topic at hand. I could see his brain grinding, opinions forming, as he sipped on his black coffee, squinting. He was likely wondering if his sweet, dejected daughter was—in fact—temporarily, certifiably crazy. And that perhaps he tragically was *not* equipped to handle the rehabilitation of her fractured state.

Could I be serious?

Oh, I was serious, Dad.

And maybe a little insane—but weren't all great people crazy, or something? Hadn't I heard that somewhere?

Why, yes, in fact, I had heard that somewhere. It was a quote from the original *Alice's Adventures in Wonderland* that I'd seen on Instagram. I'd liked it so much I had saved it. I pulled up the screenshot while Dad continued to marinate on my insanity.

I'd add the quote to my case file.

You're mad, bonkers, completely off your head, but I'll tell you a secret ... all of the best people are.

I smiled.

Was he ever going to speak?

The long silence was growing ludicrous, even for us. Maybe he was so shocked and disgusted that he'd just pretend I'd said nothing. Perhaps we would clear our sticky plates and never speak of this again.

But as he swirled one last bite on his plate, he looked right at me, at last. "I think you should do it."

I dropped my fork.

What?

"I don't have any money left, Scot. All I have is the house—and that will be your inheritance."

I lowered my eyes, embarrassed he'd even think I would ask him for money. "I know, Dad, I wasn't expecting you to—"

His hand filled the gap between us. "Of course. But I would hire you the lawyer if I could. I would. I think this is partly hilarious—partly genius."

I smirked. "*Genius*, huh? So ... you don't think I'm crazy?"

"I didn't say that." He bumped my shoulder with his. "But this is something I thought about when you were young, you know. Kingston, the princesses. Their impact on you. Some of what you are saying,"

"Seriously?"

He lifted his napkin to his lips, nodding. "Remember the year your mom left?"

I nodded.

Always.

I remembered my mom, even though there weren't any pictures of her displayed in the house anymore. I knew they pained Dad too much, back then, her pretty face staring at us from the walls, haunting and taunting us in equal turns. Her dark hair down to her stomach, her green eyes, her smile. Everything about her was high wattage, big as the sky.

Her heart, her voice, and her demons.

Her blackouts, her moods.

I never had the heart to tell Dad that I recalled my last night with Mom in vivid color. That I could still tell him about it—anyone about it—frame by frame, millisecond by millisecond, at any moment, if they ever asked.

I remembered it all.

The smell of her vanilla perfume, the feeling of her nails scratching softly on the small of my back. How transcendent her voice was when she sang to me, *Jesus loves you.*

So, Jesus loved me.

Did she?

I could tell Dad, sure, but I wouldn't. He didn't need to know that it always lived there, *right there*, the memory of her, ten times worse than my wedding day and a thousand times larger than anything else.

My last memory with her probably remained so vivid because I'd revisited it so many times. I'd learned on a podcast that the more you replayed a past event in your mind, the more it carved into your psyche. The information was intended to be a warning, for listeners to stop reliving their most painful times—but I took it as a gift. One living on in high definition on repeat.

I was afraid of forgetting her face.

That was the truth.

I feared forgetting her magical smile, and the way she played with my hair, in between the bouts when she'd disappear without telling us where she was going.

And then not return for days.

The night before she left for good, she was home, and, I knew now, sober—which was a rarity. She smelled sweet and fresh, like herself—her *real* self. There were other unsavory smells that wafted from her sometimes. Other men and cigarette smoke. Stale laundry and dirty hair, like she'd worn the same dress for three days. I pretended not to notice when she did just that; it made me too unbearably sad.

But on our last night together, my mom was clean, in every sense. All the way, deeply *there* with me, the night before my book report presentation on *Snow White*. I tried so hard not to *stare, stare, stare* at her when I had all of her with me—giving me her love and her light that I so desperately craved.

If I sit here, really still, and be really good, and read all my pages just perfectly, maybe she'll want to stay with me?

I pictured her now, on a rare night like this, looking over at me, suddenly knocked from her hazy trance, as if thinking, *What on earth have I been doing? This beautiful child of mine!* She'd say, "Come here, sweetie! Let's dance!"

And that last night, we did.

We danced.

Her smile was my spotlight as we twirled for hours—which maybe were only minutes, but I would preserve this memory in the slow motion it deserved.

That earthshattering smile.

I wondered if it was the real reason why I chose dentistry.

Did I want everyone to have a smile as unforgettable—striking—as hers?

We read, we danced, and then she kneeled to my eye level, hands on my bony shoulders. My flannel nightgown, edged in lace, touched the floor. I thought I might choke on my awe of her as she cupped my cheek with one hand and stared deeply into my eyes, our gazes mirror images of each other.

"Do you know how much I love you?" Her voice was a meadow, a song.

I remembered looking down, feeling so guilty that I couldn't tell her the truth—that no, I didn't know how much she loved me. How could I possibly? She was leaving, *always leaving*. And even when her body was here, it still usually felt like she wasn't.

Of course, I couldn't say what I wanted: *Stay here tonight, Mommy. Sleep with me, Mommy. Be here in the morning to brush my hair and pack my lunch and eat eggs with us. Teach me how to make pancakes.*

Was wanting something more than you've ever wanted anything else love?

Was a years-long stomachache love?

Was dancing and reading and hugging and laughing, believing tomorrow had the chance of being different, finally—

Love?

"Is that love?" my younger self asked God that night, quickly, silently.

He didn't answer, so I nodded, even though it wasn't the truth. *Yes, Mom. I know how much you love me.*

"Wherever you go," she continued, pressing her forehead to mine. "I'll be with you."

"What about wherever *you* go?" I blurted. I hadn't meant to. My eyes burned, and I was embarrassed to know the tears were coming. "Am I with you, too?"

And where do you go, Mom?

Where do you go?

Her eyes widened in surprise, like she hadn't expected an answer.

Was I even real to her? I wondered today. Her very flesh, birthed from her blood—or was I a doll, to play with and leave as she pleased? I was always dressed like a doll, after all—anybody could see that from my childhood pictures.

My heart ached at my dad's efforts to keep it going when Mom was gone. The messy pigtails and wrinkled skirts.

My last question to her that night, though—*Am I with you, too?*—that's when something like anger and fear flashed across her pretty face, for a moment, before her features settled back to grinning affection.

"Of course, you're always with me, my little Scotland Holiday!" She combed her nails through my hair. "Someday,

I'll take you there. To Scotland."

She was just whimsical enough to name me after a country she'd always wanted to go to. Coupled with our last time together, it felt a little *too* whimsical—so I was glad the nickname Scottie stuck when she left.

Mom took Scotland with her, forever.

The year Mom left.

The day, the hour, the second ...

I snapped from the memory, back to French toast and lawsuits, nodding. "Of course, Dad. Yes. I remember the year Mom left. I must've watched *Cinderella* every day for three years."

"Try twice a day." Poor Dad. His long work hours, scrambling for sitters, dealing with his own grief. Our stand-in nanny really was Kingston, and truthfully, she wasn't bad.

Always available, never late, and doting as a spoonful of sugar.

"Every darn day," he continued. "Over and over. And there was never a mother in the movies. I didn't notice that until after your mom left, but when I did, I thought it might be good for you—to see these princesses rise above hardship. To find happiness in the face of adversity. To find a prince, against odds."

It was a nice sentiment.

Until.

That prince turned out to be a Machiavellian toad.

"But the end is only the beginning," I concluded, exhaling. "That's when it gets hard. And the movies do a horrible job of depicting the harsher realities of human relationships."

He nodded, sipping more coffee. "Your mom and I had a fairy-tale wedding. You've seen the pictures. Hawaii with our closest friends. The storybooks show the sunset ceremony and your blushing bride—not so much your wife passing out ... or calling you to get her from jail."

I winced.

"I'm just saying. I wonder," he posed, "if all those fairy tales messed with my own approach to parenting you. Had I been more honest with you, about the world, toned down the Kingston—would you have been less blindsided by this breakup? Less totally helpless right now?"

I swallowed, bristling at the harsh truth. "Don't even think about blaming yourself, Dad," I warned in my best grown-daughter voice. "I loved growing up with Kingston. I just think they need to take responsibility for their influence. What good does it do, really, to imbed these ideas into our minds—the minds of innocent kids—before they can even form a first conscious thought?"

He cocked his head with a smile, as if I were preaching to the pastor himself.

"So, if I find a way to do this," I continued. "You're on my team?" I wouldn't take one more step without his approval.

"Without a doubt."

I smiled.

Our feast soon devoured, we both stood to clear the mess. "Are you coming to church with me?" Dad asked.

I wanted to join him sometime, maybe. But right now I needed some exercise, and yes, to interface with other humans.

It's just that I preferred total strangers and not well-meaning, cheek-pinching adults who had known me since I was seven.

I couldn't face their pity quite yet.

Plus, I missed running and wanted to find a rhythm here. Arms slicing air, breeze in my hair, preferably by the ocean. As a momentary break from my research yesterday, I'd googled running clubs in Orange County and found a group like the one I'd loved in San Francisco. They met at Fashion Island in Newport Beach at 10 a.m.

"Next time, Dad. Say hi to everyone for me."

Satiated by the huge carbo load, I skipped up the stairs two at once, dug out my trusty Asics, and saddled up to outrun my problems.

...

Chapter Six

HARRISON

I jogged toward the trim and attractive people in a half moon around the fountain. The group was unmissable. Stretching their quads and arching their backs, every one of them was the prototype of health and fitness. Probably protein shakes for breakfast, coffee undoubtedly black.

I guess this was expected given where I'd heard of them: from one of many high-end athleisure boutiques at Orange County's most luxurious outdoor mall. Morning sun cut through the blades of Fashion Island's huge lawn and dappled storefronts about to open. Early shoppers roamed with their Starbucks, some led by poofy white dogs, others by strollers that looked more high-tech than my Tesla.

I glanced again at the postcard I held, covered in bolts and flashes of "Come Change Your Life!" I'd found it buried in the bottom of a Lululemon bag, under a black dry-fit shirt I'd purchased long ago and finally worn today. I had to admit, it was the softest fabric I'd ever touched. I'd won a Lulu gift card at a work happy hour and was possibly now a believer. I'd thrown in this white baseball cap, too, and couldn't help but nod to how *great* it fit. And I was no stranger to baseball caps.

Reluctantly sold, here I was checking out OC Sprinters, Premier Running Club of Newport Beach. I would try hard to take it seriously on behalf of my (mostly) genuine interest. And the audacious claim that it might change my life.

From afar, the members all appeared around my age, vaguely millennial—but I realized as I got closer that they were not. Two lanky girls in crop tops looked more midcollege, and a few of the men boasted shiny bald heads and biceps of wrinkling skin.

My finally trying this *running club* thing wasn't entirely about avoiding the Princess of Persistence at Cardiox—but, okay, it was partly that. For as much as I loved the head-to-head nature of law, I'd never been great at confrontation in my personal life.

Despite my avoidant ways, though, I valued group fitness. And I missed being part of a team. I also needed to make some real friends in Orange County, three years later, much as I tried to deny it. I loved the weather, the pace, the space, so I should probably at least *try* the people. My assistant, Erin, was always urging me to *get out there*.

So this was me, expanding my zone, getting out to wherever "there" was.

I filled a gap in the semicircle between the two muscly bald men and three ladies gushing about infrared saunas.

Everyone seemed so cliqued off.

Maybe these weren't my new besties.

"Welcome, team, let's get started!"

Clap, clap!

My head snapped to our leader, who hopped up onto the edge of the fountain and shouted above the water flow. Clad in all black, shorts and a tank, she was short and strong with thick golden hair to her waist, the top half braided away from her severe, pretty features. Scandinavian, possibly. Blue eyes and prominent cheekbones. She meant business, for real. That much was as clear as her skin.

"Everyone, pick a buddy! Three in a group at the most. You're going to pace each other today—which you know is a five-mile run at a seven-thirty pace."

Wait.

We knew *what, now?*

And we still came?

I hadn't worked on speed in a while, and seven-thirty was rapid-fire. Ridiculous. Especially for five miles.

I gulped, scanning the group. They were nodding, stretched and prepared. I noticed a couple CamelBaks and fitness fanny packs. These people had reinforcements.

Everyone looked eager and ready, not the least of these being our teacher. And especially the bald eagles next to me, necks longs and arms hinged like wings.

Everyone, that is, except *her*.

How was I just now noticing her?

Conveniently—or alarmingly—she was the only other person standing alone, without the prop of a buddy. Part of the group, but not. Like the brother of the bride at a bachelor party.

The others clumped further into their groupings, and our fearsome leader went on.

"Good, good! We'll start here, cut back through the parking lot, around Newport Center Drive, down to Pacific Coast Highway. We'll run through Corona Del Mar, run along the cliffs—just follow me. I'll turn us around at the midway point. Are we ready?" She punched two fists up into a V.

V for vomit.

Or vulnerable.

Both.

This was worse than elementary PE, where I was always picked last, the tall oaf. Before, of course, anyone had seen the way I could throw a ball.

"O—" *Clap!* "C—" *Clap!* "SPRINTERS!!!"

Clap, clap, clap, clap, clap!

The group roared in high-pitched glee.

If I bolted now, would they notice?

"Before we take off," bellowed the leader, "I see we have some new faces!" She gestured to me and Solo Girl standing at the opposite end of the lineup. "Do you two want to introduce yourselves?"

Not really. No, I did not.

I didn't particularly want to drop dead halfway through this *life-changing* journey, in front of that gorgeous brunette, and have her know my real name.

Please don't pair us up, please don't pair us up.

Maybe she would join the two leggy college girls—and I could soar with the eagles.

Solo Girl was also leggy, but in a more compact way. Through my Ray-Bans, I had to work not to stare at her petite, perfect stems, shapely under yoga pants the tone of a chai tea latte.

She shifted her weight side to side.

Maybe she was nervous, too.

"Sure!" I heard her say. "I'm Scottie ... happy to be here. I found you guys online. I used to run thirty miles a week, but haven't run consistently in a while so ..." Her voice trailed off. Sexy, a little bit husky.

Keep talking.

"I should probably run on my own," Scottie finished, giving a shrug at me. "I don't want to slow anyone down."

"Don't be *silly*!" retorted our leader. "What do we say here, team?"

"Better *together*!" they cried in unison.

"You can run with our other newbie over here—" The leader swept her hand down to me, indicating brightly, *Your turn.*

"Charles," I blurted. "I'm Charles."

I immediately wanted to vacuum the words back in. It was a bad habit, giving my middle name, one I'd taken up in my one year of major-league baseball, when I just didn't want to be *Harrison Hayes* for a second. I'd wear a hat and a hoodie, leaving people to wonder if it had really been me—or "Charles," my doppelgänger roaming around San Diego.

Nobody knew who I was anymore in terms of baseball. Literally, no one. Sure enough, a decade eradicated fifteen minutes of fame like the crash of a ball into shoulder bone.

I batted the memory away.

I still saw lightning at the back of my eyes if I dwelled on it for more than a moment.

These days, though, I was sometimes still wary of people googling me and seeing what I did for a living. As proud as I was to work for Kingston, it usually felt like something better left private.

So today I was Charles, runner and liar.

Hi, nice to meet you, new friends!

I could've introduced Cardiox Ashley to *Charles*, but it was harder to get away with the fib when you had a sneaky, unfortunate feeling you'd see the person again.

"Scottie and Charles. Welcome! Remember, the first run is always the hardest, especially with us." Leader Girl winked. "You two stick together. Follow the wolf pack and listen up for my cues!"

I looked to Scottie, waiting for her to join me. She also wore Ray-Bans, hexagon frames on her tiny nose. Full pink lips. A smatter of freckles across her cheeks. Her dark hair hung back in an easy low ponytail. Her tummy was tight, her posture impeccable.

She was undeniably, objectively stunning.

But did she also look sad?

Even with her shoulders pulled back, head high, I sensed a touch of fragility as she sidled toward me. There was something a little concave about her core, like maybe she was currently shrink-wrapped. Smaller than usual, strained by something.

I inhaled.

Here we go.

"Hi," I offered, extending my hand.

"Hi." She smiled, taking it, revealing white teeth bright as a tennis bracelet. They caught in the morning light, glimmering, slightly softening the rest of her edges.

"You have a beautiful smile."

Dear Lord. Had I just said that out loud? Word vomit was today's soup du jour.

"Thanks," she said unexcitedly, as if she was used to hearing this but even more used to disagreeing. "I work in teeth."

I laughed; it was an odd thing to say. "Yeah?"

"Yeah." She smiled again, more softness. "Or—used to. I'm taking some time off." She didn't expound, and I didn't press. "I guess we're partners?"

"Guess so. Sorry." I grinned.

She tightened her ponytail. "Don't be. Like I said, I am rusty. Like these pants."

It seemed an *invitation* to look, so I indulged myself, for half a second.

I realized then that if rust was on trend, then I was all the way in.

"Do you mind, though?" She pulled AirPods from a slot in her pants and jiggled her phone screen at me. It was opened to Spotify.

I pretended not to notice her playlist name: *Heartbreak Hits*.

Who on God's magnificent earth would break this pretty thing's heart?

"It's hard for me to run without music," she went on. "I can put just one earbud in, if you want."

Well, *did* I want to chat up this Solo Girl, or did I want to let her enjoy her workout? I didn't want to seem clingier than her glorious pants.

"No, no—go for it." I adjusted my ball cap, grasping for chill. "I like running to silence," I lied. I'd forgotten my AirPods.

A corner of her cute mouth turned up. "Yeah?"

"Yeah." Heat spread up my face for zero good reason.

Teeth.

Maybe she was a vampire?

It would be okay with me.

Mirroring her half smile, I began to move my legs in time with the pack, cautiously thrilled about the next hour.

...

I surprised myself threefold.

One, with my ability to keep my eyes on the asphalt and not cast *too* many sideways glances at the girl who had a sum total of no interest in talking to me.

Two, with my pace, nicely in tempo with our healthy herd, even if we brought up the rear.

And three, with my willpower to not look at *Scottie*'s rear, not even once, not even almost. I should've won a medal. A trophy as tall as me.

Never mind that the winningest bald men had left us in the dust. They were speed demons. Part eagle, for sure.

There were a few moments when I even caught Scottie looking at me, in her peripheral. At first, I thought I was imagining things—but once, just past Gulfstream Restaurant, I *felt* the warmth of her eyes on me, and it killed me that I couldn't see what color they were.

When I stole a look back at her, she glanced away.

But not before I saw that smile again, right before it evaporated, and her head bobbed again adorably to her playlist.

Who broke your heart?

I'd have to scan for more clues, without being creepy. I was good at scanning for clues.

Hopefully without being creepy.

I did notice her breathing heavily come mile two, as if a giant boa were further restricting her chest. Her physique *did* remind me of Britney Spears' in her prime.

Scottie reached to wipe her brow more than once, but never slowed down. I wondered if she really was motivated by heartbreak, or just by the beats in her ears—or if maybe, *just maybe*, she also wanted to impress her new running partner.

Because I was impressed.

She was fast, doing her cheetah shoes justice.

Other than our game of sidelong visual tag, the run was scenic but uneventful. The ocean glittered in panorama, punctuated with palm trees and gulls. The picturesque strip of Corona Del Mar exuded its classic charm, old restaurants, new coffee shops.

By the time we turned around at the halfway point, I'd moved on enough from admiring Scottie to start planning the rest of my day.

Whole Foods, car wash, laundry.

Exciting!

To my delight, though, out of nowhere, as we passed a legendary local restaurant called the Quiet Woman, Scottie reached to—*gasp*—take out an earbud. The one *closest to me.* As in, maybe she wanted to *acknowledge* that we'd just covered fifteen-thousand feet of real ground together.

"I love that place." She nodded to the small restaurant. Her arms kept pumping in angles, one earbud clenched like a jellybean.

"I've never been," I admitted. Finally, not a lie. I'd heard of the place; who hadn't? Its black-and-white awning sloped downward in stripes. Rustic red brick wrapped the white facade's base in a ribbon. Flower boxes exuded the old-fashioned charm of an English village.

If you were to judge this book's cover, you would think *fairy tale* way before *bar crawl*—but the latter was where its reputation had landed.

"You need to go!" she insisted. It was the most animated she'd been all morning. "For dinner. Everyone thinks it's just a cougar bar, but they have this salad that comes on a lazy Susan … it's incredible."

She was right. Everyone did equate the Quiet Woman with cougars. Glamourous divorcées gathered late to shamelessly lure younger men, so the legend went. I'd never been inside, but I imagined amber-lit leather booths.

"What's the story," I asked, "with the name? And the headless lady?" I referred to the woman etched into stained glass at the front of the restaurant. She had no head but seemed strangely calm in her old-timey milkmaid's dress.

Scottie bubbled up even more, as if about to regale me with the story, when without any warning—whatsoever—she went lurching, tumbling, *pitching*.

Her whole body flew forward.

I watched in horror as she crashed down into the sidewalk, fall broken barely by the heels of her small hands.

She didn't say anything for a minute.

And I just stood there, frozen dumb, before spanning my hands reflexively to protect her from any more harm.

Never mind that the sidewalks were empty, or that the rest of our group was fading away, up ahead.

She didn't move. She just *stayed* there, flat on the ground. And the longer she did, the closer I watched—and then, she started to laugh.

And laugh.

And laugh.

"Are you—okay?" I knelt nervously. "That was quite a spill."

Still cackling, Scottie rolled onto her rear and sat up. She tucked in her knees and sucked in breaths. She looked at her palms, rubbed pink and raw, the only sign of her fall. "I'm fine. Totally fine." She sounded surprised. "I just feel like that *would* happen to me. Today. With"—she gestured emphatically—"you."

I smiled.

She looked at her feet, and I saw it, too. Her right shoelace had come untied, evidently, and she must've tripped on it. *Hard.* Just below her toes, the black lace had severed and snapped, loosening the whole shoe. The whole cheetah mess gaped open in disarray. She was lucky not to be hurt, I thought, my athletic injury sirens blazing to life.

I crouched and reached for her ankle. I squeezed, but she didn't flinch. "Does that hurt?"

She shook her head no.

Take off your glasses, I silently willed. I wanted to see her eyes. Their color—and if she was checking me out.

She pushed the Ray-Bans higher up on her nose.

Fine.

"Roll your ankle for me?" I instructed.

She traced a circle in the air with her toe, with no sign of agitation.

"No pain?"

"None." She exhaled. "Thank goodness."

"And your hands?" I sat back, cross-legged, and she offered them to me, palms up. I clasped her wrists. They were delicate, but not weak. She reminded me of a fox, all grace and dexterity.

Undeniably cute, but possibly savage.

I ran my thumb along the patches of her skin scraped raw, right where her wrist met her hand. I looked up then, into her lenses, which was probably a mistake, because even this, I felt in my stomach.

Her face was inches from mine.

I swallowed and lowered my eyes, leaning back on my heels. Still touching her skin. It was a weirdly intimate moment for one's first time at a running club.

I didn't want it to end.

"Hands, wrists, all fine!" She yanked them away and jiggled them in two jazz hands. "But—" She gawked helplessly at her shoe. "I can't run with this lace situation. You go … I'll walk back."

"Are you crazy? Not happening." Before I could overthink it, I reached for her foot, determined to keep the rest of this run ultra-casual. I took off her shoe and teased out the broken lace.

"What are you doing?" she asked.

"Fixing your shoe. How old are these, by the way?"

She shrugged. "A few years, maybe."

I didn't bother lecturing her that runners should replace their shoes every six months, or that *of course* this black shoelace had snapped; it was frayed to near smithereens. She should not have been so much as making a sandwich in these.

I yanked off my own white running shoe and unthreaded its shoelace. In swift motion, I laced up her busted shoe with the fresh, clean string of my own, which was not snapping anytime soon. My shoes stayed pristine at the gym, and based on the conditions of Scottie's feet, she was an outdoor runner.

I slipped her sneaker back on, cinching it tight. "There."

She stared, her face breaking into a smile. "They don't match." She stated the obvious. One black lace, one white. Nevertheless, she clicked her toes together with Dorothy umph.

I snatched her black lace from the concrete. I twisted it into a dubious triple knot that I prayed would get me back to the fountain. If it didn't, well, I'd been through worse.

I laced up my shoe with the busted black string.

Beautiful girl, disgusting shoes.

Interesting combo.

"Done," I said, satisfied, rising and reaching down for her hand.

She dusted off her hands before grabbing mine. "You know, you could've given *me* the jury-rigged lace. I'm not a damsel."

"Could've fooled me," I quipped, smiling.

Once standing, she squeezed my forearms, her fingers hot, warming me.

I still couldn't see her eyes.

"I'm totally fine," she continued. "But ... still. That was very sweet. Thank you. So much." She smirked. We stood there, air pulsing between us, before she finally slugged my good shoulder, as if she knew. "Race you back?"

Did she feel it, too?

"Not a chance, *damsel*." I bent into a deep lower-back stretch. "We will jog back at a moderate, human pace. Seven-thirty was a bit aggressive, anyway, don't you think?"

She laughed. "Well, *fine*. You saw what happened when I tried to run that fast and actually *talk*."

We jogged briefly in place before bouncing back down the road, settling into a pace that suited our equilibrium. We didn't talk much, but that second half of the run was more relaxed than the first by a mile.

And even though Scottie put both of her earbuds back in, I couldn't help but notice that she never turned the music back on.

I hoped she was thinking of me.

Stop it, man. You don't do this.

I didn't.

Not dating. Not women. Not any of it.

So I didn't get Scottie's number when we parted ways at the

fountain, where the rest of our group had long since departed and returned to their crisp autumn Sundays.

She didn't ask for mine, either, as she walked away.

To her, I would remain Charles. She could think of him when she looked down at her shoes.

Although for her sake, I hoped she didn't run in those cheetah death traps ever again.

With her final wave, before she trotted off in her rusty hotness—rust was definitely my new favorite color—I did notice something else, beyond her tight grace and mysterious air.

When she lifted her hand, I spotted a tan line on her left ring finger.

Yes, I was admittedly double-checking for clues of anything: heartbreak, commitment. I noted the thin strip of flesh, as white as her fresh, new shoelace, which was to say, mine.

Somebody loved me once, it said.

Recently.

I wondered one final time who could have broken her heart—then dismissed the thought like a foul ball bound for the nosebleeds.

...

SCOTTIE

I swerved into the parking lot of Paradise Nail Bar, predictably ten minutes early. I was known for my punctuality, and Peyton for the firm opposite. In this way, we were the best and worst friends for each other. Neither of us was ever going to change, and we knew it.

Salt and Pepper.

Blonde and Brunette.

Plus, Sunday afternoons were never not buzzing at Paradise, so by getting there early, I could square us away with a couple massage chairs.

My feet, after all, were all too massage-ready from that earlier run and wildly embarrassing spill.

And my mind was still perfectly swimmy from that big, tall drink of water that had poured right into my morning when I didn't even know I was thirsty.

What in the actual?

I was supposed to be healing, recovering, rediscovering myself on the pavement.

Not discovering *Charles*.

He kept pacing through my thoughts, and I wasn't angry about it, just—surprised, really. I truthfully didn't think another man would ever have the power to run through my veins again, let alone so weirdly soon.

It was simply a physical, chemical reaction. Pheromones. *Yes.* That guy had made me physically *feel* something—other than bitter agony and regret—and I was moved by this fact.

That's all it was.

It also seemed a cruel irony that he had such a princely name, given my new life's mission.

Not to mention his disarming chivalry.

But it was all right; maybe the sensation of being crushed in that junior-high way would be good for me. Yes, I could use a *crush*. Who didn't benefit from the thrilling blood-rush of butterflies?

Plus, I'd probably never see him again. He said he was just *checking it out.*

Checking me out, too, I hoped.

Then again, wasn't I just visiting, too?

And you could bet I'd be back for another sip of that water.

With new shoes—and double knots.

Oof.

His eyes.

So brown, and so kind. And his arms. So brown—and SO KIND.

As in, thank you, God, for the kindness of your creation. I wasn't sure I'd ever seen a man that tall and broad-shouldered.

I liked it.

A lot.

He had to be an athlete, and I needed to find out which sport.

I began a mental list of casual questions for next time. Maybe we could be *friends*.

A girl needed *friends*, right?

My phone pinged with a text from Peyton.

On my way!!!

Translation: She was filling up her iced coffee for the road—mostly creamer, artificial, fall-flavored—in her pink Yeti tumbler. She'd leave her place in five minutes. Thankfully she lived close, and I never minded her tardiness. In fact, I especially loved her today for being so darn predictable, unlike my unsteady, flailing life barely hanging by a stray cuticle.

"Two royal pedicures, please?" I told the raven-haired girl with the clipboard. I spotted two open massage chairs and looked to them hopefully, willing her to notice my plea, despite the few names ahead of mine on her list. Perhaps she could sense my desperation because she paused for only a beat before saying "pick a color" and motioning toward them, our thrones at the back of her palace.

I perused the rainbow of polishes, displayed like candy in their wall-mounted case. After much debate, I opted for a burnt cinnamon color. I flipped to the bottom of the bottle: *Schnapps Out of It*. I committed the name to memory. It looked like fall and felt like my mood.

I wanted to snap out of Charles.

And, of course, Trey.

I needed this nail appointment.

I couldn't remember the last time I'd read a magazine, so I snatched the newest issue of *Stargaze* from the fan of glossy covers on the front table. I found our seats and settled right in, ejecting my flip-flops. I sank my feet into the hot, bubbly water. *Ahhhhhh.*

This was nice.

JLo glowed from the magazine cover like the queen that she was. Honey skin and eyes ablaze, newly wed in Vegas to Ben Affleck, her one true love. I could not and would not get over this swoon-worthy reunion, this unexpected gift of nostalgia and total heat. I was only a kid back when they first dated, but their faces at every grocery store checkout stand had been a fixture of errands with Dad.

We don't deserve this couple, I thought, squinting my eyes at a red-carpet photo of them twenty years ago. How was it biologically possible that JLo looked even younger now? Ben, for one, looked older these days: more pronounced facial lines, deeper-set eyes. Signs that he'd won some Oscars, been through some life. But like JLo, he'd only grown hotter.

Charles looked a little like Ben Affleck, I realized, in the eyes and chin.

Solid, easy, super hot. More to him than what most people saw, which was already a lot. But he saved the best for those who mattered. I could just tell.

It was sexy. It was intriguing.

It was not what I needed right now.

Anyway, though, didn't the resurgence of Bennifer prove that soulmates existed? You could break up, live decades of life, and *still* end up together in the happy end?

Yes, of course, *proof*!

In my hands.

Wait.

Stop.

We don't believe in that junk anymore, remember?

JLo, in fact, was probably a much better example of love and womanhood than Cinderella. Ambitious, independent, curvaceous. And she knew how to use her voice. Although both icons knew how to dance.

My contemplations broke with the *ding-dong* of the front door. In waltzed Peyton—and there was nothing like weekend Peyton. Oversized black sunglasses and fluffy cream Sherpa sweatshirt over black leather leggings. Chic white tennis shoes and—shocker—giant iced coffee.

She carried herself and her Goyard tote with effortless, magnetic force. She made you look twice, or three times, like you might find her in a big spread of *Stargaze* and not be the least bit surprised.

I glanced down at my baggy gray graphic Def Leppard t-shirt and threadbare yoga pants I'd had since college.

Some things did not change.

Peyton snaked her way through the focused technicians and gleaming, modern salon: pink-and-silver art deco wallpaper and shiny white furniture.

She stopped in front of me and pushed her sunglasses onto her head, blonde hair tumbling everywhere. It was pulled so tightly during the week—literally and figuratively—that she released it every possible moment. The phrase "let your hair down" was written for her, she liked to say, shaking it out like a wet golden retriever.

In her typical dramatic manner, Peyton reached into her extra-large tote, which could have fit a small child.

She pulled out a binder instead.

"*I. Have. News.*"

Each word cracked like a gunshot, jerking some heads.

I stared at her, mouth agape. Only this announcement could pique my interest more than wherever Bennifer had been honeymooning.

"What is that thing?" I hinged forward, closing the magazine as my technician arrived to start on my toes.

Peyton clutched the black three-ring beast to her chest. I saw that it was stacked full of papers, separated by colored dividers.

A big case?

A workout plan?

No—of course: my new life plan. For a brief stint of time when she'd hated law school, Peyton had considered being a life coach, which honestly, she'd be great at. She had the honesty and the insight, the uncanny ability to read the room like a prophet. Occasionally this side dream resurfaced.

I'd take some life coaching right now.

"THIS!" Peyton proclaimed, so loudly that a few other ladies flitted their glances our way. She hushed her voice to a whisper. "*This*, right here, is our million-dollar case, Scotland Dolly Holiday."

Dolly.

It was my mom's name.

My face twisted into a question mark. "What are you talking about?"

"This is our Fairy-Tale Lawsuit," Peyton went on. "Meet your attorney, Peyton McKenzie, Esquire." She gave a curtsy.

I had to smile.

And she had to be teasing me.

"You're funny," I said, looking back to my magazine, feigning total disinterest and hiding my hurt.

I rested my feet on the cushion in front of me while my technician—*Sky,* said her nametag—smothered them in a towel.

This stung, if I was honest: Peyton's refusal to take me seriously. She didn't need to pour nail polish remover into my open wound.

Peyton climbed into her chair, dropping her bag but clutching the binder even more tightly. She shook her head, blue eyes dancing. She was not breaking my gaze. "I was wrong," she said, dipping her toes into the water. "I read your email—and I was up all night. *All night,* Scot. I don't pull all-nighters anymore, you know that; not even for my biggest cases. I need to look fresh in court. But I legitimately couldn't stop thinking about it."

My hands froze then on a spread of Prince Harry and Meghan Markle, another prime example of a real-life fairy tale not quite unfolding to plan.

My pulse raced a bit.

I really believed in this case.

I peered at Peyton and smacked my magazine shut. "Don't say this if you don't mean it."

"I wouldn't."

"You're serious?"

"Dead."

Peyton splayed open the binder on top of her thighs, as her own artist, *Lily*, wheeled up to pamper her feet.

"First of all, I'm impressed." She cut a look at me. "Your research yielded tons of promise. These McDonald's cases? I mean, no offense, they're *ridiculous*—but the plaintiffs *won*. That was something. It got me thinking, and then seriously considering your claims."

"I'm okay with being ridiculous." Weren't Kingston movies, too, ridiculous? Of course, they were.

I felt myself settling into the whole notion of *ridiculousness* quite nicely, in fact. I could straighten my battle-worn crown and beat Kingston at their own war.

"You want them cut down?" Sky chimed from below me. Peyton looked down at my toenails and clasped her hand over her mouth. Her eyes were saucers of horror.

"Yes—I'm so sorry," I said sheepishly. "Please cut them down."

"*Geez*, Scot, when did you last have a pedicure?" The sliver of pink at the edge of my toe's tips confirmed that it had been months.

Since the day of our rehearsal dinner, if we were keeping track.

"I've been a little preoccupied." I shrank, my face reddening. "I'm here now, aren't I?"

"Bend and snap," she quipped, and we smiled. It was our second-favorite scene from *Legally Blonde,* ranked only behind the final courtroom scene.

"*Anyway,*" she continued, flipping to a yellow divider tab. "You're onto something with the NIED claim: Negligent Infliction of Emotional Distress. In some states, the burden of proof is insane for this—and you have to show physical damages."

I glanced down in slow motion, as if scanning my body for tangible harm. If only you could do an X-ray of the human heart. Surely it would show bruising. Probably in my stomach, too. Definitely my chest. I was weaker than I'd been in a while—but feeling suddenly stronger after my morning run and the glow of Peyton's belief in me.

"In California, though," she continued, "You do *not* need to show physical harm. We can claim *mental* or *psychological* pain caused by the harmful or unlawfully inflicted damage."

I squinted. "English, please?"

"We can claim things like depression, anxiety, insomnia, fear."

Check, check, check, check.

"We may need medical proof," she explained, "but that could easily be your therapist or a doctor testifying in court. Other witnesses won't be a problem. Family and friends can totally testify to recent changes in your behavior, mood, anything unusual. I mean, thankfully, you had, like, a thousand wedding guests to witness that hot debacle."

I rolled my eyes, recalling the trauma. "Thank you. So much. For reminding me."

"Welcome." She didn't look up. "Not to mention your loss of wages, costs incurred, and general decline in your overall enjoyment of life. It's *so* sad."

"Are you trying to make me feel better, or?" Lawyer Peyton pulled no jabs, and I knew I'd have to get used to it.

"Sorry." She flinched slightly at Lily's rigorous filing. "I'm trying to see you with professionalism and objectivity."

Okay. I could take that. "And you think I have a case?"

"Can I get a longer massage, please?" Peyton asked sweetly, arching her neck. "Thank you so much. I'll pay extra." She turned back to me, and I wondered what Lily and Sky were making of our conversation. "Proving the obvious distress upon *you* and your life doesn't have me worried, Scot."

Again ... *thanks*? "*Okaaaaay*," I said, dragging the word out like taffy. "What's the challenge, then?"

"The biggest challenge," she explained, "will be proving the *extreme negligence* of Kingston. The global conglomerate, magical empire, media mogul—arguably the most beloved brand in the universe."

I chewed the inside of my cheek.

"Don't worry, Scot—I actually think we can do it." She flattened her hands on the notebook pages. "I spent all night brainstorming possible witnesses to prove just that: *extreme negligence*."

She continued, "On the plus side, everything they do is extreme. And as for the harm to you, if we make it to court—which is a big *if*—we just need to prove that the damage to you was *severe or extreme* enough that a reasonable person could not be expected to endure it."

I wormed this around in my mind.

Being left at the altar was certainly *extreme*, as was my

faith in Kingston. I could argue to the bone that the past few months—and many points in my life—were beyond what a reasonable person could be expected to deal with.

"Wow." I took a breath. "So you really ... think we can do this?" I paused. "You believe in me?"

"I believe in *us*, Scot," she corrected. "Plus, there's more. I don't think emotional distress is our only complaint here. I think it's best to go with an *everything-but-the-kitchen-sink* approach here. It's not always the smart move. It can be a sign of weakness, or lack of focus, sometimes. But for us? I think it's our game plan."

"So, I heard *sink,* but the rest just kind of swirled into dirty dishwasher—"

"Sorry, sorry." She flipped to the blue divider. "I think we might have a stronger case if we also sue Kingston for false advertising, which falls under product liability and failure to warn."

Failure to warn.

Bingo.

I perked up even more. "Now we're talking."

"Plus, that extends beyond just their movies, right? Their toys, their costumes, their books, good Lord." She adjusted her sunglasses, still perched on top of her head. "I think it would be extremely difficult to gain any traction with *intentional* infliction of emotional distress—but I think it's worth including."

"You're going to keep translating for me, right?"

She pursed her lips. "It would mean Kingston *intended* to harm you. They set out to get you, maliciously, abominably, and outrageously. Like, if Kingston executives were gathering in boardrooms devising schemes to mess with people's well-being. Specifically, your well-being, your health, your livelihood."

"They could be," I pointed out. "Haven't you heard about the social media masterminds, preying on our anxieties? Like sending diet ads to girls with a history of eating disorders?"

She gripped her throat, miming a gag. "That is a story for another day. Do not get me started on Zuckerberg."

"Fine," I agreed. "Let's throw intentionality into the sink, then."

"Yes. Good!"

As Peyton flipped through her notebook, my heart burst with pride for her. For myself. She was such a fantastic friend.

But then, I also had to voice the concern now prickling the back of my neck.

"P."

"Yes?"

"How on earth are you going to find time for this?" I tried to relax as Sky kneaded my calves. "You were just saying how busy you are. Can you really represent me? Take this on? I'm well-aware of how nuts it all sounds."

"I am 100 percent willing." She signed breathily. "Under one condition."

"Anything."

"I am busy at work. Busier than I've ever been. I've been taking Sundays as a slower workday, to sustain the outer shreds of my sanity. But I was thinking, since we did just add a new paralegal, I could give my Sundays to you, and this case, for a while."

I clapped and squealed, like a twelve-year-old girl at a Harry Styles concert. Heck. Like twenty-eight-year-old me at a Harry Styles concert. "What about your firm, though?" I asked, remembering her hesitations. "Your reputation?"

She shrugged. "What would Elle Woods do?" Her eyes glinted. "And whoever made a difference without taking a risk? Not Wade Kingston, I'll tell you that much. Plus, I think some of my female colleagues will love it. As long as it doesn't take away from my work."

"I can never repay you. Or thank you enough."

"I'm sure you'll find a way." She spread her toes, ready for hot pink polish. "There's one more thing," she continued. "You've always been smarter than me, Scot, and you don't have a job—until now. *Right now*. This is your new job. This is your life. Get ready. The work involved is going to make dental school look easy." She handed the binder to me. "I have a copy at home. All yours."

Dang, it was heavy.

"So, what next?" I asked, ignoring the implication that her profession was harder than mine.

"Next, I'll put the claim together and file it with the court."

"That sounds—easy enough?"

"It's simple, but not easy. But I can get it done soon, within a week or two."

Awesome. "And then?"

"Then, we wait. Kingston has a chance to respond, and based on their answer, the judge decides if we have a case."

She crossed her arms, leaning back into the kneads and chops of her massage chair. She rolled her head toward me. "And if we do—have a case—we start preparing for trial. Unless, of course, they offer us a settlement we can't refuse. And we can go buy the private island we've always dreamed about."

"Thank you, P.," I said throatily, my voice catching with gratitude.

"In the meantime—keep going with all that research," she instructed, waving toward the binder on my knees. "You're incredible at it. Keep building our case. Find every example, story, argument you can possibly think of. The ways Kingston built up your dreams and shattered you. The way the company's princes ruined your life."

Princes.

Prince Charles.

My mouth curled up at the memory of him dipping to help me. The length of his arms, the edges of his handsome face. I'd been a sucker for scruff through my twenties, but his smooth, angled features had weakened my knees and left me with scrapes to prove it.

I flipped up my palms self-consciously, touching the burns from my fall, already beginning to fade.

Still, there was some *physical damage* for you.

I thought of telling Peyton about the white-hatted hottie, but abruptly shook off the thought.

Not now.

It suddenly felt unimportant. Men could officially take the back seat, for as long as I could foresee.

Peyton and Scottie.

Scottie and Peyton.

We had a dragon to slay.

And we didn't need a prince.

...

Chapter Eight

SCOTTIE

Seven days later, we stood in the grand entrance plaza to Kingston Court. I was admittedly awestruck, my soles fixed to the ground like sticky churro fingers. My thoughts floated back to my many trips here during childhood, as a plucky but lonely young girl, then later, as a brainy but totally boy-crazy teen.

I remembered it with glass-slipper clarity. The royal whimsy, the frontier grit, the smells of buttery popcorn, waffle cones, and salty water rides. Grand Street's pastel-shuttered storefronts. Every elegant princess curtsy and life-sized furry-animal wave. The characters all seemed to know me, as I knew them.

Kingston Court was a community where *everybody* belonged, a place as provincial as it was powerful.

It was America. It was a dream. No one could argue that.

"How does it look exactly the same?" I whispered with a tight clasp on Peyton's elbow. "Not a single flower has changed."

"I know, right?" she said distractedly. She lifted her phone and pressed record in her dictation app, dropping her voice an octave. "*The Grand Street Train Station is impeccable and the same: classic brick, clock tower, vintage Kingston Court sign. The giant flower bed is also pristine. It's still a portrait of Rickey Rat's face—*" She took a step closer. "*—made of violas and pansies.*"

"Are you going to do that all day?" I adjusted the Rickey ears on top of my head. "*Counselor,*" I added, to clarify how thankful I was. "And are you sure we need to wear these, by the way?" Despite the picturesque setting, I was already sensing a headache.

I had no idea what adults wore to Kingston Court—especially without any kids—so I scoured the Instagram hashtags, of which there was no short supply. #KingstonFashion, #KingstonKuties, and #KingstonCourtOutfits got the most action. Turned out there were ample ways you could go with this, but no matter what, no one would judge you. Kingston Court was the land where anything goes—and where everything else is left at the entry turnstiles.

> *From this point, you leave behind the troubles of now, entering the realm of glittering magic and human imagination—where the wistfulness of yesteryear reaches toward the possibility of tomorrow.*
>
> *Today, you are here, and here, you are royalty.*
>
> *Everything is a fantasy.*
>
> *All is but a dream.*
>
> *Welcome to Kingston Court.*

While I read the plaque for the eight hundredth time in my twenty-eight years, my chest tightened with juvenile emotion.

I realized I had it memorized.

As for my outfit, I went for a plain white T-shirt, loose jeans, high-tops, and a black leather mini backpack. And, of course—per Peyton's insistence—rat ears bedazzled in black-and-red sequins. These headbands were all the rage, evidently. I felt kind of chic, I supposed. For a Kingston adult.

Interestingly, millennial moms were setting the tone for Kingston Court fashion—which made sense, the more I thought about it. They had the kids, and therefore the best reason to hold passes, visit constantly, and build up a Kingston wardrobe.

Designer Rickey and Remi Rat T-shirt and shorts? On point. Overalls and a Kingston baseball cap? Nice, ladies. Want to dress up as a character? That might be slightly more uncool, but you do you, boo!

Come as you are.

This was the Kingston ethos.

"I haven't been here in twenty years," Peyton said. "I want to wrap my mind around the whole Kingston phenomenon as we build our case." She reached up to adjust her own ears, rose gold glittering in the sun. "And, yes," she continued, "the ears are a *must*. All the cool Kingston girls wear them, and we need to blend in. We cannot look like the enemy."

"We're not the enemy *yet*," I amended, adjusting my backpack straps. Peyton had filed our lawsuit on Friday, and now we awaited our fate. "Want to get a picture?" I asked eagerly. "We can frame it next to the one of us on my tenth birthday. You know, when we're millionaires after the lawsuit."

We glanced toward the winding line for the world-famous photo op. The flower bed, the train tracks, *we're here!*

There was a Kingston photographer, if you fancied it, or you could try a stranger.

Peyton scrunched her nose. "A selfie is fine, don't you think?"

I nodded. *I guess.* "I brought my selfie stick! Too much?"

"You didn't."

My shoulders sagged by a fraction. "A regular selfie is fine."

Peyton lassoed me into a side hug and lengthened her other arm. "One, two, *weeee love Kingston*!"

I saw immediately that the photo was frameable; no one could guess we were insiders planning a coup. Wide grins, themed garb, cheeks pressed together like sisters. We looked every bit the genuine fans we embodied. No one would suspect our wizard's brew of accusations.

"The walking tour starts in front of the fire station." Peyton flipped to her Apple watch. "We have fifteen minutes to grab a coffee or use the restroom."

"I'm good on the bathroom. Starbucks?"

"*Gosh,* yes," Peyton sighed. "Do I look tired? I was up way too late again."

"As if I could tell under those sunglasses." I bared my teeth with teasing affection, referring to her gargantuan frames. Gucci, today. Black, always. "But you should stop that. We need you sharp. Sleeping Beauty-level rested."

"I know, I know." She batted a hand. "I need to use the ladies' room. Venti pumpkin spice latte. Extra whip. I'm earning it."

"Yes, you are. On me, obvs. See you in front of the station."

I sauntered down Grand Street with a set of new senses for every scrupulous detail. My research was slowly piling as high as Snowy Mountain.

Speaking of which, Snowy Mountain, I'd learned, the well-known bobsled rollercoaster, held a half-basketball-court in its peak, where employees took breaks to dribble around. Like most things in the park, the towering peak that seemed to hail from a magical, mercurial land had actually been inspired by something real: the iconic Snowy Mountains in Austria.

I'd learned also that the fairy-tale castle at Kingston Court's center—anchoring the five-hundred acres—was *Sleeping Beauty's* castle, not Cinderella's. I'd forever assumed the opposite. The artifact of European wonder—with its pinks, golds, and blues ranging from cobalt to cornflower—was inspired by the real-life Neuschwanstein Castle in Germany. Romanesque Revival, flamboyant, iconic.

Not unlike Wade Kingston himself.

The internet was light on current information about Mr. Kingston, whom no one had seen in over two decades. I'd scoured and re-scoured. After beating the unlikely odds of a major stroke, Wade Kingston had dropped off the grid at age sixty-five. Permanently and untraceably, like a fugitive.

It was all I could find.

He was gone.

But to where?

His whereabouts were everyone's guess—everyone on the planet. Entire blogs were devoted to theories on Wade Kingston's disappearance, forever shrouded in a bit of dark magic and never-ending speculation:

- » *Where's Wade? 15 Lookalikes Spotted Around the Globe*
- » *Vanity Fair's Top Ten Most Influential People of the Information Age: Why Wade Kingston Remains #1*
- » *Wade Kingston's Granddaughter Speaks Out*

Sadly, it was never the granddaughter, nor the cousin, nor the self-proclaimed high school classmate from suburban Chicago. It was the crook, out for cash, appealing to the tabloid's eternal and unabating desperation for information on Wade. Liars and fakes, all the time.

The shocking loss of America's greatest media hero, of course, had only added to the already mythical popularity of the company.

I secretly wondered if he'd been living all along inside one of the Kingston Court castle towers, like Rapunzel. Mythical royalty, captive—enslaved by his own obsession. The pressure of his own creation became too much, the stress nearly killing him.

Yet still, he could not bear to part from its grounds.

I squinted from the emerald-green door of Starbucks, my gaze on the castle beyond—half hoping for a face in a window.

There was, of course, no face.

Okay, Scottie.

It was of no consequence to my case, anyway.

And yet.

I not-so-secretly hoped our four-hour walking tour might shine some light onto one of the greatest celebrity question marks of our day.

I entered the comforts of Starbucks: signature roasts and happening energy. This one also did justice to Kingston's charm. Mahogany-framed character sketches. Pink rosebuds speckled on yellow wallpaper. Folksy chalkboards with the typical menu items. Light oak rails filed customers toward the baristas with an ornately carved Pinocchio look.

It was adorable.

But I just needed two pumpkin spice lattes.

And this line was long.

Steadily moving, though. This location, I noticed, was more heftily staffed than Nordstrom at Christmastime. Only these baristas wore buttercream-colored, pioneer-looking Kingston uniforms.

I texted Peyton.

> Bit of a line ... I'll hurry!

Line here too. NP. TY btw!

I flicked at my phone, absently tapping to the Kingston app, curious about the day's crowd index. *Average Crowds*. Not bad. Only Galaxy Mountain was closed for refurbishment, and it always gave me a migraine anyway.

My gaze drifted up to the menu—at least, my gaze *tried* to do that before snagging sharply on something.

On someone.

On someone extremely tall and disarmingly good-looking—

At least from this faraway, side angle.

I laughed then, audibly, and hysterically.

I stopped quickly, though, when the woman in front of me shielded her small children, dressed as Wendy and Peter Pan. I couldn't say that I blamed her. I was here, at Kingston, a full-grown adult, *in Rickey ears*, all alone and stifling a maniacal giggle.

But—wait.

No.

No way.

There was no universe in which this could possibly, remotely, in ten-trillion galaxies far, far away be—

Charles?

FROM RUNNING CLUB?

Was that him, in a slim black suit, with a younger, blonde, punk-pixie type in a houndstooth pencil skirt and red pumps? I liked her style—it was very *professional-meets-Queen-of-Hearts*, but—

My breath caught as he rotated his gaze to examine the pastries, or likely the fruit, based on the rippling arms I remembered in vivid convenience ...

Oh. My. Word.

It was him.

The left-side dimple and angled jaw.

Brown eyes and lashes so thick and dark that they looked Latissed.

I would have been more surprised to see Wade Kingston himself.

But there he was.

Prince Charles from running club.

I was 98 percent sure.

My instincts surprised me then, as I held up my phone to sneak a picture of him by way of a pretend selfie. I could snap it now and compare it later to my memory of him—just to fill in that pesky 2 percent doubt.

As I outstretched my hand for the shot, the mom in front of me seemed to have a surge of courage—or terror.

"Do you want me to take it for you?" she offered. She was middle-aged, with a shock of red hair, a black Kingston T-shirt and these two cute kids, her clones. Their blue eyes were round as UFOs, but I was the obvious alien.

I dropped my hand self-consciously. *Don't mind me!* Just the weird lady snapping selfies right here, all alone. Never mind the whole day ahead with magical backdrops, landmarks, and characters. *Starbucks is where it's at.*

I typically appreciated it when people occasionally offered to take a picture for me, but *why now?* Why did no one ever offer to take the picture when you really needed it, but instead put you on the spot with a side of shame when you admittedly just wanted the selfie?

I ducked then, low, hidden conveniently by a display of Kingston Court mugs that stood tall between me and Charles. Not as tall as him, but—it would do. I wasn't helping my case for normalcy but felt suddenly worried about being seen.

"Oh, that's so sweet," I said quietly to the woman. "But the selfie is fine! Ha! Thank you!"

I lifted my arm again, and the mom-of-two turned back

around, *finally*, so I could zoom into Charles in peace.

Thankfully there was no one behind me.

My heart galloped as I pressed my fingertips to my phone screen, pinching and un-pinching until I had the killer shot.

Snap.

Perfection.

The picture—and Charles' profile.

Yum.

I sprinted out of that Starbucks. Without any lattes but with this picture, which felt like important evidence.

Of what, I wasn't sure.

It didn't matter.

I'd felt the urge to capture it—and I did.

As the balls of my feet bounded down the cobblestone street, I imagined the redheaded mom phoning Kingston security.

...

I was winded by the time I reached Peyton in front of the fire station. She waited, foot tapping, with a few other Kingston fans. Our guide had not yet arrived.

I bent over, heaving.

Peyton lifted her eyebrows, more in surprise than concern. She patted my back. "Are you—okay there, Scot?" She shot furtive glances around then, hushing her voice. "Oh my gosh, are you running from someone? *Do you think someone knows why we're here?* Court records are public. It *is* possible—"

I waved my hand. "No, no. I just—encountered the weirdest coincidence of all time. I saw someone I met the other day. And

I don't even know why, but I ran. Just—sprinted away."

"Someone you met the other day," she repeated, "But more importantly," she continued, "You met a human? Aww, Scot! Given your recent state, I'm actually, like, so proud—"

"A guy," I interrupted. "A cute guy. I guess."

I spit out the running club story as fast as I could, so I could get on to the Starbucks sighting.

"W-w-*wait*." Peyton planted her fists on her hips. "This happened a *week ago* and you didn't tell me? He gave you his *shoelace*? Stop. That is maybe the cutest thing I've ever heard. I've dated a *lot* of guys—and none of them has *ever* done something that nice for me."

"That's ... kind of sad, P."

"Yeah, well, it's not like I kept them around." She flipped her sunny-blonde hair. "Anyway, let me see the pic! Gosh, you would be a good lawyer. Or private detective. If you're over the dentist thing."

"I would've told you about him, but it didn't seem like a big deal." I presented my phone with a flourish. "This is him. Who wears a suit to Kingston Court? But it was *definitely* him. I'm—almost 100 percent sure."

Peyton cocked her head. "Wait—this guy? Oh. Wow. Oh—*wow*. Is he insanely tall or is young Gwen Stefani next to him just super short?"

"He's super tall," I confirmed. "Six five maybe?"

"Well—I approve," she purred. "Mommy *likey*."

"You're not a mom." I rolled my eyes. "It's so weird when you say that."

She ignored me. "He looks *delicious*. Like—if Ben Affleck and Cody Rigsby had a baby ... it would *totally* be this guy. At least from this angle. What's his name again?"

"Charles. Who's ... Cody Rigspee?"

"*Rigsby*. I've told you before, he's my Peloton boyfriend. The best instructor. He is hysterical and just *beyond* hot. Unfortunately, he doesn't like girls, but—whatever. It's fine. He's still a sizzling plate of fajitas at Chili's on a Friday night—"

I looked at her blankly, expecting actual drool to drop from her mouth.

"His words, not mine." She snapped back to earth, clearing her throat. "*Anyway*." She stared again at the photo, my random evidence of nothing at all, when I saw something flash on her face.

Recollection, concern, or both.

"Wait a second," she said, lifting the phone. "I think I know this guy."

"What? Are you serious?"

"Yes. He is *so* familiar. But ... " She pressed the center of her forehead as if willing a memory forth. "I can't place it. I hate when this happens. My brain is like—too full. It's annoying. But I'm not getting a good vibe."

"Come on," I scoffed. Peyton was wildly smart, but she wasn't a psychic. "You can't be serious."

"No! I think—I might know him from U of A. And I'm feeling like he was a player. Maybe even a baseball player?"

"Stop."

She squinted harder and sighed, passing my phone back just

as our guide showed up in his suspenders and newsboy cap. He wore round, black-rim spectacles and a broad grin. He hardly looked old enough to have facial hair, so he didn't. His bare cheeks were rosy and plump.

"Good morning, everyone!" our new leader belted with gusto. "I'm Gus, and I'll be your walking tour guide through Kingston Court today. We're waiting for a couple more, so chat amongst yourselves for another few minutes, and then we'll get this fun parade *started*!"

"I doubt you know him," I hissed at Peyton.

She shrugged. "Maybe, maybe not. Text me the pic. I'll check my yearbook. I do feel like I'd recall the name *Charles*. And, I don't recall it. Now," she whispered, "are you ready for today? We need to pay close attention. *Soak it in*. Take notes in your phone. Remember how this place formed your psyche as a young, fragile girl. It cemented your inability to separate fact from fantasy. To you—this was real. Your undelivered promise of happiness."

I nodded, forcing myself to squeeze Charles' profile out of my mind like the last taste of toothpaste from your favorite tube.

I wouldn't mind tasting that smile.

Where did that come from?

What was my problem?

No princes were allowed in my life anymore.

I shook out my palms and rubbed them onto my jeans.

It was game time.

I needed lightsaber focus.

As the clock struck nine, Gus leapt into an animated,

impressive performance he had obviously perfected over countless tours. I'd heard before that many Kingston employees had dreams of the theater stage, and Gus fit the profile nicely. I could easily see him on Broadway or belting out a ballad. It wasn't hard to switch my mental channel to his tales of Kingston, starting here at the fire station.

"Wade's apartment was right up there." He pointed skyward to a window under a maroon awning. "He always worked with his desk light on—so after his disappearance, the company agreed to never turn it off. We've kept it on, ever since, twenty-four hours a day. We consider it a kind of vigil for him. You'll never see it off."

I could barely make out a small Victorian lantern, glowing up in the glass.

Eerie. I shivered. Maybe Wade *was* still in there. *Had anyone ever checked?*

"Wade split his time between here and LA, so he and his wife, Marian, needed a place to sleep," Gus continued, brightening in our rapt attention. "On his mornings here, legend has it that he would get up hours before the park opened and come down in his bathrobe and slippers. He'd walk down Grand Street to fetch some fresh-squeezed orange juice and a newspaper."

I smiled—the whole group did—picturing the legend padding down empty Grand Street in the twinkly glow of morning light, before thousands would flood the universe that he built for them. Where the world was small, and children were equals, where there were no rules, to-do lists, or broken hearts. Where—whether we realized it or not—at the hands of Wade, our collective consciousness was being formed into something solid as ice, but just as breakable, unable to withstand heat.

A place where a bubble was a beautiful thing to behold.

Until, of course, it burst.

My notes filled quickly with observations, ideas, and memories as Gus led us through the park. Much had changed, but more had not.

In front of the castle, I saw Cinderella and throngs of girls waiting to meet her, each so sure they were about to meet a real princess. Sparkly gown, lacquered bun, diamond tiara, and all. Most of the girls had mothers with them, their camera phones poised, like me just a few moments ago. As excited as their giddy daughters.

Near the Storybook Cruise, I saw Princess Isla in her canary-yellow gown and remembered instantly the rounds of my ten-year-old eyes as I stared, transfixed, at her beauty. She was the only princess I cared about meeting that day. She looked so much like my mom. Seeing Isla had refilled the cracks of memory that were beginning to gape—the places that held my mom's pretty features and empty promises.

Tour de Gus was full, too, of odd facts and Kingston trivia. Of how the click-clacking horses wore special shoes that made their steps even louder. How the park pumped artificial smells into the air with machines called *scentilizers*: sweet or savory, flowers or dust, cake or gunpowder, depending on where you stood. This served to elicit different emotions and maximize the experience.

The morning whizzed by, and we returned to the fire station

with full minds (history, insight) and full bellies (pretzels, lemonade).

As the group dissipated, Peyton and I hung around. I knew instinctively that she wanted to ask Gus the same question I did. We edged closer to our little newsie until no one else was in earshot.

"Listen, Gus," Peyton gushed, lifting her sunglasses so she could wear him down with her baby blues. "That was an *incredible* tour. We learned *so* much. We have just one more question."

"Anything at all," he said, shoving his hands in his pockets.

Peyton took one step nearer still, chomping her cinnamon gum. "You seem like a *real* Kingston expert. The realest we've ever met. Right, Scottie?"

I nodded dutifully, and Gus blushed under his glasses. He was Gunther from *Friends* in Rachel's glow.

"Thank you," he said. "I'm a real Kingston fan, that's for sure."

"So, as a *real, true* fan," Peyton continued, "and not as a Kingston employee, but just as a new, you know, new *friend* of ours: Why don't you tell us where you think Wade Kingston is?"

This was not his first dance, and it showed. His smile was plastic, rehearsed. "Wade Kingston," he said, "is everywhere! You just have to be paying attention."

He gave a robotic bow.

This wasn't cutting it for my lawyer.

"Come on," Peyton begged. "Surely you have to know *something*. This is your work, your life! Surely you have your own—*personal theory*, Gus."

His chest puffed at the sound of his name. "Well, of course I do," he confirmed. "But I am not at liberty to *divulge this information* to park guests."

"Gus," she pressed, rummaging into her Louis Vuitton crossbody. "Come on."

I watched as she slyly fished out a one-hundred-dollar bill and snapped it, tantalizingly, before folding it neatly and reaching to shake his hand.

Startled, Gus looked down, the debate on his young face endearing and clear. Swiftly surrender came. Kingston was noble, but cash was still king.

Gus shoved the bill into his pocket, leaning into us.

"*Fine*," he said, looking both ways before speaking. "I'm in an employee underground fan club that meets every month to share our secrets and theories. *King's Choir*, we call ourselves." He buoyed with pride. "And … we collectively have reason to believe that Wade is living at the real Neuschwanstein Castle in Germany—the one that inspired the castle palace here." He tipped his head toward the palace. "Wade was reportedly spotted around Europe many times in the early 2000s—at fairs and festivals, museums, in costume. But never after 2010—"

"The year the castle was closed to the public after one hundred years of tours," I finished.

Peyton shot me a look. They both looked impressed. I'd been doing my research.

"Exactly," Gus said. "No one has been allowed on the premises since then, and records show the ownership changed hands. He's done an excellent job of clearing his name from any documents. But—we believe he's living there, more involved with the company than anyone knows, except for the very top level of executive leadership."

Peyton folded her arms in triumph. "So you're saying he's still alive. Or at least … possibly so. Even likely so."

Gus nodded. "Oh, definitely. He's eighty-five now, but supposedly in fantastic health. The stroke really shook him up. Rearranged his priorities. He walks daily. Practices yoga. Some even say he found God."

Gus pulled back then, snapped his suspenders, and looked at the clock tower about to chime noon above the train station. "Now, if you'll excuse me, ladies—I've already said too much. I must go prepare for my next tour."

He tipped his hat, and we thanked him.

"I knew it," Peyton said, clapping. "Of course, *Wade Kingston's alive*! And we are going to find him."

"You're insane."

"And *you're* the one who lured me into this web of insanity. You want to win, don't you? Can you imagine calling Wade to the witness stand? It would be the courtroom game play of all courtroom game plays to come before it. I could eviscerate him. Shock the world. Expose the company for its origins—and the reasons that drove Wade away."

"First of all, P., of course I want to win. Secondly, that's some real confidence, even for you. And lastly—it's one thing to win this little lawsuit. It's another thing *entirely* to track down the Most Wanted Man in the Universe."

"I hate to tell you this, Scot." Peyton arched a brow. "But if we have a case, your suit is *not* going to be little. Not if I have anything to say about it."

I loved her certainty, but it filled me with nerves.

What might a big case do to me?

I shivered in the fall chill, eager to change the subject. "If you find Wade Kingston," I replied, "I will treat you to Starbucks for the rest of your life. But like, for real next time. No more running from hot enchiladas in suits."

"*Fajitas*," she corrected, her lips pulling into a smile. "Promise?"

"Promise."

For the rest of the afternoon, we let ourselves slip into kid mode, forgetting about the lawsuit, our research, my broken engagement, her workload.

We rode the fastest rides with our hands erect, let cotton candy melt in our mouths, waited in line for a picture with Sleeping Beauty.

We didn't chase the exit till nightfall.

As we did, tree lights glimmering, horse-drawn carriages clopping, salted caramel ice cream dripping onto our tongues, I glanced back again at the castle, once more eyeing the tallest tower with its arched window, thinking of Wade.

And of the *other* guy who got away today.

Okay, fine: of the other guy from whom I'd sprinted away as fast as I could.

Who was he, anyway?

Magically, I realized, I was not thinking of Trey.

...

Chapter Nine

HARRISON

I tapped three times on Cooper Hollister's office door, forever a gateway to nothing interesting and everything I didn't love about working at Kingston.

In theory, I enjoyed my job, on purpose and principle. But my direct boss seemed fixed, as ever, on his mission to make me miserable. While my work-life balance was awesome, the actual tasks lately had become more tedious than counting Cooper's passive aggressive insults.

I pushed his door open. Cooper didn't look up. The perpetual mess on his desk stressed me out and was yet another reason I stayed away from him. But more than anything, it was his energy.

Tan mediocrity at its finest.

That was his essence. Leathery skin and flat, beady eyes. Cartons of takeout filling the trashcans. Legal files piled like leaves instead of primly lined in their drawers. He seemed keenly driven toward *average*, if not unhappy. I didn't want to be cruel; it was just the plain truth.

I projected a deep *ahem*. "You wanted to see me?"

Past the mess, the room wasn't hideous. One large window loomed behind Cooper's back with a big view of Kingston Court, the loops of Rickey Rat Rollercoaster in panorama. On the grounds below, park guests marched like ants, determined to get their daily ticket's worth of fulfillment.

I loved Kingston Court, and even got to pop over for occasional lunch breaks and legal field trips. Park litigation technically fell to a team of its own, but Kingston Court was sued at least once a week. The team could never keep up with the caseload, so the work spilled into our group sometimes, and I didn't mind. We were typically asked to scan the scene of a "crime." Armed with our legal pads, Erin and I would go check out the slippery curb or the handsy duck or the trashcan that toppled "randomly" onto a lady.

Right.

There was also the time an ice sculpture injured a woman, and the man who claimed to tumble accidentally from one of the gondolas strung in the sky. Both of those cases were ages ago, the gondolas long since removed, but they lingered as reminders that Kingston Court had to stay lawyered up.

I was always happy to help. It felt like a perk of the job, honestly.

Plus, Kingston Court had a Starbucks.

Cooper graced me finally, now, with a cursory glance. "Come in, Hayes. Have a seat." His golden hair was plastered into its usual hefty side part. He seemed focused on something specific, which was unlike him. Typically, he was all over the place—his grimy fingerprints everywhere and nowhere at once—but the papers in front of him had locked his attention.

As I stooped into one of the pine chairs facing his desk, he sucked in a breath, studying me.

"So," Cooper started, voice gruff. "I hear you want more—*responsibility*. Around here." He pursed his dry lips. "That you don't think I 'share the workload' as well as I could." His air quotes reaffirmed that he wasn't thrilled with me, as if I couldn't tell from his tone. "You think that—shall we say—you could do my job better than I do."

I didn't let myself flinch.

Yes, yes, and yes.

It was all true, I reminded myself.

Don't let him get to you.

And *thanks*, Abel Iverson. Seamless. Smooth. I tried not to be disappointed. Yes, this was a *foolproof* way to foster team unity and boost my direct supervisor's faith in me. Stir up the pot and throw in some fire for fun.

I waited a beat.

"I think you're amazing at your job," I lied, keeping my voice even. "But—yes, Cooper. I do believe you could trust me with more hands-on work. I thought it was time to express myself when my annual review asked me"—I mimed quotes of my own—"*if there was anything I would like to express to my direct or indirect supervisor about my current position here at the Kingston Company.*"

Cooper pulled on his chin, the silence heavy between us.

"Fine, then," he said, stiffening in his seat. "That's what I thought. Just wanted to confirm."

That couldn't be all.

No fight? No more digs?

He dragged me here to *confirm?*

No way.

I waited.

And waited some more.

"And?" I leaned back, crossing my ankles.

"Well ... I suppose there is something more." Cooper thumped his fists on the desk in a steadily building drumroll. "The thing is, Hayes—I have a case for you."

"A ... *case*?" I echoed. "A case." It was not growing more believable with each repetition.

I'd never had my own case before. Not here, not ever.

I watched him shuffle through the papers in front of him, before slipping them into a folder. Nodding, he handed it to me. "Yes, Hayes. A *case*," he confirmed. "You're familiar with the word?"

I considered this. The possibility of a case; not his snark. I felt equal parts thrilled at the prospect and terrified by the catch—because clearly, there had to be one.

I flipped through the folder of evidence, looking for skeletons. It was, after all, October. "Familiar, sir."

"Great then! So—here's the deal." The edges of his mouth curved up diabolically. "Some broad is suing the Kingston Company for breaking her heart. And I thought—what better *way* to give Hayes more *opportunity* than with a *special* lawsuit like this?" I could tell he'd been waiting to spill this, like ink from his sticky black tentacles.

Of course.

He was throwing a frivolous suit in my lap as payback for wanting more.

This was low, even for Cooper, but what should I have expected?

Don't. Let. Him. Get. To. You.

I cracked my knuckles as loudly as they would pop. I'd been waiting for this—for any chance to exercise my capabilities—and I would rise to the challenge. I would not show him my hand. I would not reveal my high-pitched annoyance that this mean clown juggled my fate.

"Wow, that's—really *something*." I thought I'd heard every desperate claim in the book, but this seemed a fresh hell entirely. "How did the company ... do that, exactly? Break her heart?"

"Well, the plaintiff's question would be: how *didn't* we break her heart?" Cooper grinned evilly, loving this. "We made her believe in fairy tales, of course! We built her dreams up—and left them to die. Naturally, she has a sob story." He gestured to the folder of documents, now my responsibility. "She claims Kingston is liable for false advertising because our films, products, and characters have *exceedingly and repeatedly* fallen short of our company's promise to her—which was, of course, happily ever after."

"You can't be serious."

"I am very serious."

"And we need to respond?"

"Yes, but—there's no *we* here," Cooper corrected. "You and Erin. I won't have anything to do with this." He laced his fingers comfortably around his red neck. "If the case goes to court, outside counsel will come in—but we both know the chances of that are slimmer than your hipster tie, Hayes."

I swallowed.

Irritation swelled in my chest, and I pulled on my tie. I *loved* this tie, a Christmas gift from my grandmother. Black and red stripes, *Rickey Rat's colors*, she'd effused with what remained of her wispy voice. She was born the same year as Wade Kingston. I'd only met her ten years ago, after my injury, when I felt the first pangs of wanting to track down my blood relatives. A bifurcation in your life plan will do that. The fact that she shared my Kingston love was sweet reassurance that she was family.

I flung open the folder, and sure enough, the plaintiff was suing us for everything Cooper had flippantly rattled off. It was a real *fairy tale* of a lawsuit, all right. Just as tall and fantastical. This whole thing was an insult to my intelligence and my time.

There was no way it had legs.

It didn't even have toes.

I'd file our demurrer, rebuffing each claim, and we'd cleanse our limbs of the mess. We'd douse the spark of a PR fire before it could even breathe.

I would handle it, crisply and capably, without so much as cracking my knuckles.

I cleared my throat, scanning the claims, surprised to see it had come from Cashion & Baker, one of the biggest law firms in Orange County. My eyes dropped to the name of the lawyer, Peyton McKenzie. Why did that sound familiar?

I then saw the name of the plaintiff: Scotland Dolly Holiday. Come on, now. Was that a real name? She was probably middle-aged and deeply single, warmed at night by her feral cats and collection of housekeeping magazines.

I cleared my throat. "No problem, boss," I said through my teeth. "I'll get going on this."

"Any questions? *Concerns?*" Cooper reached to the ceiling in an indolent stretch. I thought to myself that he'd make a great prototype for a Kingston villain in one of the newer cartoons with a corporate-world enemy: a second-rate lawyer meets aging Ken doll with a hefty splash of Mr. Scrooge.

Who put this man in charge?

"Nope." I glided out of my chair with a flash of my teeth, thankful to flee and exhale the frustration lodged painfully in my airway. "None whatsoever. Thank you, boss. It's a real *privilege* to finally have my own case."

Like heck it was.

I felt his black eyes burn holes in my back as I finally rolled mine to heaven.

...

Back in my stark-white, lackluster office, devoid of any windows to speak of, I skimmed through the myriad of Peyton McKenzies on Facebook.

I knew that name; *I just knew it.*

There were dozens of them, apparently, speckled all over the globe.

At long last, I landed on one with whom I shared twenty-seven connections.

She wore a black blazer and hot pink blouse, shiny blonde hair to her collarbone. Sapphire eyes and a heart-shaped face. Objectively pretty, but not my type. It was quite a professional headshot for a profile picture, but then again, people my age rarely used Facebook anymore. Many kept it only for business, so this made sense.

I clicked to enlarge the photo, staring, willing my memory to cough forth the information.

I scanned to her details, which were minimal, but all that I needed.

Boom:

Education: *University of Arizona*
Residence: *Irvine, California*
Work: *Cashion & Baker, Associate*

I gulped.

I would've been a senior at U of A when she was a freshman. I didn't know her well, but I knew her face partly because it was the face shared by nearly all of her Kappa Kappa Gamma sorority sisters.

Except for my ex-fiancée.

Maybe the only brunette in the house.

It was also possible to extremely likely that I'd seen Peyton around the political science building. I chose the major because it was easy to juggle with the demands of being an athlete—but Peyton had likely, apparently, been one of the students who was also prelaw and maybe double-majored in business.

Truthfully, and unfortunately, I wasn't very nice to Peyton—or to women in general—before I started dating Marissa in my last semester of senior year. Marissa was my only real girlfriend, ever. At least the only one to whom I'd ever given a title.

She was also my only ex-almost-wife.

If Peyton knew me in college—from the blurry parties, tailgate rackets, and athletic-center-to-Greek-system gossip hotline—chances were fair that she probably didn't like me very much. I wasn't proud of that person I was.

Arrogant, brash, and curt.

Insecure, lonely, and drunk.

Good for Peyton McKenzie, though. She was a lawyer for a top firm and hadn't aged a day from the eighteen-year-old freshman I blearily recollected.

She looked good. She seemed well.

I wondered if she'd stayed in touch with Marissa.

Regardless, the important thing now was that I could file my legal opponent into the appropriate mental box: Peyton McKenzie might remember me from another life, might think I was a jerk, might *still* think I was a jerk when I kicked her butt to the courthouse curb with my retort against her client's outlandish claims.

But suing Kingston for such a ridiculous reason?

Come on, now.

In a haste, I typed "Scotland Holiday" into the Facebook search bar, but only one appeared. She lived in Australia and looked maybe twelve.

Oh well.

As I should have suspected, my plaintiff was so antisocial that she didn't even do social media. I checked out of the browser and opened a brand-new document.

None of it mattered, anyway.

I spread open Cooper's folder once more.

These claims were doomed as a snowman in summer.

Even if they wished on a shooting star, I would not see these ladies in court.

...

Chapter Ten

SCOTTIE

"*Scottie!*" snapped a familiar voice. "Wake up, *now*."

Facedown, I clutched my pillow in a hug, groaning. I cracked opened an eye to assess whether I was dreaming. Nope.

Very much awake.

Peyton had cozied my desk chair up to my bedside, where she now double-fisted two coffee cups. "PSLs," she chimed. "Triple shots."

Morning poured in through the blinds, painting shards of sunshine on her high ballerina bun. She wore her round tortoiseshell glasses. We called them her Harry Potter frames.

"Thanks, H. P.," I grumbled, accepting the caffeine.

"Don't mention it."

I squinted.

Peyton's glasses meant only one thing. I peeled my other eye open.

Business.

"*Peyton?*" I dragged out the syllables in a scolding. "What are you doing here?"

"I'll give you a minute." She stood up tall in her pumps. "You're going to need it."

"It's not even Sunday," I whined, burrowing deeper into the covers.

"Well, you're about to see me a lot more frequently than just Sundays."

Huh?

She traversed the length of my room, back to my vanity, her voice and energy softening as she neared it. "You still have these pictures up?" She painted her fingers over our faces at prom.

I sipped my coffee. "You know my dad. The emo king. Plus, we're pretty adorable."

"You're not wrong. We're the cutest."

I wriggled into a sitting position, swigging more of the sweet, spicy latte while Peyton kept pacing the room.

She pivoted to face me again as I reached absently for my phone on the nightstand. "*NOOOOO!*" she shrieked in hysteria, at unreasonable volume and speed.

I startled, spilling some of the steamy brown liquid onto my favorite T-shirt, my softest one, *USF Dental School* in navy letters on cream-colored cotton.

Stretched like a blanket on top of me, Payton managed to yank my phone and toss it to the foot of my bed before I had one fraction of a chance to guess what the heck had just happened.

I stared at her blankly, befuddled, her face mere centimeters from mine. We were practically making out.

I knew my look said it all: *EXPLAIN YOURSELF, LADY.*

Peyton unpinned me and rolled off the mattress, reperching herself in the chair. I rubbed at my shirt's new stain, annoyed and disoriented.

I didn't even know what time it was.

I *believed* it was Thursday.

Peyton emitting a nervous cough. "Well, Scot," she began measuredly. "I have good news, and I have bad news. Which do you want first?"

Nerves bubbled up in my stomach.

News.

No matter the kind, it almost always meant change. And I had faced so many pivots lately. "Who let you in, anyway?" I glanced around cautiously.

"Your dad," she said. "Gosh, I love him. And I can't believe he never remarried. You know? He's just so handsome and good."

"If you say *Mommy Likey*, I'm going to dump this on you." I pointed threateningly at my beverage.

She stuck out her tongue. "Eww. Handsome in like ... a Dennis Quaid way, not in a Brad Pitt way."

"You will never be over Brad Pitt, will you? Can you believe he's, like, in the dad category now?"

"Nice try," she scolded. "You're not avoiding my news. Plus, Brad Pitt will always be Tyler Durden to me. So—do you want to smile or cry first? The choice is yours."

I exhaled. "Sounds like I'm about to do both."

"Let's smile first, then. Take one more sip. And a really deep breath."

I obliged, savoring the slurp of autumn and bracing myself.

I repositioned the pillow behind me, ensuring I had proper support for this.

I gulped one more breath and nodded.

Speak.

Peyton rolled back her shoulders, lifted her chin, and fiddled with the arm of her glasses. She clapped. "The plaintiff's claim has succeeded, Scot! I can't believe it."

I squinted and jiggled my cup. "No legalese until this is drained, please."

"Well, get used to it, Buttercup," she continued. "Because we have a case. *We are going to court*! They're taking our case, Scot! Can you even? The Kingston Company filed their objection and the judge—are you ready?—*denied it*. The judge didn't take every one of our claims, but"—she punched the air like a cheer captain—"we did it. We are suing Kingston for emotional distress and false advertising. Starring *Y-O-U*."

I brought a hand to my mouth as shock filled my throat.

"We did it?" I whispered, suspending my belief cautiously. I had to be sure I was undeniably, irreversibly, *unequivocally* not in a dream. "It's happening? They think—we have something? That we have actual *grounds* to sue them for what we claimed?"

Peyton nodded violently, grabbing my hands. "That's right. We're doing it, Scot. You and me."

Without warning, my memory floated back to the handful of times when my mom sat in that same seat, sun rising, warming me in her glow. Brighter than any shard of the morning, but never staying past noon.

I swallowed and shook off the ache, recalling that there was more news. "So … what's the bad news?"

Peyton rose and sidled to the end of my bed. "How do I put

this?" She scooped up my phone and tossed it gently onto my lap. The motion was firm; her eyes were soft. "You're kind of ... famous, Scot." She paused. "I'm right here as you take it in."

My heart jackhammered. I snatched the thing and pressed the side button. The screen glowed fiercely, blinding me with notifications.

Friends, people, everyone, had been, as they say, *giving me space* since the breakup. And even more since the move.

But. Here. They. Were. Now.

Here they were.

Finding, infiltrating, *exploding* my space to the heavens.

Everyone, it seemed, that I knew.

Bridesmaids, coworkers, acquaintances, aunts and cousins and numbers I didn't recognize. Thankfully had I closed all my social media accounts after the wedding, or the apps would've been flooding me too.

My vision blurred as I tapped through the texts:

OMG, are you okay?

Wow, Scottie, this is INSANE!!!

I wish I thought of this. Rooting for you!

How did they get a wedding picture? At least you look gorgeous!

I know you hate me, but I really think we should talk.

That last one, of course, was from Trey, but helpfully he included a link. It was very *him*, to include a link, I thought. Semi-thoughtful and predictably gentlemanlike, even as the devil himself. I clicked on the article and felt the headline churn in my gut:

» ***Young Woman Sues Kingston for Making Her Believe in Fairy Tales***

"No."

No, no, no.

I peered up at Peyton, whose eyes confirmed, very much, *yes*. The story had been leaked and splashed across the United States of America. Maybe even the world. I skimmed the article violently, prowling for details.

> Could the Kingston Company be liable for peddling a false promise of happily ever after? According to 28-year-old Scotland "Scottie" Holiday—left at the altar by her wealthy Bay Area groom—the media giant is purportedly guilty of this violation, and more.
>
> California-based Holiday has filed a lawsuit claiming Kingston has caused her "expensive and irreparable" damages through its "films, characters, plots, products, and other entities"—specifically with their false advertising of "perfect" endings and "unrealistic and incomprehensibly shallow" representations of romantic relationships.

> In the lawsuit, filed Oct. 15 with the Superior Court of Orange County, Holiday cites more than 30 examples of harmful material in Kingston productions. She is requesting $5 million in reparations for "substantial" financial losses and "unquantifiable" personal injury. She is presently taking time off from her work as a pediatric dentist.

I squirrelled back into the cave of my covers, reeling. I loved how they tacked on that I was a dentist, an afterthought, barely an asterisk, with an emphasis on my time off. Of course, an educated, sane, rational woman would never dream of suing the almighty Kingston Company.

I wasn't stupid; I knew how this lawsuit could be perceived. *Jilted woman, desperate, alone, can't earn her own money so goes after Kingston with a frivolous lawsuit.*

It was an easy spin, the cheap take, the juicy angle.

It also wasn't me.

Perhaps I hadn't thought this all the way through—never considered our case beyond the prospect of being accepted into the court, let alone the possibility of media hype. The idea had felt so simple and small, Peyton and I over pedicures.

How many people had read this?

I searched for the number of social media shares: 128,000 retweets already.

It was only 8:08 a.m.

Weren't eights supposed to be lucky?

I wasn't exactly Twitter-savvy, but I managed to find the digital trail, pleasantly flattered to see some of the captions shared with the article. Many echoed my friends' supportive texts, but these words were from total strangers:

> OMG THIS GIRL IS MY HERO
>
> It's about time!
>
> Fairy TALE caught between Kingston's legs?! Oh, snap!
>
> I always thought The Little Mermaid was fishy...
>
> Get Britney Spears' lawyer on this. SO GOOD
>
> Mad at Kingston? #SameSame
>
> Damsel in Discovery
>
> #IStandWithScottie #HottieHoliday
>
> #FreeScottie

Was I already a hashtag?
Was I already *several hashtags*?
I couldn't be.
Trending.
I breathed.

My smile drooped, though, when I saw the other side of the argument.

My haters appeared to be the minority, but still, their mean tweets sent a chill up my back. The thought of people who didn't know me, deciding from behind their tiny screens that they hated me ... it was haunting. I'd seen the harm trolls could inflict.

So far, though, I didn't see anything too offensive:

> Aww, a beautiful wealthy white dentist? I feel so bad for you. Privileged much? YAWN.
> Let us live!!!! Kingston 4eva!!!!

How was this spreading so fast?

Peyton was silent, her mouth a neat line.

We held a quick conversation without any words.

This is bad.

Yep, pretty bad.

My anxiety started to settle, though, as the initial blast of shock to my system subsided.

I decided to google myself.

Just as I feared, the usual top hits were buried. No Dream Pediatric Dentistry, no half marathon results, no LinkedIn profile to be seen. Every trace of my former life was buried under a mountain of headlines:

» **Happily-Never-After: Kingston Gets Served**
» **Young Woman Claims Kingston Ruined Her Life with Fairy Tales**
» **Is Kingston the Villain of Its Own Empire?**

On the plus side, everyone was calling me young. Twenty-eight felt ancient in, say, TikTok terms. Maybe I wasn't quite *cheugy* yet, Ugg boots be darned.

I saw that many of the articles featured the same picture of me on my wedding day. And thankfully, I loved the picture. My brown hair cascading, full gown trailing, dentist-white smile shining. Candid in the meadow behind the bridesmaids' house, right before the ceremony.

Pain bloomed in my chest at the memory of what I hadn't known in that moment.

But who would've leaked the photo, and why? I had no clue. My photographer? A greedy guest? Did the press pay big bucks for photos of plaintiffs in high-profile cases?

I plunked down the phone on my bed, unsure what exactly this meant for me. Or for the case, for that matter.

I smothered my face with my hands. "I'm everywhere," I muttered through them.

"To put it subtly, yes. You are *everywhere*," Peyton confirmed.

"When … how … I don't understand." I couldn't wrap my brain around how *anyone* had grabbed ahold of this story so mind-blowingly fast.

"I found out late yesterday that we were approved for a trial." Peyton shrugged. "I was dying to call you immediately, but decided to wait. I wanted to tell you in person today. Court documents are public record, so someone must've caught wind of our case and been lurking around, waiting for details. Unfortunately, it happens. Especially with companies the size of Kingston."

"Why don't any of the articles mention you?"

"My law firm is listed toward the end, in some of the articles," Peyton explained. "But I won't be the face of this case, Scot. You're already out there—like *all the way out there*—and the story has been live for"—she thumbed her phone—"three whole hours."

I moaned.

We sat unspeaking for several more minutes.

"You okay?" Peyton tried.

I sighed.

How did it *feel*, really *feel*, to have *thousands* of people reading about me right now?

Millions of people, no doubt, by dusk?

I squeezed my eyes into slits, breathing.

I was still here.

I was still healthy.

I was still (mostly) whole.

I still believed in our case and wanted to fight for it.

"You know what? I'm okay," I answered honestly, surprised by my own sense of calm. "And you?" I steeled myself for a legal monologue.

She cocked her head thoughtfully, though, blue eyes fixed toward the street. "To be honest ... I think it's exciting." She seemed hesitant with this admission, and I considered that she might've been waiting to see my reaction before showing hers.

"I think this case could be huge," she went on. "If we gain national—maybe even worldwide—attention, it could be amazing for both of us. Everyone will be taking us seriously. And most of all, we'll be fighting for something we believe in. For *truth*. For better stories. For women."

She paused. "It's also nerve-racking. Kingston is going to bring the heat, and the media will be circling." She thumbed the H on her Hermès belt. "We absolutely need to take you shopping, by the way. No more 'breakup du jour'"—her hand swept the length of my body—"or whatever you have going on lately."

I hugged myself defensively. "I love this shirt!"

"You can keep the shirt. You just can't *wear* it, outside this bed. You need to live up to those fabulous wedding photos. The public is watching you now."

"This is suddenly feeling very O. J. Simpson," I mused.

"Oh, please. You're not a criminal. You're a hero." Her mouth curled. "But I'm kind of your Robert Kardashian."

"The *best* best-friend-lawyer." I slugged her. "Speaking of the Kardashians, you know Kim passed the bar. You think she'd want in on this?"

"She wishes; she's only passed the Baby Bar so far." Peyton grinned. "But maybe she could help with your fashion chaos."

"*Hey.*"

"We'll get you a whole new wardrobe," she breezed, "and then we have work to do. Serious work. Discovery begins now."

"Which means what, exactly?"

"Piles of research, digging through files, building our case. And *coffee*. Gallons of coffee. Discovery is the time between now and our trial date, which we'll receive in the next couple weeks."

"Research. Coffee. I can do that. Like dental school. But without the cadavers."

"Oh, there will be dead bodies. Trust me." She smirked. "First up, we'll need to prepare you for the deposition, where the Kingston lawyers will grill you. On the record. For hours. Nothing's off limits. Literally, nothing."

"Um … that sounds terrifying." I shivered, flicking mentally through my life's highlights, considering what might be relevant to the case. Exes, probably. Mental health, surely. Experience with Kingston, most definitely.

"It's nothing scary," Peyton assured. "At least not with me at your side."

The image seized my heart with tender emotion.

"What do you say?" Peyton raised up one palm with authority and touched her pretty belt again with the other. "Let me be your knight in shining Hermès?"

I saluted her. "I thought you'd never ask."

...

Part Two

Chapter Eleven

HARRISON

Everyone wants to know what I thought—what I *really* experienced cognitively—when I first heard about the lawsuit that would tilt humanity's fantasy world on its axis. The case that would dig under the almighty skin of the Kingston Company. That would cut through every one of its layers.

Timeless, thick, and protective.

Castle walls covered with pixie dust.

People ask as if my answer will change. As if maybe one day, I'll reconsider, revise my report of the past, of that first fated day in Cooper Hollister's office when he passed off the case to me.

Why, yes, folks. Now that I've had more time to ponder, I had it wrong! I really sensed that this off-the-wall lawsuit would not only proceed to court, but snowball into an international news story, full-company panic attack, and make-or-break moment of my career. Definitely. Affirmative. I saw the avalanche coming.

I didn't.

Which was, arguably, why the case became what it did. Nobody was on guard. Who in their ever-loving mind would have taken those ludicrous claims seriously?

Maybe you would have.

I should have.

After all this time, the only interesting tidbits I hold from that day are that I suspected my boss was using the case to spite me (he was)—and that I assumed Scotland Dolly Holiday was an antisocial weirdo (she wasn't).

She was Scottie from running club.

But you knew that already.

Also, don't get too excited.

I wasn't thrilled to learn it was her.

Disgusted was more like it. "What a waste," was my exact thought—and this apparently wasn't the first time a man made this judgment of her.

But I'm getting ahead of myself.

Additionally, don't get me wrong: I had something to prove when Cooper tossed me that case, however outlandish. I poured my entire brain into the official objection we filed. Point by point, I dismantled the cringeworthy claims.

We never promised you anything, woman.

What possible proof could you have in the way of damages?

And what about the people who have loved fairy tales for centuries, despite the million little unhappy endings faced in their lives, every day?

What I didn't grasp at the onset is that my brain wouldn't be enough for this case.

It would demand my heart.

Shoot.

What responsibility *does* a global brand have when it wields power over the formative psyche and our collective imagination?

Maybe there *was* proof of damages.

And, yes, *what about* those people?

The believers, the dreamers, the kids?

More than anything, what did I believe—*truly believe*—about Kingston?

Fairy tales?

Myself?

Everything changed for Scottie, but I tell you, it changed for me too.

Anyway, back to the story. Let's get into the moment when things got real for me. After all, what's a good Kingston story without a sidekick? Squawking, dancing, sometimes even stealing the show.

I'll walk you through the day I met mine.

Or rather, the day I became one.

...

I drummed a tune on my desk with my fingertips, unable to focus. I was sweating through the layers of animal fur I was regretting like a bad tattoo.

It was the Thursday before Halloween. Cotton draped over doorways in spiderwebs. Friendly skeletons and candy cauldrons bordered the hallways.

In company tradition, we were all dressed up as Kingston characters. Later this afternoon, employees would welcome their children and families for trick-or-treating and costume voting. My assistant, Erin, was Tinkerbell, all glittery green, and our two other team attorneys were Tweedledee and Tweedledum: red suspenders, pillowed bellies, tiny flags stuck into their hats like golf pins. Cooper never participated in the festivities, which surprised no one.

I usually loved this day. The giddy kids, the first festive air of the holidays filling our space. I'd won the costume contest twice in the past, scoring four tickets to Kingston Court each time. Thanks to Erin, Halloween in the office had slowly become as festive as the park's Haunted House. It was the spookiest time of the year and it showed.

On me, today, it *shouted*.

Nothing said "HAPPY HALLOWEEN!" like a two-hundred-thirty-pound warthog the size of a door. It was my kind of costume. Goofy, brave, and compassionate, Pedro the Warthog was known for having no worries and lots of jokes. Today, though, I had every one of the worries and absolutely none of the jokes.

Except for the huge one on me.

Because we were going to court.

We were going to court.

I didn't know how it was true.

This ridiculous Holiday woman and her cry-me-a-waterfall joke of a case were proceeding beyond our walls.

Frankly, I was in shock.

Judge Craig Davidoff—plus the local Orange County court and juries, in general—were known for being pro-Kingston. How could they not be? This was their turf, their theme park, their playground. Wade Kingston started everything here in Anaheim: the movies, the magic, the madness.

Not only did Kingston lawsuits rarely proceed to trial; they even more rarely were won by the opposition. The unspoken rule was baked into the understanding of Southern Californians, like their sunshine and cheeseburgers. Even the most litigious of souls knew the deal: good luck suing Kingston, basically. Better luck still if Judge Davidoff sat on the other side of your plea.

Rumor had it Judge Davidoff used to golf with Wade Kingston. That they'd dine after hours with their wives inside the theme park's most lavish restaurants. The two men were supposedly friends, even if they sometimes battled in court. There was respect, trust, and justice.

Kingston "just so happened" to usually win.

So, naturally, I was still trying to scrape my jaw off the floor after learning early this morning—via an email from Cooper Hollister, no less—that Judge Davidoff had dismissed my rebuttal. We would "chat more ASAP."

Even worse, I had to digest this reality with all the dignity of a cartoon pig.

The kids better *love* this costume.

Those tickets were *mine*.

Maybe I'd even send them to Gym Ashley, instead of showing up for our date next week.

My office phone trilled, piercing my daze.

Cooper Hollister.

Of course.

"This is Harrison." I leaned back, scratching my neck.

"Hayes," he clipped. "As you know, our outside counsel

will come in for this—*case*, if we can call it that. I don't want you to sweat it."

I glanced down at my fuzzy inferno.

Too late for that.

"Brent Callahan will be lead attorney, and you'll be second chair," he continued. "We need him for power, but you for optics—when the time comes. Kingston, devoting one of our own. Put everything else on hold for now. Don't answer any calls from the press. PR is drafting a statement."

Press?

Seriously?

In a show of agreement, to only myself, I pushed aside the mountain of papers in front of me. I didn't hate that my other minutia could be dismissed for now. "Yes, sir."

"One more thing."

"Yep?"

"Brent is on his way here."

I gulped, and stood, a hairy cyclone of panic. "Wow. Um … okay." Brent Callahan, famed Kingston lawyer and savage whip. "He's coming from LA, though, right?" I frenziedly calculated that I had maybe forty-five minutes before Brent arrived from his downtown office. If I prayed for green lights and broke every speed limit, I could drive home, change into a suit meant for humans, and still return in time.

Barely.

But maybe, just maybe.

Cooper spat a chuckle so loud I could hear it from down the hall. "He'll be here at nine thirty."

My jaw pulsed.

I gripped the phone tighter.

And he was telling me *now*?

I had twenty minutes.

But *of course* Cooper would send me to meet Brent Callahan as a buffoon. This meeting could've waited until this afternoon, and he knew it.

"Cooper," I hissed, "I'm dressed up as a *warthog*."

Another laugh croaked. "Yes, I saw that. Great *team spirit*, Hayes. Good luck with the costume contest!"

Click.

I covered my sweaty animal face with my palms.

Paws?

Should I at least go hunt down some clothes, or stay committed to character like a towering idiot? I breathed in and felt to the horns on my skull, and decided Pedro was staying. If I embarrassed the company, it was Cooper's fault, not mine. Plus, Brent Callahan was a shark. The human animal of all human animals. He could handle it; I was confident.

Plus, *we* were paying *him*, last I checked.

Reluctantly I jiggled my mouse, squinting into my desktop screen. I opened the case folder I'd saved apathetically to my desktop. I hit *print* on the papers I needed, suddenly missing last year's Halloween office day terribly. Eating candy, dressed as a merman, not a care in the world.

For a Holiday, this gal sure seemed like a grinch.

...

If you're going to be a warthog, at least be an early warthog, I figured.

I sat at the far edge of my favorite conference room, smooth walnut table reflecting the overhead lights. The glass of the huge, windowed wall gave the same view as Cooper's office. The theme park, the people, the Kingston fanatics—who one day might feel so deeply scorned they would sue us.

You never knew what was coming.

Or who.

Water bottles: *Check.*

Documents: *Check.*

Legal Pads: *Check.*

Self-respect: *Feeble.*

Body: *On fire.*

Time: *9:26 a.m.*

Five minutes later, I smelled Brent Callahan before I looked up to see him. Pine and ocean: pure man. No wonder the women loved him, according to rumors. He smelled fantastic from ten feet away.

I wouldn't say he smelled sexy, but I might even say sexy.

I rose, shame pounding me like a boulder at the sight of his trim suit, designer, obviously expensive. His light brown hair cut tight on the sides was longer on top, professional and hipster at once. The angles of his face sharpened forward, like a fresh pencil. He looked like a hunter and felt like a spear. He was handsome. This guy had shed blood in his time. That much was clear.

He traversed the room and extended his hand. "Brent Callahan."

As if I didn't know.

As if everyone, everywhere didn't know.

I shook his hand with my costume mitt, hoping he'd see beyond my disguise to the promising young colleague beneath, even if it required imagination. Collegiate athlete, ambitious lawyer, and yes, fun-loving pig! I was willing to put it all on the line for Kingston, at least. Look, proof! If anything, I was serving a first impression he'd never forget.

"Harrison Hayes." I gestured to the length of myself. "It's Halloween here today."

He scanned me quickly but thoroughly as a document. "I noticed," he deadpanned. To my surprise then, he thrust one hand into a pocket, procuring a fistful of candy and littering the pieces on the table between us. "Good to meet you."

Mostly Reese's and Twix.

Good taste.

Naturally.

It was a buffer, this candy.

A show that we were on the same team.

I pointed to the chair at the head of the table like I was presenting his throne. "Shall we?"

Brent took the seat, promptly uncapping a pen with his teeth. He blew the plastic top-piece onto the table. *Power move,* I thought, not caring whom or what is touched by your spit.

"Have you read the articles?" he started. "The case is everywhere. Already."

"Not yet," I admitted, spreading my folder open. "I've been reviewing everything that we have. Trying to grasp where this goes from here."

"Well, it's going somewhere *fast*." He scraped words onto one of the legal pads. "This is a big brand's nightmare—and a small reporter's dream. The fans are going nuts, and so are the haters. But stay away from all the noise, for now. I want a pure start, you and me."

I nodded.

Okay.

I wouldn't have pegged Brent Callahan for a purist.

"Listen." He stabbed the pen behind his ear. "I've been defending Kingston for over a decade. There's something inherent to their cases that's absent in most big suits."

"And that is?"

I waited.

"That is—" Brent mimed a two-handed explosion.

He paused for impact.

"*Emotion.*"

What?

Many lawyers argued the opposite, that feelings shouldn't muck up a case. I nodded, though, encouraging him to proceed.

"Kingston is more than a company," Brent continued. "More than a media empire, more than a rat who's become an international star. Kingston—for many—is more like a belief system."

I knew that and thought it often. People *loved* Kingston. People *hated* Kingston. But no one was untouched by Kingston, whether they knew it or not. "Agreed," I said. "I see that, every day."

"People think I'm a great attorney because I'm the villain." Brent helped himself to one of the water bottles. "They say I have no soul. That I've 'commodified' Kingston, that I defend the brand like it's a cold-blooded corporation. That Wade Kingston wouldn't approve."

I laughed. "You're telling me that's not true?" I challenged. Brent was intuitive, brilliant. He had to know his reputation preceded him. "At least partially true?"

He paused. "Partially, maybe. It's just not the whole truth."

"What is, then?"

He downed half his water in one gulp, crunching the bottle. "The secret sauce, Hayes, is that I believe in the Kingston Company. I love this brand with my blood." He thumped his chest with a fist. "And because of that, I can make a jury believe, too. If they don't already believe. Home-court advantage is real around here."

"And you're telling me this, because ..."

"Because you have to believe too."

"Believe in..." I scratched my perspiring head clumsily. "What exactly?"

He outstretched his arms. "Magic."

I laughed.

But he didn't.

Also, how did his hair stay so firmly, exactly in place? I wondered what product he used. Probably magic, I realized.

Wait, was he messing with me?

Or was Brent Callahan actually trying to *fairy godmother* me? Was this how he thought we would win?

Through so-called *belief*?

Of course, I believed in Kingston. I was dressed as a warthog, wasn't I?

"I'm a huge Kingston fan, Mr. Callahan," I responded. "Obviously, I believe in the company."

"Do you, really, though? Because your objections to Ms. Holiday's claims were ... unimpressive, frankly. I didn't sense you were fighting with blood."

What was with all the blood? Should I go grab an IV? Start feeling for a good vein? Prick my finger and then sign a contract?

"Did you read her claims?" I shot back. "She's a joke."

"See, that's another problem." Brent folded his arms, arching back. "You probably think I'm an arrogant jerk, but I'm not. Or at least—I'm not *only* an arrogant jerk. No one is only one thing. You need to put yourself in the plaintiff's shoes. Glass slippers. Whatever it takes. *Their* shoes, whatever they're wearing. *You go there.* You figure out how to care. Or at least, how to see their point of view. You can't beat the opposition without understanding them. It's a dance. It's a ball."

He did not just compare our case to a royal ball.

"A dance," I repeated sarcastically.

"Yes." He flipped his pen, leaning forward again. "You gun for the jury's emotion—the judge's, too—without revealing yours. *You don't care*, in that courtroom. But of course—you do. You care more than anyone. And you're going to remind every single person how much they care, too. Because this is Kingston. And that"—he thudded his torso again—"is the magic."

Was it just me, or was he speaking in riddles?

It made sudden and incredible sense to me that Abel Iverson had found Brent, all those years ago, as a young associate in big law and appointed him as our legal front man.

I thought of the small swan in Abel's office. Kingston lawyers had a reputation for being venomous. But were they all secretly softies hoarding glass figurines? Was truly *caring* their secret weapon?

I wasn't buying it.

Yet.

But this was certainly one pep talk I hadn't seen coming.

"Should we talk logistics?" I suggested, eager to flip the channel on this conversation.

"Yes." Brent fished into his briefcase. "We'll start framing the case, building evidence. I've started our list of key witnesses. You'll handle the depositions. And research. I'll let you dig into our girl."

I pulled a face. "You mean Holiday? *Woman*, right?"

Brent angled his head. "Late twenties? I suppose. Very attractive. Objectively speaking."

"No way." I frowned, picturing cats, dust, and tea.

Brent retrieved a headshot and slid it to me like an air-hockey puck—and my stomach flipped immediately with fighting emotions.

Fury and lust.

Doubt and delight.

Confusion and comprehension.

I thought of my now-mismatched shoelaces, and of my futile attempts at forgetting that face.

Those freckles and lips.
Her eyes are green.
Objectively attractive indeed.
What a beautiful waste.

...

Chapter Twelve

SCOTTIE

With all my trips to Kingston Court as a kid, I never once noticed the silver block of an office building located directly across the street from the park's south end. Then again, the structure looked new: shiny and abundantly windowed. A contrast to Kingston's old-fashioned roots, but a modern, appropriate nod to prestige and invention.

I tilted my head back in awe. "So, this is it."

"This is it." Peyton patted her black leather briefcase, as if in a last-minute check. We were more prepared than two Girl Scouts. Peyton had even dragged me to every nook of the mall last week, in blazing pursuit of new outfits.

"You need to look *hot* and *confident* for these proceedings. For all of it," she'd insisted. "You're a feminist icon now."

Truthfully, I didn't know how to handle the media hype. So I'd concluded it was best for me to pretend it wasn't happening. I needed to stay focused, anyway. I was just on an adventure with my best friend, *tra la la*, two schoolgirls who still loved to play. Just now with bigger stakes and true risks. Not to mention real money.

Lots of it.

No more pastel Monopoly bills for us.

Between Nordstrom (obviously) and Express (underrated

severely, according to Peyton), we had assembled a wardrobe fit for a plaintiff, one who needed to "look viral-meme-ready at all times," as Peyton kept reminding me. Pencil skirts and pretty blouses, one pantsuit and a pair of spiky black pumps. I'd wobbled in the heels at first, standing there in front of the dressing room mirror, missing my lab coat.

"You are *fire*." Peyton had circled me like a hawk. "Your body's insane. Those legs! If I run, will I get a thigh gap? No—rewind. We need feminist thinking. Fixing wage gaps, not thigh gaps." She stroked her chin. "Practice walking in those at home, okay? Take the stairs. Do the dishes. Get cozy."

As we dropped seven hundred (real) dollars and sipped on our coffees (black Americanos this time, game on), Peyton had prepared me rigorously for my deposition.

Listen carefully.
Tell the truth.
It's okay to say, 'I don't know.'
Do breathe.
Don't ramble.
Listen to me.
Only answer the actual question at hand.

Days later now, I sucked in uneven breaths, attempting to *stay calm* in front of the Kingston offices. The sun shimmered brightly on the building's facade and blinked through the fountain flowing in front of us. To our right was an iron statue of Wade Kingston and Rickey Rat, elevated on a stone pedestal, both smiling and waving and—

Scaring me, just a little.

Were we really taking them on?

You bet we were.

Peyton snatched my hand and pulled me past the iconic figures. Two sets of best friends facing off.

Ready as we'd ever be.

...

I tried my best not to gawk at the views from the conference room—Kingston Court in full glory—or to freak at the video camera. Peyton had explained that there'd be one, but I guess hadn't fully considered it.

There was just so much to remember.

Breathe, listen, pause, think, don't overthink, don't miss a beat ...

Oh, and it's all on tape!

Awesome.

Help!

Facing the crystalline window, we took our place at the giant table and waited for Kingston's attorney.

"What do you know about their lawyer?" I whispered, eyeing the camera lens.

Peyton fished into her briefcase and pulled out a folder. "They appointed someone in-house. To support Brent Callahan, the top attorney from their big LA firm."

"Male or female?"

"Not sure."

"Young or old?"

"Probably old."

"You don't know anything about our mortal enemy, do you?"

"They've kept it on lock. Which is smart. But we'll know in about thirty seconds."

And know, we would.

As if in slow motion, the door to the room peeled open and a large, square physique filled its frame.

The afternoon glare caught the chrome of the doorknob, momentarily blinding me.

Playing tricks on me.

I flinched.

Heart racing.

Whew.

For a second there, my vision had eclipsed and betrayed me, and I could have sworn I was seeing him, again—

I mean, seeing him somewhere beyond my imagination where he annoyingly kept running laps.

I thought I was seeing my Prince Charles.

By chance.

Again.

Peyton suddenly slapped her palms on the table at a deafening volume. I swear I could feel her eyes bulge.

Huh?

Then I sensed her freeze cold, right as my sight cleared up and clicked into place. We both stood then, rapidly, urgently, assertively, speaking at the same time.

"Harrison Hayes?" Peyton barked.

"*Charles*?!" I squeaked.

There was no questioning it now.

Hot Running Guy was standing before us.

"Ladies." He gave a tight bow that meant business and adeptly avoided my gaze.

Nooooo, I whined in my head, taking him in. *No, no, no.*

He was supposed to be *uglier* than I remembered, not dreamier. Whenever he popped into my head and I wanted to swat him away, I'd been distorting his looks in an act of self-preservation. I mean, I knew I'd never see him again, and it stung. So I'd been adding some zits, receding his hairline, shrinking him down a little.

No dice.

He was a vision.

Hotter than fire.

His skin, his hair, his sheer size.

Wide-shouldered, square-jawed, and—

"You're so *tall*," I gushed accidently.

Oops.

I barked a fake cough as a cover-up.

He still refused to look at me, shrugging. "Must be the suit."

It was funny, but he didn't smile. He would be tall in anything. A gunnysack, a raincoat.

His boxers.

GAH!

Pull your mind from the edge.

"He is tall, isn't he?" Peyton crossed her arms violently, glowering across the table. "And I just now, finally, figured it out." She snapped her fingers. "He really *takes up a room*, doesn't he, Scot?"

I flicked my gaze from Charles to Peyton, back and forth, like a metronome.

"So ... you *do* know him? The guy from running club? And Starbucks?" I dropped my voice. "It's him, P. My guy."

"He is *not* your guy," she hissed. "This is ..."

I fixed my eyes back on Charles, only to meet his for a millisecond. He looked away fast, and my stomach dropped.

His eyes were still soft—but his face was flint.

And I didn't like it one bit.

There had been an openness to him on our run that had endeared him to me immediately. He had been sweet; I'd been the aloof one. I had been guarded. Now he was, too.

He stood now, in fact, like a soldier protecting his kingdom.

Which, I supposed, he was.

"This is *Harrison Hayes*," Peyton finished. "Captain of our college baseball team. Chief womanizer and jerk-hole. And, apparently, Kingston attorney-at-law." She all but stuck out her tongue.

"That's ... quite an introduction." Harrison took a step, thrusting his hand out to me. Eyes still everywhere else.

"You ..." I inhaled, glancing between them again. "So ... your name ... isn't Charles?"

"Afraid not." His handsome mouth tightened. "I use an alias sometimes."

Oh.

Okay.

We were cocky now.

Who does this guy think he is?

"Smart," Peyton chided. "You should probably keep a safe distance from, you know, the person you really are."

Which was—who, exactly?

I was so confused.

He gave me his shoelace like a total sweetheart but lied about his own name?

This wasn't adding up.

Choose your words wisely from the moment we walk in the room, echoed Peyton's deposition instructions inside my mind. She should probably take her own advice, but at least one of us could play nice.

Nice-ish, anyway.

I sucked in a breath and leaned forward, into the tension. "All right then ... Harrison." I swallowed. "I'm Scot—Ms. Holiday. Nice to ... meet you."

If that's what you'd call this charade.

Harrison grabbed my hand as my organs melted inside me—but his firm refusal to look in my eyes was annoying me to my core.

Speaking of core, I bet he had a nice one, if his gorgeous build was a hint. I'd always loved baseball players. Any ball players, really. I thought of his big arms, pumping and heaving, next to me, on our run.

His thumbs on my wrist again.

What's. Wrong. With. Me.

I was the enemy now, I reminded myself.

Of course he would look at me differently.

Or refuse to look at me at all.

As my vision widened, beyond this bizarre barrel of lies, I noticed that next to Harrison on one side stood the punky blonde girl I'd also spotted in Starbucks. Sapphire eyes, white blouse, houndstooth skirt, crimson heels matching her lipstick. Chopped shag suiting her perfectly. She was cute. Younger than Harrison by a decade, at least. I wondered if she was in love with him. How could she not be? Then again, his whole workplace vibe was not exactly enticing.

Work-Charles Harrison seemed ... overbearing. Stoic. Harsh, even.

"This is my legal assistant, Erin Stark." He presented the blonde. "And this"—he gestured to his other side, to an older woman with silver hair spun in a braid—"is Helen, our court reporter. She'll be recording the deposition today."

Smiling warmly, Helen lifted a palm. She wore a baggy tan sweater and square glasses over green eyes. She had a calming vibe, which we clearly needed here. She pointed down the table to her big, clunky machine.

"Peyton McKenzie, Cashion & Baker." Peyton extended her grip to the women but ignored Harrison's hand suspended in air as if it smelled of old fish. She sniffed disgustedly.

Ignoring her rudeness, Harrison took his seat and we followed his lead. "Thank you, ladies, for coming here." Even his voice was different today, so dignified and direct.

Has he kept my shoelace, too?

Will these distracting thoughts ruin my testimony?

"I trust," Harrison started, "that Peyton here has explained to you how a deposition works, Ms. Holiday."

I nodded, smoothing down my black satin blouse and settling into my seat. The Rickey Rat clock on the wall chimed eleven. I'd been warned we could be here till nightfall.

"We'll have lunch brought in," Erin added.

"That's nice," I said.

Or was it nice to feed your own prisoners?

"My client is ready to answer every question you have for her." Peyton clasped her hands on the table. "Assuming, of course, Mr. Hayes, that Kingston has taught you how to be a gentleman since your college days."

Harrison's mouth cracked into the slightest smile. "I think it's best if we keep all"—his eyes finally locked into mine—"*prior personal encounters* ... out of this case." He glanced to Peyton again. "Don't you, Ms. McKenzie?"

"Oh, please, don't *Ms.* me," she scoffed. "Call me Peyton and let's get on with it."

Oh, boy.

This was going to be *fun*!

But I wouldn't let "Charles" unnerve me with his icicle treatment. No. He would not win this game. He wanted to sweep our *prior personal encounter* into the past?

Well, great.

What encounter, then?

I had enough of my past to throw at him. And Peyton to make sure he'd drown in it.

"Let's definitely get on with it," agreed Harrison.

Erin poised an eager hand over her notepad, and Helen likewise hovered over her stenograph.

"Are you ready, ladies?" Harrison asked.

They nodded.

He picked up a clicker and pointed it at the video camera. The small green light strobed in time with my heart rate.

Flashing.

"Could you please state your full name for the record?" Harrison held his pen breezily, his focus on me now.

Finally.

I was the subject, at last, of his unsplit attention.

And I wasn't sure how to feel about it.

I could really use three Advil and another Americano.

I rubbed my temples, refusing to care that Hot Running Guy had lied to me. I would not care that he was Superman-handsome or that his actual name was hotter than smoke. *Harrison Hayes.* It was even sexier than *Channing Tatum* or *Harry Styles*—and this heartthrob had touched my skin.

"My name is *Scotland Dolly Holiday*," I replied, peering bravely into his face. My goal was a poker face to shame Lady Gaga's. "My friends call me Scottie."

"Which clearly you're not," Peyton inserted. "Her friend."

Again, he ignored Peyton, folding his giant arms, eyes on me. "Thank you, Ms. Holiday."

I really wish he wouldn't call me that.

"And you're aware that you're being deposed today in the case of Holiday v. Kingston?"

"Yes." I swallowed.

"Have you ever been deposed before?"

"No," I replied.

"You are under oath," he continued, "and required to answer every question to the best of your ability. Is that clear?"

"Clear. *Sir.*"

Two could swordfight with ice.

Harrison clipped right on. "And finally. Is there any reason—such as unusual stress, a physical or mental condition, or being under the influence of any substances—that would prevent or limit you today from giving truthful answers to my questions?"

The fact that your second impression leaves something to be desired?

I hate that I love your brown eyes?

I'm keeping your shoelace forever?

"None, whatsoever."

I darted my eyes to Erin, then Helen. Both were submersed in recording, while Peyton was poised like a pit bull next to me, ready to pounce if Harrison crossed the line. She might as well be holding a shield.

"And lastly, if you need clarification on any question, at any point, you need to look to me—and not to anyone else," explained Harrison. "Do you understand this?"

We were in a contest now, staring each other *down*. I thought of the theory that any two strangers could fall in love if they held eye contact for long enough.

His brows arched, and my stomach flipped.

Why was I sweating when this arctic AC could keep a snowman alive?

I thumbed my gold paperclip-chain necklace and cut my eyes to the ceiling. "I understand this fully."

Peyton's knee knocked mine under the table, and I was thankful.

I'm here, too, she was saying. *Do not let him intimidate you.*

"Let's get into it, then." Harrison flipped a page of his notepad. "I'm going to gather a lot of background information today, so if some of this seems tedious or repetitive, please bear in mind that it's part of the process. In general, my questions will fall under the categories of personal background, injury, and damages. Understood?"

I nodded.

"Let's start, then, with your childhood." He flattened his tie and proceeded fluidly. "Where'd you grow up, and with whom?"

"I was raised here in Orange County," I replied. "In Irvine. Mostly by my dad. My mom left when I was six."

"Where did she go?"

Where did she go, exactly, and how much would I pay to find out? If I won this lawsuit and had the money, I'd track her down at any cost. I'd already made that vow. "I don't know. Where she went."

"And presently? Are you in touch?"

"No." I looked over Harrison's shoulder to the theme park below, twinkling even in the daylight. "I don't know where she went. I haven't known in twenty-two years."

He bit his fancy pen, pausing. "What was she like? Your mother."

I sighed. "She was beautiful. Just ... exceptionally stunning. And magical." Like a Kingston princess, but all grown-up, huge eyes and billowing hair. *One who just so happened to binge drink and sometimes forget to come home.* "But she was also depressive and ... unpredictable. Free-spirited. Or at least, she thought she was free." My voice quieted. "I knew she wasn't as free as she thought. I think she was chained to ... demons she couldn't see. Still, though." I paused. "She had that X factor. She was mesmerizing. I remember loving her smile." Whimsy and disaster, wrapped into one. That was Mom.

"Do you miss her?" Harrison asked.

I glanced sideways at Peyton to see if she'd interject, but her gaze was deadlocked ahead. This line of questioning felt so ... *personal.* But maybe that was the norm.

I nodded yes. "I miss her very much. I think about her more now, actually, than I did as a kid."

Harrison cocked his head, scribbling something. "Interesting," he observed. "Why do you think that is?"

"Probably," I said slowly, "because she was around my age now, twenty-eight, when she left me forever. I try to ... I don't know. Put myself in her place, maybe. Imagine what kind of woman leaves her six-year-old daughter and never comes back. Never checks on her. Never once tries to make contact, or even wish her a happy birthday. You know?"

Harrison's jaw flinched, which it hadn't yet. And trust me, I would've noticed. It was an almost imperceptible twitch—but I saw it. Even if I didn't know what it meant.

A flicker.

Emotion, maybe?

The man was a human, folks.

"I simultaneously miss her," I explained, "and, if I'm honest, feel scared of her. Resurfacing, someday. In ... me."

I caught another wince of his features. Maybe he simply hadn't been banking on such brutal honesty out of me. He jotted something else with his pen.

I strained to see, with no luck.

"Let's shift the discussion now." Harrison raked his dark hair while sifting easily through some more papers. He was a natural at this, no doubt. "Specifically, let's talk about Kingston and the company's role in your childhood. Clearly, you're here." He held out his arms in an eagle-wide span. If he wasn't suddenly smirking so hugely, I might've imagined them hugging me. "You obviously feel that we played a crucial part in your upbringing."

Classy enough.

Fairly put.

But he wasn't finished yet.

"And from my understanding, Ms. Holiday, you're upset you didn't end up a real princess, with a diamond-encrusted tiara."

There it is.

"Objection!" snapped Peyton.

"For what?" Harrison's eyes narrowed.

"I don't know. Making fun of my plaintiff?"

He half rolled his eyes. "Fine, I'll—rephrase the question. Ms. Holiday." He coughed. "How would you describe the role of Kingston films, characters, and storylines in your childhood?"

Peyton's interruption had jolted me, but I breathed and straightened right up. I was intelligent. I was grounded. I was abundantly capable of returning whatever balls this player pitched at me.

What *did* Kingston mean to my childhood?

Everything.

And I would tell him so.

I explained that Kingston had often been my babysitter, via videotape. That Kingston had filled in as a parent when my dad had to work. That Kingston was the only child therapist I ever saw, when I could've really used professional help with my grief. That Kingston's characters were like playmates to me—and their lack of a mom, a mirror and balm for my brokenness. That the princesses had been my heroines and my friends.

From my earliest memory, I told him, Kingston movies had supported me and entertained me.

And then, when my mom left, the stories made me *believe* that I could also rise from my heartache to achieve anything. I could change the world if I wanted. There was nothing I couldn't do. I was promised my happy ending, no matter the odds.

I believed in the impossible because Kingston told me to—and during my most tender years.

If I wished upon a star, my dreams would flourish to life.

As a child, to me, it seemed simple.

As an adult, today, it seemed cruel.

It was a bold-faced lie.

I exhaled and left it at that.

Harrison licked his lips and slanted a look toward the camera. He took several beats to respond. "I see," he drawled finally.

Erin and Helen were both scrawling copious notes.

Peyton patted my knee. *You're doing so great. Keep going.*

Harrison whirled his fingertips like a wheel. "Now ... let's fast-forward a bit, Ms. Holiday. Where did you go to college and what did you study?"

I jolted at the quick shift in topic.

College.

Okay.

I cleared my throat. "I went to UC Berkeley for undergrad. I majored in biology and minored in art history."

"Interesting combination." He flipped his pen like a baton "Why art history?"

"Why *not* art history?" I shrugged. "I love art. It informs everything. Even dentistry."

"I guess we can agree on something there." He looked up at me through dark lashes. "Who's your favorite artist?"

"Van Gogh," I said easily. "He was so ... tortured. In so much emotional pain. But he picked up his brush and made beauty out of it."

Harrison jerked.

Again.

Was there some sort of Morse code I should be assembling from his reactions?

"Yes. Thank you." He cleared his throat once again, now done with the art topic. "And for the record, can you confirm your highest level of education?"

"Of course. I earned my DMD from UCSF." I laced my fingers together on top of the table, hoping to look as impressive as my degrees. "That's a doctor of medicine in dentistry."

"I know," he defended. "And ... that's a great school."

I nodded. "My top choice."

"Did you have a residency requirement?"

"Two years for pediatrics."

His eyes darkened. Another reaction?

He wasn't very good at hiding his feelings.

If only I knew what they meant.

"Impressive resume," he noted, appearing to ruminate on my credentials. "So—would you then, Ms. Holiday, consider yourself to be an *ambitious, independent, capable* woman?"

Peyton lifted her hands in a *stop* motion. "Objection! Leading the witness."

I remembered this meant he was trying to put words in my mouth.

"I'm not leading her *anywhere*," Harrison said, not looking away from me. "I see no problem with asking a dentist if she considers herself a success. It's relevant information. For assessing her mental state and tracking her biographical history."

Peyton's frustration was palpable.

She folded her arms in a hefty pause, finally nodding with hesitation.

But I didn't know what to say.

What was the right answer here?

"Yes," I voiced finally. "I would ... consider myself to be an *ambitious, independent, capable* woman, Mr. Hayes."

Right?

I think?

Did I just mess up?

Harrison brightened.

Shoot.

I definitely just messed up.

"And yet." Harrison practically beamed. "Your life was destroyed to smithereens when some pretty boy broke your heart."

"Are you kidding me?" Peyton yelped. "You know this is being recorded, right? *Unprofessional* much?"

Harrison seemed unfazed. He might've even been thrilled. "I'm trying to point out—rather easily, might I add—that Kingston hasn't exactly kept your client from *reaching for the stars*. Or whatever she felt she was promised."

"But your *company of employment*," I interjected, "*Mr. Hayes*. Is the global entity that insisted my worth would arrive in the form of a savior on a white horse. Correct? I'm ambitious, independent, and capable, yes—I'm a *doctor of dentistry*—and *still* I was duped by Kingston. I'd argue that isn't my fault. Innocent children are Kingston's key target, are they not?"

"I'm merely *saying*," Harrison pressed, "that I'm struggling to see the real damages here. I wasn't expecting someone so—" He whipped a hand chaotically in the air.

Erin's pupils were popping out of her skull.

Helen had stopped typing altogether.

What, Harrison?

Someone so smart?

Someone so pretty?

Say it!

What did he think of me, really? He seemed to hate me here, but I wasn't sure. The intermittent intensity of his eye contact and the repeated *body flinches* were totally throwing me off.

"Shall we discuss my client's mountain of debt, night terrors, and crippling depression, then?" Peyton barked, livid now, standing. "This feels like you're wasting our time."

"How about a lunch break?" Erin stood, too, waving her phone like a peace flag. "Mendocino Farms is here. *Yay*! I'll ... um ... be right back."

All of us saved by the cowbell.

"Yes, recess, *please*," Peyton hissed. "Do you have a conference room where we could regroup in private?"

"Follow me, Counselor," Erin said. She looked to Harrison with silent reproach, like a mom commanding time-out. "We'll give you ladies an hour."

...

One hour later, full of chicken sandwiches and superfood salads, we resumed our spots in Harrison's line of fire.

We had needed that break.

We were recollected, refueled.

I loved that my lawyer was fiery, but I assured Peyton that she could *calm down a little* already. Harrison was getting to her more than he was getting to me. Nothing had shocked me yet—except for, you know, who our opposing counsel had turned out to be. Then again, Peyton was the one who knew how this typically worked.

I would admit that there was a *vibe* in the air.

A palpable vibe.

Harrison, Erin, and Helen were already seated and ready, back in the conference room. Kingston Court still hummed with life in the distance, so ignorant of the arguments it had ignited, right here, across the street. Kids laughing, lovers kissing, crowds smashing together in line for a chance to meet royalty. I envied every one of them in that moment, their bliss of still believing in magic.

In believing something at all.

My heart ached suddenly, deeply, as I looked around at what I was doing here.

But I remembered that I was fighting for every girl down there in a princess dress, each one more achingly innocent than the last, utterly naïve to the hollowness of her dreams.

Harrison's loud cough slapped me back into business mode. "How was your food, ladies?"

"Delicious," I managed. "Thank you."

Erin flashed her Crest-Whitestrips-white teeth. "You're welcome."

Harrison scooped up the remote and pointed it at the tripod again. "We're back," he announced. "Resuming the deposition of plaintiff Scotland Dolly Holiday."

The rest of the interview floated along rather peacefully—which seemed to surprise us all.

Harrison eased from the edge of his seat and stuffed away his audacity. He kept things professional and productive for the remainder of the long day. Maybe Helen and Erin had lectured him during the break.

I preserved my cool, too, even while splaying my life on the table in detail. My wedding day, the traumatic aftermath, my debt, and my hiatus from work. There were follow-up questions along the way, but most were free of judgment and hellfire. The smoke had at last stopped streaming from Peyton's ears, too.

By five o'clock, though, I was spent.

I needed us to be done.

As if on cue, Harrison closed his folder and arched his back in a deep stretch. I was oddly used to his eyes on me by hour six. Whether by choice or default, he had relaxed as well. He'd even grinned sporadically and occasionally, revealing his wit. I tried not to notice how his straight, sparkly smile played against his pillowy lips.

"I have just a few more questions for you today," he said.

Look away from his mouth.

"You think there's anything left?" I thrust out my arms coyly. "Have at me."

"Well, then."

Eyes. Lips. Skin.

Stop.

"What ... do you want, Ms. Holiday?" Harrison paused. "What do you want, now?"

"Like, for dinner, or—?"

One dimple made an appearance.

A dash.

At some point I'd crack this code.

"Generally. Next. In life. What is it you really want?"

I heaved my deepest sigh of the day, sinking into my seat. "Well—what does any of us really want?" I lifted my shoulders. "I guess ... I want to feel valued. Respected, accepted. Loved and cherished. For who I really am." I pursed my lips, wondering if he'd catch the dig. "I want to be happy, and—" I paused. "I don't … ever want to be abandoned again. By someone I care about."

"And you believe," Harrison proceeded slowly, "you *truly believe*, Ms. Holiday, that the Kingston Company played an emotionally, physically, and *psychologically destructive* role in your pursuit of this happiness?"

I chewed the inside of my lip.

"Yes." I nodded firmly. "I do."

I wouldn't be here if I didn't.

He exhaled. "Well, then—" He waited, maybe debated, with a tilt of his head. "I have one final question for you today." He tossed one last look at Erin and Helen before spitting it out already.

"What do you think …" He paused. "… of me?"

Huh?

Stop it.

"Objection!" Peyton yelped. "Highly—*extremely*—irrelevant." She let her forehead fall to her forearms folded on top of the table. "We were doing so well, Hayes."

His mouth quirked. "She still has to answer."

I flicked my eyes between the two lawyers.

He was not serious.

Was he?

Peyton shrugged. "You actually … do," she surrendered, "have to answer him. He can ask you whatever he wants, within reason. And it's not technically inappropriate or unreasonable. Just—good Lord. Keep it brief."

I blazed my eyes into Harrison's, lifting a brow. "What do I think of you … today? Or when I first met you?"

I heard Helen stop typing and felt Erin freeze.

They both looked at the camera.

"Well," Harrison responded. "Either. Both. It's a very *interesting* situation, us having met before, which I suppose we can acknowledge briefly."

"All right, then," I drawled. I noticed a pin-thin scar just above his left brow, and two moles along his right jaw. In intimidating situations, I always found it helpful to tally someone's small imperfections.

Unfortunately for me, Harrison's just made him hotter.

But I forged on, feeling brave. "Well, to be honest—I think you're a really nice guy who makes the whole world think you're a jerk. I think you have aced that game. I think you're probably very good at pretending like you don't care. Pretending to be—someone else."

He winced, but I wasn't done.

"When no one's looking, I think you're probably wonderful. When everyone's looking"—I tossed a look at the camera—"I haven't decided yet. I guess my answer, Mr. Hayes, *for the record*, is that I don't know what to think of you. I mean, I *barely* even know your real name." I winked at him smugly.

Peyton had assured me multiple times that *I don't know* was an answer. I felt pleased to use it at last.

We were done here, for now.

My answer was truthy enough.

I did not need to add, *You're the hottest guy I've ever seen. And an obnoxiously fantastic lawyer.*

...

Chapter Thirteen

SCOTTIE

"*Coming!*" I flung open our front door to see Peyton poised on the welcome mat, peppy and pretty in a butterscotch yoga ensemble. The long-sleeved top gave a flash of her tummy, taut as a tambourine. She wiggled a long white box of my favorite donuts.

"You didn't." I seized the treats with both hands.

She strode past me, jingling her keys. "I figured you might be hungry—with the baby and all."

I looked at her quizzically.

"You know. After Harrison Hayes *impregnated* you with his stares."

Oh, Peyton.

Peyton and her way with *words*.

"I've been in a lot of depositions, Scott." She huffed. "And I can tell you—that guy wants you."

I rolled my eyes and opened the donut box. "You're insane. He does not want me. He wants me *dead*. You felt the tension in there."

"Yes, the *sexual tension*, exactly. They felt it from outer space." She plopped her huge tote on the tan velvet couch in the living room before taking a seat. "I saw the way he was looking at you. Let me tell you—that was not normal. My job is usually *very* professional. Swear."

I shrugged. "Felt fine to me." Mostly fine.

I was just glad I'd had the chance to share my opinion of him, for the record.

I unpeeled a maple-bacon donut from tissue and curled into a chair. "Happy Sunday!" I toasted her with the treat. "What's on the docket today, Boss?"

Sunday meetings were our new tradition. Breakfast, caffeine, then case work till bedtime. Punching in DoorDash or whipping up smoothies whenever we needed a boost. Peyton's high-rise office was always an option, but we'd settled in here nicely. We never said it aloud, but I think we both cherished the comfort and the nostalgia. The thought of our younger, playful selves and how proud those girls would be of us.

"So. Much. To. Do." Peyton sighed. "We got the trial date. Are you ready? It's January 10, Scot. As in—*this coming* January. As in, exactly *eight weeks*."

"Really?" I didn't know if this was long or short.

"Yes, really. And it's unheard of—a date this soon."

Oh.

"Lawsuits like this can take years," Peyton explained. "Companies like Kingston find a million reasons to push them. Courts, too. Someone either wants us to win—or wants us to lose. This isn't much time, for either side."

I considered this.

Two months seemed like enough time to me. I couldn't imagine carrying the weight of a lawsuit for years, like the queen,

Erin Brockovich. But if she could fight like she fought, then we could do this.

I squared my shoulders. "Then we better get started."

In unison, we pulled our computers onto our laps and started tapping in silence, letting the sugar and coffee beans work through our veins.

"Morning, worker bees!" My dad filled the archway that separated us from the dining room. "Can I get you guys anything?"

"Morning, Mr. Holiday!" Peyton chirped, breaking her focus to greet her favorite man on the planet. "I think we're fine, but thank you *so* much."

I held out the donut box like an offering plate. "Old-fashioned for the old-fashioned?"

"I'm good, too—and thanks for that." He winked, lifting a thermos custom designed with snapshots of him and me, *World's Best Dad* in black font. I instantly felt bad for calling him old as I remembered him unwrapping it at my rehearsal dinner. He'd cried, actual waterfall-tears. He really was as good as they came, his battered brown Bible tucked carefully under one elbow now. "Heading to brunch after church." He smiled. "I'll see you girls later. Don't forget to take breaks."

"Breaks are for wimps!" sang Peyton, eyes locked back on her screen.

"Tell that to God," said Dad. "Resting on the seventh day seemed to work out for him ..." His voice faded into the hallway and then the garage.

"Bye, Dad!" I called.

"Don't do anything we wouldn't do!" Peyton yelled.

Once his Bronco had rumbled into the street, Peyton looked to me. "Do you think he'll ever date again? Find love? Get married?"

The thought was so hopeful, like an old hymn. On one hand, the thought of him finding love again thrilled me. Someone to join him at church and to weeknight dinners at the Cheesecake Factory.

On the other, the notion of another woman, any woman, so much as accidentally bumping his precious heart and leaving a mark—well, it was more than my own heart could handle.

Especially these days.

"I hope so," I answered honestly. "I keep telling him to get on the dating apps."

"My gosh, he would *slay* at the apps." Peyton's blue eyes rounded. "When we're done with all of this, let's help him. In like ninety days from now when we actually have a second to pee."

I double-clicked on my case folder, which was filling up daily with documents. One by one, color-coded, like gumballs. I inhaled. "Do you want to go first, or me?"

We'd fallen into this practice. One of us would present our latest findings and arguments. Daily we were grinding away at the case, independently but together. Building. Grain by grain, our castle was forming. The dynasty to send Kingston crumbling.

"You go," she said. "I have a witness update. And something else—interesting."

"Truly interesting or weird-interesting?"

"Surprising-interesting."

"Okay, well, now I'm intrigued. You go first."

She sipped her coffee, flapping her hand at me. "No," she insisted. "I want to hear what you learned at the library."

Yesterday I had sent her a selfie from the Newport Beach Public Library, where I'd unearthed my gold. In the picture I was air-kissing a stack of nine books, every one supremely relevant to our mission impossible.

Now I pulled one of the heftiest books from my bag, lobbing it into the air. Peyton grabbed it with a thud.

"Um, what is this *brick?*" she inquired. "It literally weighs more than you."

Golden swirls and stars embellished the border of the canvas green cover, with four words stamped in the center: *Grimms' Complete Fairy Tales.*

"You are holding the source material for the Kingston Company's greatest hits." I gave a bow in my chair.

I'd always known vaguely that the Kingston Company didn't come up with the fairy tales with which now it was nearly synonymous. But if I was serious about winning here, I knew I needed to clarify my understanding.

And so, I did.

I *more than* did.

It only took me two twelve-hour days at the library.

While Peyton rifled through the book's pages, pausing where I'd stuck Post-its, I gave her my expert summary.

I shared what I'd learned about Mr. Wade Kingston, visionary and businessman, from the earliest days of his company. Rather than creating original stories from scratch at the onset, he had focused instead on retelling stories already known by the world. He built on the familiarity and the fantasy.

European folklore, fables, novels.

These were his inspiration and muse.

Bambi, *The Adventures of Pinocchio*, and *Mary Poppins* were full-length novels for children, published in 1923, 1883, and 1934, respectively.

Snow White, *Rapunzel*, and *Sleeping Beauty* were folk tales from Europe, compiled in 1812 by the Brothers Grimm. They thought the stories represented the German people in an important way—illustrating the strength of children and families surviving hardship. The brothers wanted to preserve the oral tradition of these tales forever.

The Little Mermaid and *The Snow Queen* were Danish fairy tales written by Hans Christian Andersen. They provided inspiration for some of Kingston's best-loved princesses and their stories.

"What people don't realize," I continued, "is that in some cases—most cases—Kingston *drastically* changed the original fairy tale. The Kingston 'magic' is real. I understand gearing content for children. But how far is too far? Wade Kingston essentially omitted the darkest evil, the weirdest subplots, and often—"

"The unhappy endings."

"Ding-ding!"

I told her that *Cinderella* had a version that even predated the Grimm brothers. Published in 1697, that *Cinderella*, from Charles Perrault, was most widely known today. The glass slipper, the pumpkin, the fairy godmother. Kingston's version, of course.

"Grimm, however, made basically *everything* grim," I explained.

I told her about their *Cinderella*, in which one of the stepsisters cuts off her own toes to try and make the shoe fit. I told her about *The Frog Prince*, in which the princess throws the frog against the wall in frustration—and that's how he turns into a human prince. That it was never a kiss. I told her about Grimms' *Snow White*, in which the evil queen requests her lungs and her liver—not her heart—from the huntsman. And that the queen eats them, salted and boiled.

I told her that Kingston left all this out.

"It's all very *Game of Thrones*." Peyton lifted the book to her face. "Nothing like a little cannibalism."

"I didn't even tell you about the original version of *Sleeping Beauty*." I winced. "Let's just say the king could've used a lecture about consent. The princess was impregnated *in her sleep*. Can you even? I could go on and on about the disturbing content in the original versions of these stories. And Kingston just … ignored it all. Or at the very least, most of it."

"Negligence."

"Exactly."

She bit her top lip. "Irresponsible erasure of original, historical content that we all deserved to grow up with." Her gears were turning. "Fairy tales were perhaps originally intended to convey a realistic message—one of beauty and pain—even through its fantastical measures. A promise—but a warning, too."

"Yep," I said. "And to be fair, Kingston always includes a bad guy—we can't ignore that. But it's like they took these powerful, complex European stories and watered them *way, way* down for an American audience. With no acknowledgment that sometimes, evil *does* win." I broke for a bite of donut. "Even though—let's be real—some of those Kingston villains are terrifying."

"Right?" Peyton shivered. "The *Snow White* witch and her facial warts." Nothing scared her more than bad skin. "This is good, Scot. We need a solid witness to take the stand, though. A Kingston critic or European lit theorist, maybe. The smartest scholar or cultural commentator we can find. Can you work on that?"

"One step ahead of you." I beamed, pulling a sheet from my folder. Blanket of red hair, fair skin, spindle-sharp olive eyes. I'd done a double take to make sure it wasn't Jessica Chastain. "She did her doctoral thesis on the Kingston Company's treatment of fairy tales. How the company has manipulated history and literature, and therefore, our children. Basically, lied to the world."

"Fantastic. And a woman? Even better."

I stacked the rest of the books in a tower between us. "If you want to look, they're all here."

"Perfection." She reached for the Perrault. "I'm seriously so impressed. Anything else?"

"A few little things—but, you go. I want to hear your *surprising-interesting* information."

"Well, before that, let me update you on our witness list."

She rattled off the names and titles of everyone we were after.

There was my therapist from San Francisco, who could attest to my mental health history. Colby, the roommate who'd witnessed my emotional plummet right into Hades. My dad, whom we would need to approach with care, but whose testimony would be crucial.

Most ambitiously, but perhaps most importantly, Peyton was determined to get in touch with the higher-ups at the IRAA: the Imagination Recalibration Authority of America. This regulatory association was Kingston's most longstanding enemy, battling them incessantly over content, ratings, and appropriateness of material.

While much of the world believed in Kingston's positive impact on imagination, the IRAA held steadfastly that the company's films were debasing youth, dumbing down dreams, and propagating negative stereotypes. If we could get an IRAA member, Peyton insisted, we might have this thing locked. We needed their loud mouths and deep pockets on our side of the aisle.

Additional witnesses would likely arise, but Peyton would begin the depositions next week, in person and via Zoom.

Now it was my turn to gawk. "Wow. You really know what you're doing."

"Obvs." She swigged the rest of her coffee. "Now, I'll get to this last thing. Which maybe I've hyped too much—because it doesn't technically even have to do with the case."

"What?" I gasped, slapping my heart with my hand. "Peyton McKenzie? *Wasting time*? Can you go get me a parka because I think hell just froze."

She ignored me. "Well, it does have to do with the case—and it doesn't."

"Go on."

"As part of the case," she started, "like I told you, I was given access to *everything*. Kingston documents, records, and emails. Dating back *years*. Like literally, all the years."

I nodded.

"Well, I sorted and searched through emails until my eyeballs hurt. I was looking for anything. *Everything*. Mostly any sign of misconduct. Something to incriminate Kingston. Any indication that there's a bad guy pulling the strings. Some sordid master agenda or the tiniest hint of foul play. Or—fine—any sign that Wade Kingston is out there, somewhere, discoverable."

"And?" I probed.

"And, *nothing*."

My posture sunk, but Peyton forged on.

"It's no surprise that they'd cover their tracks immaculately if there was something to hide. I was hoping to find something big. *But*." She yanked open her laptop again. "After Kingston came up squeaky clean, I don't know—I guess I got curious about your baby daddy."

"Can you please not call him that?"

"He was just such a *monster* in college."

"Seriously?" I curved an eyebrow. "That's pretty harsh, even for you."

"He went through Kappas like pop rocks, Scot. The whole baseball team, just—*barf*. He does seem to be fairly upstanding these days, in comparison. Despite his lying. And inability to keep his eyes in his pants."

"Yeah, I did not need that visual."

"I'm *trying to* tell you that I wanted Harrison Hayes to be our biggest villain here. Office flirtations, porn subscriptions, fudging on his billable hours ... *something*." She stopped clicking and presented her screen to me. "But *unfortunately*, my digging revealed that my beast might have turned into—less of a beast. And you need to know as much as you can about Harrison Hayes, Scottie. Because the more you know, the less he'll have the ability to intimidate you in court."

She was right.

This jived with my hunting-for-scars theory.

I snatched the computer. In the "from" column of an email inbox, over and over, gleamed the name I'd become too familiar with.

Harrison Hayes, *Harrison Hayes*, *Harrison Hayes*, into infinity. Dozens—maybe hundreds—of emails. Surely, he sent countless emails on average every day.

But these were all to the same person: a Caleb Waters.

I scrolled down, down, down.

"What am I looking at, exactly?"

"Open one of them."

I clicked on the one subjected, *Swing Hard This Weekend!*

CIF PLAYOFFS!!!!! I'm so bummed I can't be there today. I'm cheering you on! No matter what happens, we'll celebrate soon. California Pizza Kitchen and batting cages!

And then the one that said *See You on Saturday!*

Can't wait to see you, buddy! And don't worry. Your first tux always feels a little awkward, but we'll get you looking like Bond. I just can't believe you're Homecoming Prince! It's a testament to your kindness and character. I'm so proud of you.

I opened another message Peyton had flagged within the same folder, a reply from Harrison to CASH—Court Appointed Special Helpers—an organization I knew helped children in foster care by connecting them with a mentor and scholarships. The email included the summary of Harrison's annual giving last year.

Fifteen thousand dollars.

And the name of Harrison's mentee: Caleb Waters.

Surprise swelled in my belly, teasing its way up my throat. He *was* part sweetheart, after all. Maybe even more than he knew. I gave my instincts a silent thumbs-up.

"Harrison is a ... *mentor*? For *foster youth*?"

"Apparently." Peyton sighed. "Rather *inconvenient* when you're trying to hate someone. But now I'm wondering—why? I mean, lots of lawyers donate time and money to charity. But this is some high-key involvement. Right? And fine, if you're going to twist my arm, it's pretty, unbelievably sweet. Makes me wonder, though. Why CASH? Why Caleb?"

"I'll look into it."

"Are you sure?"

"Of course." My curiosity was red-hot. "Can you forward these emails to me?"

"Yes, I'll put them on a drive for you. They'd take until next year to send."

"Cool."

The doorbell sang, jarring us both.

Eager for a stretch, I sprang to my UGGs. I was still getting away with wearing whatever I wanted at home. Cheetah leggings and an oversized chunky black sweater today. "Coming!" I sang, unprepared for the scene awaiting me.

Young, fit, and blond, a Nordic-looking gentleman greeted me at the door. His clipboard and khaki polo said business. "Peyton McKenzie?"

I stole a look backward. "She's—here."

Unseasonably hot morning sun drenched a U-Haul truck that was backing into the driveway. In slow motion, I watched the truck park, before another young guy unlatched the rear door and rolled it all the way to the top.

Boxes and boxes—*file boxes?*—were stacked inside to the ceiling. Two more workers hopped out of the truck's cab and beelined it for the rear.

"I'm so sorry," I said cluelessly. "There must be some mistake. We didn't order anything." And my things had arrived from San Francisco three weeks ago.

Peyton materialized beside me, snatching the clipboard. "Yes, thank you so much ... *Finn*," she read from his nametag, winking. "I'll sign for this."

I looked at her in befuddlement. "What in the world?" I hissed.

Her cheeks flushed scarlet, a rarity. "I'm so sorry, Scot.

I should've told you—but there's no way these would fit at my office, or my apartment and"—she shrugged—"I didn't think you'd mind, so I gave them your address as our location headquarters."

"You mean my *dad's* address."

Finn cleared his throat. "Err—where do you want the boxes, Ms. McKenzie?" The small troop in khaki had lined up behind him, arms full.

Peyton looked to me.

"Ah." I thought fast, sucking in air. "The garage, I guess. I'll open it for you. Give me a moment." I held up a finger, hating that my sweet dad wouldn't even complain when he had to park his baby Bronco outside.

I pivoted back to Peyton, brows high.

"They're files from Kingston," she explained.

"*All of them?*" I was slack-jawed, incredulous. "Every one of those ten million boxes?"

"Yes."

"And we need to sort through—again, *all of them?*"

"I told you this would be lots of work, Scot."

I pointed back to our case materials, already heaped high in the living room. "*That*," I retorted, "is a lot of work. *This?* This is just insanity. We'll never make a *dent* in that. And what if there's something important in there, that we miss?"

Finn shifted uneasily, hacking a cough.

"Just one more sec," I apologized to him.

"There might be something important, sure, but don't worry." Peyton seized my shoulders in a confident square. "It's called a document dump. It's an *intimidation tactic*. Kingston is trying to bury us. We can't possibly read through everything—and they know it. We're going to find everything that we need. Somehow. I promise."

I let my arms dangle down at my sides like two dumbbells too heavy to carry. "*Fine.*" I turned toward the garage. "But I'm not tackling these alone."

"Hey!" Peyton called over my shoulder. "Maybe we'll find Wade Kingston in there!"

She'd better hope.

...

Chapter Fourteen

HARRISON

If I'd survived that deposition, I could survive anything.

This is what I told myself on the way to meet Gym Ashley, at last. It was Sunday night—two days after that inquisition of nightmares—and hard to be mad at the restaurant choice. Malibu Farms at Lido Marina Village. Delicious food, oceanfront views, and a rustic farm ambience. The young girls at Kingston lived for this place.

I, meanwhile, lived for any break from the office or from my own head lately.

Thankfully Kingston had managed to keep my name out of the press. So far, anyway. Our PR team was made for a crisis. As usual with big lawsuits, the news articles popping up daily cited Callahan & Lucas generally as our defenders. But I was the one entrenched, overwhelmed—more than I'd ever been as a lawyer.

The stakes were mounting, along with my stress.

As I trotted down the steps of the parking garage to the strip of restaurants and shops along Newport's harbor, I hoped to breathe in some peace. I felt my shoulders relaxing as I passed the bourgeois boutiques and eateries. Lots of shiplap and flower walls. Instagram photo ops everywhere.

I noticed a mural scripted onto white brick: *Let Your Dreams Set Sail.*

Ha.

Watch out for Scotland Holiday.

She might sue you if she gets shipwrecked.

I wasn't exactly proud of my behavior inside that conference room—but I meant it when I told Erin later that I couldn't help myself. I didn't understand it, necessarily, but something like passion or anger kept surging inside me.

Yes, Erin said reassuringly. *We saw that, but it's okay!*

Wanting to win, wanting to fight—and, yes, maybe also wanting Scottie in some abstract way I couldn't seem to identify. I thought I'd despise her for what she was doing, and certainly, part of me did.

How could someone so wildly smart be pursuing something so dumb?

But then there were those apple-green eyes.

Sharp, sexy, and smart.

Completely alarming.

Pulling me into a glare-off that throbbed like a drumbeat under my suit.

And then she would say something totally stupid that yanked me back into reality—into the *actual* world—in which this girl was dragging my company insultingly through a circus.

In the end, though, I thought the deposition went well.

Right, Erin? It went okay?

I'd begged for my assistant's affirmation, honestly. This was still my first case. We got what we needed, I thought, didn't we? Honest and forthright answers from our attacker?

Yes, Harrison. Erin's smile was pure perk and Pollyanna. *It was tense at times—but sure, great! You got the answers we needed, and that's what matters!*

This morning, I'd returned to running club for the first time, since the one time, not-so-secretly hoping I'd run into Scottie again. Which might have been professionally questionable at this point, but I didn't care. My heart had sped with my feet when I approached the group—and slowed when I saw that she wasn't part of the half circle.

In retrospect, I realized Scottie might've sprinted away from me, anyway, after our showdown. But how could I not be curious? Would she ignore me again, stuff in her earbuds and look away? Or was there a chance I had sparked her intrigue in the same weird way she'd sparked mine?

No.

Not happening.

I could not have a crush on my plaintiff.

Not even an angsty, complicated, not-exactly-normal-crush situation.

I would have to forget it.

Maybe Gym Ashley could help with that.

Across the airy, bright restaurant, brimming with white oak tables, attractive couples, and candlelight, Ashley waved at me. Her usual ponytail was nowhere in sight, replaced with long, lemony waves. She had *great* hair, I noticed. The princess job made even more sense with it down. Her tight black dress was a moody contrast to the bubblegum aura she emanated at the gym.

I liked it.

Maybe most of us were two different people inside the gym and out.

Ashley stood as I neared her, the fall ocean breeze floating around us. She flung out two arms for a hug. She was a tall girl, maybe six foot in heels, but I still had to dip to squeeze her.

"Hiiiiii!" she squealed, wringing my neck. "I am *so happy* this finally worked out. Can you even? We're here! We're, like, *not* in our workout clothes."

She was high-strung but didn't seem nervous. This must just be her personality. Her brown eyes were big. Her smile was warm.

"I'm glad you kept asking," I fibbed, taking my seat, camel leather on metal. She scooped into the bench across from me, and I mirrored her smile.

"Well, it's hard to get your attention when you're so in the *zone*." She tapped her fingernails onto the menu. "Mister Treadmill over there. But we made it. Cheers!"

"Cheers," I said, lifting my water glass.

I asked her to tell me more about work—translation: to remind me of every detail because I'd forgotten. I wished suddenly that I'd remembered, though. She was a very sweet girl, and I found myself hoping for chemistry. I wasn't feeling the sizzle, but maybe I could ignite it.

Ashley told me she taught kindergarten at a public school in Costa Mesa. She explained that every single one of her students lived below the poverty line, and that for 95 percent of them, English was their second language, Spanish their first.

"Do you speak Spanish, then?" I asked.

"*Si, Senor.*" Her accent rolled flawlessly, unexpectedly. "*Y tu también?*"

"*Un poco.*" I laughed a bit awkwardly, flushed, and impressed by her. "I wish I knew more. I'm half-Cuban, actually."

She cupped her glass. "I see that. So handsome. Mom's side or dad's?"

I swallowed, appreciative of the compliment but wishing against further questions. "My mom's."

"Where do your parents live?"

Already?

Dang it.

It wasn't the main reason I didn't date, but it was for sure on the list. My family of origin was hard to describe in new social settings. The balancing act was a delicate one. Don't be a total, lame downer, but also don't sound callous or flippant.

The depth of my answer also depended on who was asking. Ashley seemed truly interested, so I'd tell her the truth.

Or most of the truth.

"My biological parents died when I was three. In a car accident," I began. "But I was raised in the foster system, and I had a great experience. And I didn't find her until my twenties, but now, I'm really close to my maternal grandmother. She reams me for not knowing more Spanish." I paused, exhaling. "Her name is Rosa, and that's what I call her. My Rosa."

I hadn't shared this much in a while.

Ashley blinked. "Oh. *Wow.* That's, like—wow, I'm so sorry, Harrison." She gulped some water and gently set down her glass. "So, you went into the system right away? No relatives offered to take you? Tried to adopt you? I'm—so sorry if that's insensitive, I just—I have a lot of students in the system. My heart. You know?"

I did know. "No blood relative was equipped to take me, ah, unfortunately. No. But truly, I loved my two foster families."

It was a half-truth.

I had loved one of my foster families.

The candle on the table flickered between us as I thought back to my summer between junior high and high school. I was placed in a new foster home that July, after my first foster mom, Ruth, fell unexpectedly pregnant with twins. She had pale hair and a long, thin face. Fine wrinkles that made me feel safe. She wrote poetry and drove a station wagon.

When she told me I'd be moving on to another family, she wept as she shook both my hands, there at our marble countertop, home of a thousand egg breakfasts. "We love you *so much*, Harrison. We know you'll be happy with this new family. We are so *lucky* that we got to raise you until now. Your big brown eyes as a little boy—your tee-ball swing. We always knew you were something. We're always a phone call away."

Ruth meant her promise with every breath, at the time. I chose to believe that. But ultimately, she couldn't fulfill it. Twins at age forty—on top of the four they already had—swallowed the rest of her time and her love. She called me on my first two birthdays away from them—fourteen and fifteen—but by sixteen, she had forgotten.

She didn't call.

Nobody called.

It was the first night I ever got drunk and kissed a girl I didn't know.

My next and last foster family had been horrible. Rick and Georgia, six foster kids, in it to cash the checks. I shared a room with two other boys. We never spoke to each other—just grunted around in our macho adolescent silence. The beige tract home smelled of urine and sour milk. Rick yelled, Georgia nagged. Nobody was invested in me, whatsoever, at that point.

Except my lawyer, George Gunn.

Every foster kid who rises to shine has a great lawyer behind them. Few people realize this, and I only knew because I had gotten lucky. Somebody needed to negotiate and communicate between the social worker, the foster system, the families, and me. Fight for my rights; make sure I was okay. With George in my corner, I could survive just about anything for four years. He kept me going. It was the countdown to college. I tallied the months in pencil on the wood of my bunk bed.

My first foster parents might have abandoned me—but at least they had given me baseball. I made varsity as a freshman, which was everything for my social life. I mowed lawns for extra cash and spent every dollar on private coaching and batting cage hours. I didn't love much, but I loved baseball.

And I was good at it.

Baseball was my ticket out.

Until it took me out.

"You okay?" Ashley waved her hand like a windshield wiper. "You look like you went somewhere for a second." She flicked her head upward, and I saw our waitress standing there, pen angled, hair-thin brows raised under a blunt raven bob.

"Ah … sorry. Just thinking about what I want here." I gave the menu a once-over. "I'll have—the New York strip steak, please? Medium rare."

"*Yum*," Ashley purred. "I also ordered us the nachos to share. They are to *die* for."

"Well, here's to our funeral then."

"May we rest in *cheese*."

I laughed. It was the kind of bad joke I loved.

I tilted my head and thought for the second time how much Ashley looked like a Kingston princess. The big almond eyes and her sweetness. She was a natural.

"I want to know," I said, offloading my menu to the waitress, "what it was like being a princess for Kingston. Cinderella and Rapunzel, right? I want to know all the secrets."

"*Me* tell *you* the secrets?" She laughed. "Doesn't being a Kingston lawyer mean you're in some creepy inner circle of trust? Plus—aren't *you* going to tell *me* all the dirty details about that gorgeous girl all over the news? The one suing you guys for not granting her genie wishes?"

Shoot.

Scottie was gorgeous, wasn't she?

And Ashley was paying attention.

I coughed into my napkin.

"Unfortunately—I am not at liberty to discuss details of the Holiday case." I was thankful for the honest excuse. "But, yes, that may be true," I confirmed. "About the circle of trust. The innermost core of Kingston can be a bit creepy." I knew about every secret passage and tunnel in the amusement park, plus the intensive hiring criteria at every level. The hidden Rickeys, the best churro carts, how the Haunted House really worked.

"I'll tell you what I know," I offered, "if you tell me?" The words came out more suggestive than I had intended, but Ashley was gulping them down.

She hinged forward conspiratorially. "Deal. Ask me anything."

I leaned back. "Anything, huh?" What did I want to know? Or suddenly, I wondered—more importantly—what information might be potentially helpful to my case? I had a real-life princess here in the hot seat. "Was Kingston good to you?" I heard myself asking. "As a company—and an employer?"

She narrowed her eyes playfully. "Are you asking me as a lawyer or as my date?"

I smiled. "Your date. Off the record, Your Highness."

Wistfulness clouded her eyes. "Well then," she started. "It was the best. Like the very best. It was a dream. The princesses had some catfights. Don't get me wrong. There's a lot of estrogen in those wig rooms. And there's a serious hierarchy, for the parades and the trips—the shifts and the ranks. But what workplace doesn't have politics, right?"

She could say that again.

"Kingston made my dreams come true." She paused. "Cheesy—but true. I made some of my best friends for life. I got to be face-to-face with every walk of humanity. And" —she shrugged, looking young—"I got to be a princess when I grew up."

The waitress presented our nachos, a steaming, colored pile of toppings and crispiness.

"That's really a whole thing for girls, isn't it?" I scooped a chip covered in pico de gallo and sour cream. "Princesses, I mean."

"Of course," she affirmed. "It's like we can't even help it. We just grow up—wanting to be one." She procured an extra-decadent piece of the nachos. "And the feeling of little girls *believing*—with their whole hearts—that I was the *real* Cinderella?" Her voice lowered, chip in the air. "You know, three different times, I got to meet a little girl through the Make-a-Wish Foundation. Spend the day with the family. Give them a private park tour. And ... you can't put a price on that. To be someone's dying wish."

"I can't imagine you can." I was growing impressed by this girl, even if I wasn't feeling the fire.

"So—what's your deal with Kingston?" she probed. "You grew up loving princesses, too?"

I laughed. "Not exactly. Though if I had to choose: Isla, all the way, every day."

"Thanks a lot," she said, reaching to slug my shoulder. "The only princess I *wasn't*."

"Wow, I did *not* mean it that way," I said honestly. "Did I mention how much I have always loved Cinderella?"

"It's fine, it's fine. Isla and I are still the dearest of friends. But really—I want to know what it is for you, about Kingston. We both know that you don't last long at the company unless you really buy into it all."

This was true, to a degree. "I don't know, exactly." I swallowed. "It was never about the royalty for me. I didn't grow up wanting to be a prince, or even rich or powerful. I just—"

What, then?

I'd never been asked this before.

"If I'm being totally honest." I paused. Why not be totally honest? By this point I felt almost entirely safe at this table, with nothing I could think of to lose. "I can't remember my parents' faces. Before their accident." I let that fall before I pressed on. "I do remember my mom's voice, though. It was so beautiful. I remember her singing Kingston songs while she rocked me to sleep. Especially 'Love is Never Lost.' But so many more, too."

Ashley rolled her eyes indulgently. "So. Many. Good. Songs. Too many, really."

"Agreed." I folded my hands on the table. "Then, when my parents died, through my childhood, I became Harrison the Foster Kid. I didn't shake that until college. And Kingston films were a comfort to me. Genuinely. The characters felt like my friends. I know that sounds lame."

"Not to me." She pointed up to her head, as if to an invisible crown. "Princess here."

I laughed, thankfully, and a little sadly.

I'd realized as I'd said it how true it was—the importance of the characters to my formation. I remembered the boxy TVs and their curved, static screens, coming to life with something I could rely on.

"The coming-of-age stories," I said. "Those were the ones that resonated with me the most. *Pinocchio*, *Hercules*. Their persistence and hope, you know? Kingston's newer work is incredible, too, but I don't think they will ever beat the originals."

Ashley nodded. "One hundred percent."

"It's almost like those stories became part of me, you know?" I shot her a half grin. "They're like—braided into my psyche."

I coughed, hoping to dismiss some of the sentimentality suddenly filling my voice.

"Anyway. When I decided to leave big law and find something in-house," I explained, "Kingston was the first place I looked. Keep wishing, as Cinderella would say."

"And dreaming," she echoed in a soft song.

Of course, her voice was even prettier than her hair.

It reminded me of my mom's.

Our food appeared then like a magic trick, and we continued to chat and munch with companionable ease.

My steak was insanely good, and judging by her soon-empty plate, Ashley loved her salmon too. We each ordered coffee and our own dessert.

It was a wonderful night.

But as I watched Ashley stab at her gluten-free carrot cake, I couldn't keep my mind from wandering into another land.

How is Scottie going to play this?

She can't really think she might win.

I bet she always orders the chocolate.

Brown eyes are great, but—

Green.

Ashley, however, was truly a gem of a human. A princess well worth her crown.

I scanned my mental Rolodex of eligible buddies who would drop everything for a chance with a girl like her. I could easily help find a guy for her, down the line, maybe. I would explain politely to her, once again, that I wasn't looking for anything romantic right now.

I was, however, looking for something else.

I was hunting for witnesses. For tried-and-true, supremely well-spoken Kingston aficionados, in fact. For people who made believing look brilliant.

To my own surprise, I also wouldn't mind a new pal, if she was game.

"Ashley," I said, forking my grilled chocolate cake, "how would you feel about the possible opportunity of testifying for Kingston in court?"

...

Chapter Fifteen

SCOTTIE

I rubbed my temples. My afternoon Americano hadn't tasted as good as my morning one. Bitter espresso, unsweetened, round one, wasn't bad.

Let's work! Let's drink! Let's go!

Now I was just feeling agitated and maybe a little paranoid.

Should I just wash it down with a Frappuccino?

Probably not, I decided, my jolted limbs admittedly shaking.

Camped inside my favorite Starbucks, the one bordering Fashion Island, I sat back. The lofty white ceilings, pearly subway-tiled walls, and caramel-colored leather upholstery made the space feel more elevated than the average chain.

The proximity to the Newport Beach Public Library was also convenient. I'd started the morning there, picked up some more books, and found myself here, submersed in caffeine and research, again. Both things officially expanded into infinity for me these days. There was literally no limit to either.

It was wonderful.

It was the worst.

And now, already, it was 5:30 p.m.

I'd worked hard on this November Wednesday, and I felt pleased. Plus, my stomach was starting to rumble like a stampede of wildebeests.

Before retiring, though, I scrolled back through the Word document that held today's project, an assignment from Peyton. More like a challenge, really.

As a building block of our case, she wanted me to start tracing my romantic history, as far back as I could remember with court-worthy clarity. Of course, she could help fill in some of the gaps, because she was there for all of it. What were best friends for if not remembering to hate every male who'd ever so much as cut you off in the lunch line?

Then, further still, Peyton wanted me to compare each man who'd broken my heart to a different Kingston prince.

"If we can identify the problematic behaviors of the most popular Kingston princes, the boys we were brainwashed to worship, then we have tapped into a whole new arsenal of powerful evidence," she'd argued passionately. "It's already a *big* case. We've identified our high-level complaints. But if we can also make it a *small* case—drill into some ultra-specifics that Kingston won't see coming—we can catch them off guard. Not to mention appeal to every juror who's been dumped by a jerk."

"You want me to compare my ex-boyfriends to Kingston princes," I repeated flatly. "Are you being serious? Because I can't tell. This is equal parts truly inspired—and completely ridiculous."

"Do I need to keep reminding you who begged me to take this *inspired* and *ridiculous case*?"

"Fair enough." I sighed. "Should I, like, draw parallels in a flowchart?"

She snapped her fingers. "Yes. A flowchart would be fantastic."

So.

She was serious.

As always, though, Peyton had counseled me prudently on the chart idea. I gazed with pride upon the diagram I'd sketched in my notepad. Turned out my exes did have some Kingston prince counterparts. You might even say I'd worked my way through the royal roster.

I grinned and cringed simultaneously as I read my naughty list:

Aladdin → Jace Anderson, Eighth Grade

In junior high, I met my first boyfriend, Jace Anderson. He had raven hair and blue eyes. He asked if I'd be his girlfriend in front of the cafeteria vending machines and an audience. He smelled like first love and Acqua di Giò.

Jace was the first boy I ever touched, or rather, who touched me, and made me want to touch him back. I remember him grabbing my hand and feeling the heat in my belly, thinking, *Oh! This is fun. This is why people hold hands.* We were on our way to history class when those first butterflies flapped to life.

Jace, unfortunately, was a pathological liar.

Not about anything malicious. I wasn't even angry, at first.

They were just *so weird,* the lies.

I'd never known who he was.

He said he lived in Newport Coast—perhaps the most luxurious and expensive coastal gated community in Orange County, filled with mansions and sea cliffs. He said his house had a pool with a water slide, that he had one younger sister and two golden retrievers. His grandfather invented Pringles, he said. Both of his parents were "doctors."

It all sounded neat to me. I wasn't impressed by the money; just a little by the potato chips. He had them in his lunch every day, which was convincing. I mostly appreciated that I could talk to Jace about anything.

Not for one second did it occur to me that someone would make up a life story. Try to be someone they weren't. I wasn't exactly the golden girl on campus, anyway—someone you needed to lie to. Everyone knew my mom was gone and that none of my clothes fit quite right.

Jace, in reality, lived in an apartment with his dad, mom, and three little brothers. His dad worked construction and cheated on his young mom, who stayed home with the kids.

Jace did not come from money. He was bussed into the Irvine school system because his public charter was full. His main food groups were Top Ramen and Oscar Mayer. No relative invented those brands. Jace didn't have any sisters or an infinity pool; there were no purebred dogs.

But Jace was kind. Whip-smart, so funny. He had soft hands and pretty eyes, especially when he wore blue.

So, no, Jace wasn't rich—but the frustrating part was that I didn't need him to be.

We were *twelve*, for God's sake.

I just needed him not to lie.

Maybe it was a fluke, I thought. Maybe I'd help him change. Wouldn't that be cool? I was already crazy about him when one of his friends ratted him out to me. I confronted him without hesitation. He apologized, seeming contrite, and I forgave him. I assumed at this point that I knew everything Jace was hiding.

I did not.

Jace was also holding hands with a redheaded sixth-grader named Kelly.

So, I broke up with him.

Permanently, this time.

What I didn't know then is that if a boy lies to you about one thing—especially *who he is*—he will lie to you about anything. As my dad would tell me years later: "If a man will cheat on his wife, he'll cheat on his business partner."

Trey's private equity firm better watch it.

KINGSTON PRINCE PROBLEM #1: *Aladdin* communicates the message that dishonesty is okay. False advertising, an option. Pretending can reap great reward. The truth comes in many colors, like a magic Arabian rug. One that might lift you up to the sky, before dropping you on your head.

What does it say about Jasmine that she marries a chronic liar, and we cheer her on for it? Why do we assume that her future with Aladdin has any foundation at all? Chances are if you marry a guy who likes to get bendy with the truth, he might like to get bendy with other things, if you know what I mean.

The Beast → Weston Ford, Sophomore Year of High School

Jace Anderson admittedly ruined me for a while. *No boys*, I swore to Peyton. I was becoming obsessed with my studies anyway. Especially science. I liked that it was objective, unlike English, which you could analyze and criticize a million ways.

"But that's the beauty—the point!" insisted Peyton. "I

love hearing different perspectives and then arguing mine to the death."

Her profession had always made sense.

Tenth-grade English class, though, was where I found my next flame, where Weston Ford sat right in front of me.

What I found most intriguing about Weston is that he was the unhappiest, angriest boy I had ever met. *No one's* that angry, I'd think, staring in wonder at the back of his midnight hair sculpted into hard four-inch spikes. Black T-shirts, always. Silver chains, too. Vans shoes and press-on tattoos. Sometimes he'd sneak in an iPod, and I could *not believe* the gnashing and wailing. Like a mother, I worried for the guy's hearing.

Weston wasn't attractive, at least not in the traditional California-boy sense. Acne scars muddled his cheeks. His eyes were black as tar. I'd never seen his smile.

But there was something about him.

He was the smartest one in our class. His insights were complex, impressive. He waxed so poetic about *Animal Farm*. His black-and-white checkered backpack was stuffed with great books. I was his captive audience, looking always for good. I occasionally complimented him on his class commentary.

So, when he asked me to the homecoming dance, I didn't hesitate.

Weston was amazing—in there, somewhere.

I was sure of it.

But Weston was not amazing in there.

And I would learn it the hard way.

Weston was, as we all knew, angry. But surely good, too,

I kept insisting. *We all have good inside of us.* I would always believe that.

But something or someone had wounded this boy so completely, so deeply, at some point, that it was going to take a miracle or a mother to heal him.

He arrived to pick me up drunk, for one, wearing his Beetlejuice suit. I hated lying to my dad about anything—but I shoved Weston away from our doorstep and back toward his truck before my dad could see. None of my friends had ever even tasted beer, while Weston had a flask of moonshine stashed in his pocket.

Throughout the night, then, Weston kept sliding his hand up the slit of my red dress—over, and over, and over.

It was making me sick.

In the car, during dinner, on the dance floor, unresponsive to my repeated and unmistakable *slaps*, he persisted.

Finally, I looked at him by the punch bowl, eyes burning, heart racing. "I'm going to ask you one more time to stop touching me."

"Come on," he slurred. "Nerd."

"That's not very nice," I said.

"Oh, please," he yelled, and, right as the music hushed between songs, "YOU'RE SUCH A TEASE!"

I ran to the bathroom, crying, where Peyton found me.

"Scottie, I'm *so sorry*." She lovingly patted my updo. "I never should've let you go alone with that creep. Come on. We'll share my date."

Peyton didn't say what she could have. That I always believed the best of people, which didn't always mean believing the best of myself. That I couldn't change a boy any more than I'd changed my mom.

But it was okay. I talked to my English teacher that Monday and asked to be moved to the other side of the classroom. I told her I'd rather not explain why.

Weston and I never spoke again.

My heart clenched that April when, one day, he didn't come back to school. We were told not to ask questions.

KINGSTON PRINCE PROBLEM #2: Of all the early Kingston films, *Beauty and the Beast*'s core messages are arguably the most positive. Don't judge a beast by his cover. Genuine love can transform. We all need human connection.

But they should have added: Don't assume that *because* a man is not conventionally good-looking or popular that he is automatically good. Or that, if he is unkind, there must be a jewel within him that it is your calling to find. And if he screams at you and keeps you a prisoner? Run like the wolves out of the forest. No matter how dreamy his book collection.

That was the end of Weston, my personal beast who wasn't anything more. I hadn't yet identified Trey's Kingston counterpart, but I was working on it. In the meantime, my organizational chart listed three more suitors:

The Prince of* The Little Mermaid → *Will Simpson, Junior Year of High School
- Prom King Prick: Encourages you to become part of his world, but not before abandoning your own self. Swim away, fast. Never sacrifice your voice for a man.

The Prince of Sleeping Beauty → *Sam Fox, UC Berkeley Quarterback*
- Football Dragon Fighter: Falls for you at a party, declaring he's "never seen anyone more beautiful in his life." *You're so mysterious,* he says. Turns out he wanted someone to stay nice and quiet. Fast asleep? Even better. Not happy at your first display of a personality. He didn't want a girl. He wanted a mime. Goodbye!

The Prince of Cinderella → *Harrison Hayes, Esquire*
- Running Club Rogue: Lights you up from within and even saves the day with your shoe, which is so on brand. Promptly acts like you never existed. One "dance" does not equal love. Anyone can be sweet for forty-five minutes. Watch out for this one. *Watch close.*

I folded up my laptop, suddenly starving.

...

Chapter Sixteen

SCOTTIE

Ravenous, I left Starbucks in search of sustenance, meandering the brink of the posh outdoor mall. Twinkle lights curled around the trunks of palm trees like candy cane stripes. Christmas music was starting to echo from storefronts. The holidays were swirling to life, with only two weeks till Thanksgiving.

I decided Whole Foods would do. Peyton was obsessed with their salad bar, and she usually wasn't wrong. I could avoid the long restaurant waits and pick up some groceries, too.

Chilly air and fresh produce welcomed me. I wandered into a random aisle lined with cereals I didn't recognize. I picked up a small bag of granola.

Seven bucks?

Not happening with my new budget.

Whole Paycheck was a joke for a reason, apparently, and I didn't exactly have one right now.

I sighed.

Better stick to my man Trader Joe.

Still determined to see what the salad bar fuss was about, I set out to find it, admiring the displays on my way. Pumpkins of every variety. Gorgeous fall foliage arrangements. Ice cream brands even more foreign to me than the cereals.

On the far side of the store, I stumbled into it finally, and my Whole Mouth dropped open.

This was more, really, like a *salad experience.*

I counted the salad bars—five—each boasting a formidable holiday feast of their own. Steaming brussels sprouts, cubed sweet potatoes, seventeen kinds of lettuce. Pick your protein, fresh fruit, fancy cheese.

Peyton. She always knew.

I pulled a medium box from the brown cardboard tower. I let the sumptuous smells guide me. Maple chicken and brown rice. Roasted carrots and crisp arugula.

I could get used to this.

Hot, nutritious, delicious dinner that I didn't have to cook. Neither did my sweet dad. And only $8.99 per pound screamed a deal to me, especially for this place.

"I'd go with the pumpkin seeds," said a throaty voice over my shoulder.

My serving spoon froze in the air, hovering indecisively over pumpkin and sunflower.

"The pumpkin seeds are bigger—plus seasonal, and more flavorful."

I swallowed, dropping the spoon in a clatter.

Red filled my belly and crept to my cheeks.

It was embarrassing, really, that I knew *this voice*, instantly and already.

Tall, dark, and thick, like a chocolate bar.

The expensive kind.

Bitter and sweet.

Infuriatingly so.

I whipped around, backing into the counter, nearly dropping my dinner. I didn't say anything. I couldn't say anything.

"Sorry." Harrison's face spread into a handsome smile. Teeth gleaming, eyes crinkling, jaw pulsing, under the same white baseball cap he'd worn to running club. "Didn't mean to scare you."

I scanned him up and down before I could stop myself. He had the *best* legs, I noticed. Strapped with muscle and shape. He wore a black shirt and gray shorts. His shoelaces matched again, and my heart sank a little. They were both white as bleach—no black one in sight—tied responsibly in neat double knots.

Why was I disappointed?

"You didn't," I lied. "Scare me, that is." My eyes flitted over his face again. I was determined to keep them fixed above his giant collar bones, which reminded me of a dinosaur's. A very good-looking dinosaur.

So tall.

So solid.

So hot.

Even when he'd been angry, he'd been insanely hot.

"I've just—never been here before," I managed. "To the salad bar, anyway. Peyton is always raving about it."

His face clouded. "Peyton. Ah. My biggest fan."

I smirked. "Something like that." He held a gargantuan salad box of his own, mounted with more food than I'd imagined these things could carry. I flicked a nod. "Are you seriously going to eat all of that?"

"Probably." He shrugged. "Peyton's right—about this one thing, anyway. There's no better salad bar on the earth."

I glanced around nervously. "Are you allowed—to be talking to me?" I whispered. "Aren't there rules against us communicating?"

He took a step back, politely. "I mean, I shouldn't be contacting you directly or trying to get you alone ..."

Shame.

Gulp.

He continued, "... but if I see you in public? Sure. I'm allowed to be cordial. I can ... *acknowledge* you."

He said the word *acknowledge* like it meant something else.

This was so confusing.

Face burning hotter, I turned to resume my creation. I picked up the buffet spoon and heaped on a pile of sunflower seeds just to spite him. I tossed him a backward glance, hoping he noticed.

He took a step forward again, and I felt it.

Stupid butterflies.

"What are you doing here, anyway?" I pretended to look distracted by more of the million toppings before me.

He joined me, to my right, as if his box had more room. "I'm here for running club. There's a night run at seven. Just grabbing dinner first." He reached for the grilled veggie tongs. "I noticed you haven't been back."

I shoveled some feta. "I've been a little busy."

"Yeah, me too. Working nonstop. Thanks for that."

"Anytime." I glanced over at him and, sure enough, he was looking at me, too. Our eyes clicked into each other's, and I thought of the deposition.

Of all the personal things he now knew.

I lunged away, toward the salad dressing.

"I promise I'm not following you," he reassured, trailing behind me. "I just need some dressing, and then I'll be done."

I halted in front of the dozen-or-so vats of liquid.

Did there have to be *so* many options?

"The honey-mustard is delicious, if you're into sweet, but their balsamic is one of the best."

"What are you, the Whole Foods salad bar tour guide?"

"Well, you look like you need one."

I grabbed for the ranch—anything he hadn't mentioned. "Do you come here a lot?"

"I do. It's the best place for a reasonably priced, huge, healthy meal. I eat a lot."

"I bet you do." I smirked. "Do you ever cook?" Even as I asked it, I didn't know why. Other than the fact that he'd look good at a stove, and I was picturing it.

"Sometimes." He stood next to me, loading up on honey-mustard. "Only for people I like."

Do you like me?

Or would you if I weren't suing you?

Will you watch while I walk away?

I breathed.

Determined to stay super cool, I folded up my salad creation, the box shaped like Chinese takeout. The truth was, Harrison knew things about me now, enemy or not. And once again, he was being semisweet away from the office.

I sauntered to the register, wondering if he'd trail behind me or not.

As the silver-haired cashier confirmed my total of $12.99—*what a steal*—I heard that voice again, vibrating behind my ear. "Are you eating here or taking yours to go?"

If I was honest, I'd planned on eating it in my car. I'd hated eating alone in public since the wedding. I didn't used to mind. In fact, I used to enjoy it. Lately, though, it felt sad.

I looked to the left, to the corner of a dining area with floor-to-ceiling windows, a full bar, and tables sprinkled with a few customers.

I shrugged.

"Maybe here," I thought out loud, surprising myself. Food *did* tend to leave a stench in my car.

I lingered while Harrison paid, feeling uneasily sure he'd fall into my wake again.

Sure enough, I claimed a seat next to the window, and Harrison dropped his things at the table beside mine.

I shot up my brows.

"What?" he asked.

"You don't think this is—*a bad idea?*" My voice had dropped to a hush again, as if we were being watched.

"What, eating?" he practically shouted.

"Eating *together*." I hung my bag on the back of my chair.

"We're not eating *together*. We're eating alone. In near proximity to one another. I mean, legally. You want some water?"

I sighed, dipping into my chair. "Yes. Fine. Sure. Whatever."

Watch out for this one.

As he fetched the drinks, I opened my salad and willed this happenstance to feel normal. Of course, it was anything but. My life would likely never feel normal again, and I should accept that.

I scooped up my phone and tapped to Twitter, my latest unconscious habit. I couldn't keep myself from stalking the strips of new quips:

> Kingston's Holiday Horror, Oh My!
> Trial Date Set for Princess Plaintiff
> Damsel in Dentistry Drills into Kingston

They were still using old pictures, but I knew when the trial started, the cameras would aim at me like cannons. I'd been keeping a safe, low profile recently. Home, library, Starbucks. Still no mention of Harrison's name anywhere in the press, only Kingston's big firm. I wondered why, but I didn't want to ask.

There were, however, other things I'd like to ask.

Harrison reappeared and I grabbed a cup from him, a few drops of water splashing onto the floor. He took the seat at his own table, but on the opposite side of me, so now we faced each other, diagonally. I watched him settle with focus in front of his salad. He was slightly too big for the chair, and I wondered if he was slightly too big for most chairs. It was cute, his legs tucked into a position that looked both awkward and as normal to him as skin, like a boy outgrowing his Lego table, undaunted.

We ate in silence that should have been strained but felt surprisingly easy.

I finally rattled the quiet. "I know we probably ... shouldn't talk about the case. So ... I won't. Do that. Talk about how I'm suing you."

He nodded, chewing, eyes up and blank.

"But can I ask you something else?" I continued.

He swallowed. "Sure. Why not?"

My thoughts tumbled into an exhale. "Why does Peyton hate you so much?" I fondled my fork handle above my sweet potatoes. "Were you really that bad in college?"

Harrison sipped his water, unflinching, then paused for at least a full minute. "I was." He nodded. "That bad. Until my senior year."

"When you met Marissa."

He froze. "Peyton spares no details, does she?"

"Does any good lawyer?"

"Guess not." He wiped his palms together. "But like you said. Marissa doesn't have anything to do with the case."

I shrugged at him, daring, *So, tell me, then.*

"All right," he agreed. "I'll give you the short version. But no follow-up questions. Fair?"

"All's fair in love and lawsuits."

He gave a *humph* and started talking.

His full lips spilled forth the story, while I darted looks between them and my sweet potatoes. From his first day at the University of Arizona, I learned, Harrison Hayes was well-known on campus. He didn't share this boastfully; just rationally, like he was reciting math facts. He was a top baseball recruit and strong student, known best for his fire-fast pitch. He'd learned as a teen that girls liked him—and this was to his surprise. He'd always felt too gargantuan for his own skin. Too big, and too much, to be loved by anyone for too long. This included the string of make-outs and first dates that he crammed into his college schedule.

I refrained from asking about his family.

I gathered slowly that he'd given his time and energy away pretty freely—mostly to baseball and women.

But his actual heart, not so much.

When senior year came, with the MLB draft in sight, Harrison decided finally to slow the drinking and speed up the good choices. He changed his habits dramatically, started sleeping more, partying less.

He liked it.

He started enjoying some of his classes, not to mention his new clear mind and surge in energy. He didn't miss the hangovers, admittedly. He even began to feel bad for the way he had treated so many girls and—contrary to what Peyton thought she knew—he had made a secret list of them. And, eventually, started *apologizing* to the girls he had hurt, one by one, when he could. Not in any huge-deal way, just in a "hey, that was lame" kind of way. But he always saw in their faces that it was due.

"Really?" I asked, surprised. "You did that."

"Really." He nodded. "I did that."

He didn't so much as look at another girl until he met Marissa, in January, he explained.

Marissa was a sophomore transfer, midyear, right into Kappa. When he talked about her, his eyes darkened slightly but undeniably. He didn't gush about their happy days together—just stated plainly that she was a gorgeous brunette from Los Angeles and a business major. They had a general ed class together, astronomy, one they both needed to graduate.

Harrison and Marissa fell fast and crazy, like college kids. They dated for the next year, during which Harrison was drafted to the San Diego Padres for a huge five-year contract. Playing in the pros was his one and only dream. He proposed to Marissa on home plate after a game. He loved her—he did—and he'd never really loved anyone.

This was stated, also, like fact.

Then, two years into the pros, bottom of the eighth inning against the Angels, Harrison went to bat. Bases loaded. Padres ahead by two. It was their game to lose.

The pitcher's arm cranked.

The ball released.

The navy sky exploded to white.

Harrison felt a gunshot inside his shoulder.

Who let a gun past security? was his first thought. Of course, it wasn't a gun. It was his true love: the ball.

Life as he knew it had ended there, he explained. His career halted that day, despite two expensive surgeries and months of physical therapy.

Marissa had stood by his side, for every appointment, each up and down—until it was confirmed once and for all.

He would never play baseball again.

"I don't want to believe she wanted me for the baseball," he said. "That kind of injury would be hard on any relationship.

But, yes, it was pretty awful when she didn't stick around."

Yeah.

I knew what that felt like.

"That *is* awful." I shivered. "You didn't have to tell me all that, by the way. But—thank you. I'm so sorry."

"Well, I know a lot about you. Feels fair, I guess." He smiled. "I just want you to know—maybe even for the sake of the case—that I'm not the same guy Peyton knew. I've been through a lot. Eaten the crap sandwich, as they say."

I scrunched my nose. "I hate that saying."

He wiggled his brows. "I thought you might."

"Have you had any contact with her? Marissa? Over the years?"

"Oh gosh, no." He waved a hand. "She's married. Has a few kids, I think. Still lives in San Diego. I'm happy for her. Not meant to be."

Harrison scoured his salad box clean, and I came close to finishing, too, shoveling, quietly riveted by his stories.

We stood simultaneously and walked side by side toward the exit. He gave me the right of way and I strode past him.

He smelled so unbelievably good.

Musk and warm wood.

"You know, you're actually not that horrible—when you're not being horrible," I acknowledged coolly as I felt his heat.

He side-eyed me. "Please don't tell me that's supposed to be a compliment."

I smirked. "It's as good as you're going to get."

"Fine."

"*Fine.*"

"Punk." He couldn't stifle his smile, his one dimple carving deep.

When we reached the parking lot, we stood in the limbo of saying goodbye to someone you knew better than a handshake, but not enough for a hug.

He opted for the high five.

I reached up and slapped his high hand, holding mine there a beat too long.

To my shock, he folded his lengthy fingers into my own.

Stop!

Don't.

Stunning me further, he pulled me to him—not inappropriately close, but close enough that I had to look up at him, towering.

He tilted my chin, tentatively, with his other hand.

It should have felt awkward.

It didn't.

No, it did not.

I looked in his eyes, through those dark lashes, then at his lips.

Kiss me, I willed abruptly, silently.

Kiss me!

"Bye, Scottie."

He released me.

Patted my head.

The darn head pat.

He jogged away.

...

I floated home with the light evening traffic down Jamboree Road, my head still swimming in the hot pool of Harrison's eyes.

What in God's name was that moment?

I didn't want to overanalyze it out of fear that it wasn't real. I'd hold it loosely, like the best cotton candy from Kingston Court.

My phone vibrated from my cupholder, startling me, glowing with Peyton's name. I wasn't sure if I should tell her what happened—not yet anyway. "Hi, P.!"

"Well, you sound chipper."

Did I?

"I am. I got so much done today."

"Your homework went well?"

Starbucks felt like a year ago. "*So* well. *So* many bad boyfriends."

"Good, good," she said. "Okay. Are you sitting down?"

I glanced down at my lap. "Yes. Yikes. Why?"

"No, no. It's good news. Insane news. *I-don't-even-know-how-to-tell-you-this* news."

My chest pitter-pattered. "Spill it."

"I got a call today, Scottie. From the Imagination Recalibration Authority of America. The big guns. Our kill shot."

"No." I breathed.

"Yes, 100 percent. I talked to their president. They want to file an amicus brief."

"Amica-huh?"

"They want to—basically, chime into the lawsuit, on our behalf. They're working on a statement in support of our case, which they'll submit to the court."

I squealed.

"I know," she continued. "But there's more."

"Go on."

She paused. "Scottie—they want to take over the case. Bring in their lawyers. Pay us—*a lot* of money, and handle everything from here. Between the media attention and Kingston's response, they see this as a huge opportunity for their organization. Their chance to take down Kingston, once and for all. Change their content. Change the world."

I should have felt pride, relief, and overwhelming gratitude. Wonder and awe that our little-case-that-could had managed to garner this kind of attention.

Why did I feel nauseous instead?

This was *our* lawsuit, our bona fide baby. My broken-winged flight to justice. Peyton and Scottie. Scottie and Peyton.

Holiday vs. Kingston.

Scotland Holiday vs. Harrison Hayes.

Bringing in the bomb to end all bombs?

That didn't feel, well, *fair*.

"Scot, did you hear me?"

"Yes, yes, of course. I'm just—processing. Wow!" I tried so hard to sound happy. "I can't believe it. But what does that mean exactly? What about all our work?"

"You'll still be the key witness. Your claims are everything. The crux of it all."

"And—what about you? What would this mean for you?"

She hesitated over the line. "I'll be done with the case, Scot. I'll get back to work. But I will be *abundantly* taken care of—trust me. And you'll be in the hands of some of the best lawyers in the country."

"But what if I don't want to be in their hands?" I blurted the words.

Static crackled.

"Come on, Scottie. Stop."

"I'm serious. We started this! What if I want to finish it? Can't they just file their amica-bobbidi-thingamajig to support us?"

"I think this is more of an *all-or-nothing* offer, if you know what I mean."

"Well, maybe I don't want their offer at all." I sounded like a brat, pouting. I knew it. But then again, I also saw the validity in my stance. We sat in the tension, red brake lights strobing around me.

My eyes hurt.

My head hurt.

Maybe my heart did, too.

"Let's sleep on it and talk in the morning," Peyton offered. "This would be enormous for my career, just so you know. And you would be set for life. If financial restoration and my best interest are your goals, Scot ... well, then. I think this is it."

...

Chapter Seventeen

HARRISON

Waves licked the shore as we perched lazily on top of the dune, our toes covered in the dry sand. Moonlight burned on the seafoam. Her pretty head fit like a mitten into my shoulder. She looked up at me, biting her lip.

Green eyes on fire. Teeth bright.

I leaned down to kiss her, to taste her.

I think I'm falling for you. She whispered it into my teeth. Then her mouth covered mine.

She tasted like vanilla and mint. Like heaven.

Like her.

"Hellllllo?"

Erin's voice startled me to attention.

Did she have to be wearing *green*, of all colors, today? She held a folder tightly to her silky shirt, which was the color of emeralds.

Or eyes.

Scottie's eyes.

Good Lord.

I needed to stop reliving the dream that wouldn't leave me alone. I went to sleep thinking about Scottie after our Whole Foods run-in—and sure enough, she came to me in the night.

And periodically through every day since.

Which sounded so gosh-darn creepy.

Was I a creep?

Why couldn't I stop thinking about my plaintiff?

Then again, it's not like she wasn't the planet around which my days currently spun.

I needed some coffee.

Yes, *coffee*.

I coughed dryly into my fist. "Sorry, Erin, I was, uh—distracted."

"Obviously."

"What do you have there?"

"*Well*," she said proudly, shining. "I might've taken a little initiative."

"Oh no." I pointed a finger. "Last time you took initiative, we didn't have paper cups here for over a year."

"I still can't *believe* that didn't stick." She rolled her eyes. "It's embarrassing. Kingston needs to lead by example. We have over two hundred thousand employees."

"But only two hundred in this office. It's not *that* many paper cups, when you think about it. Don't you ever just not feel like cleaning a dish?"

"Not really, Hayes. I care about our planet, thanks. And the day we're too busy to rinse a cup is the day—"

"I know, I know. Plus, look!" I held up my mug, shiny ceramic embossed with Kingston Court's silhouette. It was the runner-up prize I'd earned for my warthog Halloween costume. I was still fully bitter. "I'm about to go fill this up."

Erin stepped toward me, snatching it. "I'll do that for you. You need to get to work."

"That's true." I sighed. "Now, what did you want to tell me?"

She presented a flier. "Look what officially opened today."

I grabbed it, skimming the fancy font:

Creating Kingston:
The Fine Art of Animation

Royal balls, singing birds, gilded clock towers … for the first time, explore behind the curtain of Wade Kingston's mythical genius and sources of original inspiration. Don't miss this powerful exhibition at the Anaheim Convention Center, directly across from Kingston Court. Explore the influence of French elements and European art on the Kingston Company's groundbreaking stories, characters, and productions.

Seventy-five pieces of art from eighteenth-century Europe will be displayed—paintings, sculptures, tapestries, gowns, and more. In juxtaposition will be one hundred original Wade Kingston drawings from the company vault, which showcase his obsession with gothic architecture, medieval Paris, and decorative design, as well as surrealism and natural movement.

The exhibition marks the 50th anniversary of Kingston World's grand opening in Orlando, Florida. For more information, visit www.creatingkingston.com.

"I remember hearing about this." I glanced at my calendar. November was flying. "I can't believe they're releasing work from the archives." The Kingston Company *never* cracked open the vault. Not even for the twentieth anniversary of Wade's disappearance last year.

"Right?"

"We should go. Maybe in a few weeks when this case calms down."

"Calms down?" She cackled. "I don't think that's happening until the gavel comes down."

I groaned.

She was right.

"Was there something else?" I peered at her skeptically. She didn't tend to come here without an agenda. Kingston events were a frequency, but usually didn't warrant a pop-in.

Erin plopped into one of my office chairs. She gazed around. "You need some snacks in here."

"Snacks? What, like peanuts? Werther's candies?"

She shrugged. "Either. Both. Something for your visitors."

"So, for *you*."

She folded her arms. "Are you ready to hear what I did, or not?"

I leaned back, rubbing my eyes. "Can you get my coffee first?"

"No. I'll be fast."

"Fine."

She handed me a sheet of paper speckled with data, a line separating it into halves. They looked to me like receipts.

"What am I looking at?"

"You, *Counselor*, are looking at ticket stubs for two VIP tickets to the Creating Kingston exhibit!" She clapped ecstatically. "I sent the tickets to Scottie and her lawyer. Anonymously, of course. They can use them anytime between now and New Year's."

I slapped my forehead. "Tell me you didn't."

"Oh, yes. I absolutely did." She clutched her folder to her chest like a gold medal. "Scottie was an *art history* minor, remember?"

"Yes, I remember." I remembered *everything*, unfortunately for me. Especially how Scottie looked in rust-colored workout pants.

And how she kissed in my dream.

But this crossed so many lines. How did Erin not realize this? Or even worse, how did she not care?

"Erin." I pressed my forehead. "Do I really need to tell you this? Gifting items to the opposition is *highly* unethical and *unbelievably* inappropriate."

Her face fell. "But—why?" Her wonder was genuine. "If juries can go on field trips to Kingston Court, why can't our plaintiff take a jaunt somewhere helpful?"

"That's—well, that's different."

"How is it different?"

"I don't know. Ask the state of California. They permit jury field trips in certain instances. Like when the scope of evidence is too large to be presented in court."

She stood. "Exactly! Those girls need some pixie dust. You can't *tell* them how magical Kingston is. You need to *show* them.

Didn't you ever, like, take Writing 101?"

"Erin."

"*Harrison.* No one will ever know who sent them the tickets," she promised. "I covered my tracks. I really think this could help us. How could they not be inspired by seeing Wade's true inspiration?"

"You covered your tracks. So, you *knew* you were doing something wrong."

"Not wrong," she insisted. "Just—creative."

"They probably won't even go," I realized out loud. "They'll probably think it's a prank."

"But *maybe* they'll go," she said. "And *maybe* they'll feel the magic. And Scottie will realize what an imbecile she is being."

"She's not an imbecile," I said before thinking.

Erin raised an eyebrow. "No?"

"I mean—yes. Of course. She's being absurd and dramatic with this whole thing. But Brent Callahan says that we shouldn't disparage the other side. It's not helpful."

She squinted at me disbelievingly. "If you say so. Where is he, by the way? The famous Brent Callahan is a lot less involved than I thought he'd be."

You and me both, Sister.

But we finally had a meeting scheduled later this afternoon. I looked at my watch. "He'll be here in a few hours, actually. Now, I'm happy to get my own coffee, or—"

"No, no," she said, raising my mug. "I got it." She paused in the doorway, crossing her ankles. "Am I in trouble? For sending the tickets?"

I exhaled.

Of course not. If forced to at gunpoint, I might even admit that it was a clever move. And something I might get disbarred for, so—better coming from her.

"No," I told her. "You were just trying to help. I appreciate the imagination."

Wade Kingston himself might approve, after all. So I guessed I could, too.

...

Brent Callahan glided into the conference room. I said silent thanks that both of us were suited up this time. Men in black. Boys who believed.

Water bottles, case files, snacks.

Erin—fine—had inspired me.

Snacks for this meeting.

Remembering Brent's Halloween munchies, I'd found some M&M's last minute, stashed up high in the office kitchen.

I was ready today, despite not knowing what Brent would want to discuss. I'd let him take the lead.

Second chair, I reminded myself. I was thrilled with our progress and eager to hear his updates.

This time, Brent had brought his own water bottle, which was more of a tank. Its titanium bottom clanked on the table. He sat at the head of the table again, while I assumed the chair at his right. He looked at me cold, unblinking. Fresh haircut and a red tie. He had the first scruff of a beard.

"I like the facial hair," I noted. "Looks great."

"Thanks," he said. "Girlfriend likes it."

Brent Callahan had a girlfriend? Seemed like news. I swallowed my curiosity.

"Speaking of girlfriend." He narrowed his eyes into daggers, aimed for me. "There's no natural way to ease into this."

I bristled.

My mind circled.

Ease into what?

Brent rummaged into his briefcase and pulled out a manila envelope.

Just like in the movies, but in no case I'd ever touched, he procured from it a stack of photos.

Black and white, voyeuristic, as if they'd been snapped by a night stalker.

Oh, fun!

Who were we spying on?

Trey, Scottie's ex, came to mind; one of our critical witnesses. I was awaiting his written deposition responses. Frankly, though, I wasn't expecting much. From what I'd gleaned, he was a predictable private equity prep boy. Princely, minus the charm. Plus, his secrets were spilled already. Scottie had seen to that.

One by one, Brent dealt the pictures in front of me, like an unlucky poker hand.

I gulped.

Scottie and me in front of Whole Foods. *Buddies.*

Scottie and me high-fiving. *Close buddies.*

Scottie and me lacing fingers. *More than buddies?* Scottie gazing up at me while I cupped her chin with my hand, our faces inches apart. *Are they going to kiss?* This looked bad. *So bad.* What in the name of all that is holy could I possibly have been thinking? But more importantly, who in the God-loving earth would have taken these pictures?

"It's not what it looks like," I said lamely.

"You think I haven't heard that before?" He leaned forward, eyes darts. "Listen, Hayes. I'm going to give you the benefit of the criminal: innocent until proven guilty. And these pictures don't necessarily prove anything. So, tell me. Are you sleeping with her?"

"*Gosh*, no!" I shouted, too loudly. "Really. That's—that's not me. I mean, it's me in the pictures, but—sleeping with Scottie is not something I would do. I ran into her at Whole Foods and … we ate near each other. We talked. I was polite. We said our goodbyes. That's it."

"You're touching her face, Hayes. And it looks to me like you want to touch more than that."

"Why do you have those pictures?" I challenged, not liking this one bit. "Are you having me followed?"

"Not you, smarty-pants. *Her.* We sent our best private investigator to just—track her a few days a week."

I didn't like this, either. "How come? You don't think I'll get what we need?"

"She's suing the Kingston Company, Hayes. And in case you didn't notice, the world is watching. She's beautiful. Smart. Sympathetic. We need to know *everything*. And you're lucky I'm the one with these pictures, which I'm promptly going to burn. If anyone else had seen you two together? I need you to know what's at stake here."

I nodded, sweaty, raking my hair. "I swear, nothing happened."

"Fine. I'll choose to believe you." He gathered the pictures. I felt like a teen in detention for making out behind the bleachers at lunch—only I didn't even get the actual kiss.

"If you're lying to me, end it now," said Brent. "I'm not telling Cooper. Or anyone."

"Thank you," I practically stuttered. "For that. Thank you. So much. I won't go near her again."

"Are you confident you can proceed in this case without compromising your professionalism and loyalty?"

"Yes, sir." I swallowed. "Without a doubt."

"Great. Then this conversation never happened." He snapped open his water, dragged a long sip, and flared a villainous grin. "Let's go over our witness list."

...

Three days later, the Friday before Thanksgiving, I was still chilled to my skeleton over those photos. Over being *this close* to losing, well, everything.

For the second time in my life.

Brent's rebuke had been the icy splash of water I'd needed. I hadn't dreamed of Scottie again, awake or asleep. I'd run twenty miles in three days. I'd stay away from Fashion Island until the case closed.

I made plans to see my grandma Rosa in her retirement home on Thanksgiving. She was lucid, but frail. We'd play Scrabble and eat a good takeout feast—which would *not* come from Whole Foods this year.

I was properly spooked.

Staying away from all Scottie haunts.

As I plugged in my phone and climbed into bed that night, my phone double-dinged with an unfamiliar number.

I couldn't think of anyone I knew with a 415 area code.

Anyone, except, maybe, Scottie.

My stomach flipped, and I tapped.

First, a selfie in a white ruffly top and jeans. Her pretty face was a present. The cute freckles on her tiny nose, a gothic castle painting behind her.

Why are you texting me, Scottie?

It seemed uncharacteristically bold.

Second, a message:

> Stole your number from Peyton's files. She'd kill me. Delete this! Just wanted to say thanks for the tickets. I mean, you're not winning the case. But nice to see the magic that wrecked my life. The art is beautiful. Punk. Xx, Scottie

I was sweating in my cold sheets. I might have to sit on my own two hands, but I would not text her back. But I did write replies in my head.

> You really shouldn't be texting me. Please don't do it again.

> Wish I could take credit. That was all Erin.

> You sure about this lawsuit thing? MARRY ME!!!!!!

I snapped off the light.
Swipe.
Delete.

...

Chapter Eighteen

SCOTTIE

Tomorrow was Thanksgiving, but the law didn't sleep.

Peyton swerved her black BMW into a parking slot marked for guests. She powered off the car with a button, her blonde locks blown into a sheen. Her black suit was fierce and flattering. She cut me a look in the passenger seat. "Are you ready?"

I assessed my own outfit one last time. We'd picked it out on our shopping spree a few weeks ago. The sleeves of my camel blouse billowed like clouds and tightened around my wrists. The fabric cinched around my neck in a circlet up to my jaw. It reminded me of a coffee filter and made me feel like a queen. I wore black pants and high pumps.

I told Peyton yes, of course, I was ready.

Deep down, I wasn't sure.

My first response to the IRAA's offer had been: Nope. Absolutely not. Thank you so much, but—*no, thank you.* I appreciated the overwhelming support, but this case had begun so personally for me and had only grown closer to home. I knew Peyton would battle Kingston with all her power—which, frankly, I'd learned, was a lot.

More importantly, I knew Peyton was fighting for *me*, as a human being and her best friend. At the end of each grueling day, she still cared about my well-being more than anything else. More than a victory, more than justice, more than her reputation.

To the imagination police, I wasn't a person. I was a potential pawn in a war and a convenient publicity splash.

But then, things had changed.

They offered us $7 million.

"That literally *can't* be right," I'd said to Peyton, befuddled, crouched over takeout sushi on top of my bed. "Why in the world would they pay us that kind of money—more than we want from Kingston—to take over and do all the work?"

"Like I told you, Scot." She'd sucked a piece of hot edamame into her bright-white teeth. "In the words of the great Eminem, they got *one shot*. Once in a lifetime. They've been trying to take Kingston to court for decades. They never make it to trial. Kingston comes back with a settlement offer they can't refuse—or the court throws the claims in the trash."

"Does this mean they think I can win?"

"Of course it does."

Then she'd shown me the amicus brief they'd submitted already to Judge Craig Davidoff, in a move that meant they were serious. On the plus side, this documented piece of evidence was now part of our case, no matter what. The jury would review every line of the ten-page argument. The introduction alone was amazing:

AMICUS BRIEF FOR THE CASE OF HOLIDAY v. KINGSTON, PRESENTED BY THE IMAGINATION RECALIBRATION AUTHORITY OF AMERICA

INTRODUCTION

Submitted on behalf of America's future, our brief supports plaintiff Scotland Dolly Holiday. Herein, we remind the Court of the powerful role of entertainment in shaping our youth. We implore the Court to consider a world in which more than a single entity—namely, the Kingston Company—controls our collective dreams and imagination.

Is it right that the whole of mythologies, epics, and tales lie currently in the hands of one corporation? And what of the message communicated by this singular, homogenous voice? Might we benefit from a veritable buffet of creative interpretations, ideas, viewpoints, and anecdotes?

Meanwhile, where is the man who started it all? Is the King himself even aware of the grand-scale authority with which his empire has been endued—extending, truly, to the ends of the earth? Is Wade Kingston hiding—perhaps—from his own creation?

We implore you, Court, to consider the devastating effects of the Kingston Company's ubiquitous content—story interpretations and original productions alike—not only on Ms. Holiday's psyche, but on the billions of youths beyond her. The children behind us, before us, and with us now.

May we consider a recalibration of our consciousness—an elevation of our dreams, communal and individual.

May we redefine the scope of the "fairy tale" and be willing to examine the shortcomings in our pre-held ways of defining our heroes, as well as our happiness.

Seven. Million. Dollars.

Peyton said she wouldn't take more than two of it. So that left me with $5 million and no more burden of proof.

Poof.

Burden.

Gone.

This was everything I was asking for, tied up like an early Christmas present.

So why couldn't I sleep at night?

And why was Harrison part of those trancelike hours now— those tender, twinkly, unbridled moments between consciousness and sleep? Day slipping into night? Harrison's hand slipping into mine? Him closing the gap of that kiss right in front of Whole Foods?

There had also been the gift of the art exhibit tickets last week. Utterly extravagant if not completely unallowed. They'd arrived at Peyton's office, by mail carrier straight to her desk, along with two long-stemmed red roses.

Five words had sparkled in gold on the envelope: *Do you believe in magic?*

Peyton told me she'd fumed when the gift arrived, almost dumped them right in the trash.

"What an *insult* to my role in this case—to the law! I should report him to the California Bar Association."

But then she'd shoved the invitation in my face, and I'd begged her to go.

"Didn't we go to Kingston Court for this reason?" I pointed out. "To *wrap ourselves up* in the Kingston phenomenon? What better way? Be serious. Can you think of a more incredible opportunity than submersing ourselves in the original inspiration?"

Peyton was still fixed on finding Wade Kingston, but every new try at tracking him down had proved more of a failure than the last.

Europe? No. Montecito? No luck. Sipping tropical cocktails out at sea on a Kingston cruise ship? Maybe, actually, but how could we ever know?

She'd just about given up.

And she'd finally sighed when I wouldn't relent about the two tickets. "*Fine*. We'll go to the exhibit. But Friday night. And I only have an hour."

I knew she ended up thankful for my persistence. The exhibit defined enchantment; we both had to admit it.

In one room, baroque-style homeware and furniture hung invisibly from the ceiling, a nod to Kingston's *Beauty and the Beast*. Ornate teacups, upholstered couches, and a giant gold-encrusted wardrobe were suspended in an impressive trick of the eye.

In another space, one entire wall featured a digital rendering of the original Neuschwanstein Castle—which transposed every three minutes into the castle at Kingston Court. The effect was impressive and mesmerizing, a compare-and-contrast for the ages.

Each display of European art was complemented with sketches by Wade and his early animators, preserved carefully under glass. I felt transported to somewhere almost holy, beholding versions of Kingston castles from the cutting room floor. Drawings of churches, rodents, and royalty. Etched by the king in his chain-smoking nights, no doubt.

I wondered if Wade knew these artifacts had resurfaced, and if so, what he had to say about it.

"Harrison Hayes is a *sketch ball* for sending us here, but—fine. This is cool," Peyton allowed.

I still hadn't told her about our sort-of dinner. Togetherish.

I didn't know what the IRAA's takeover would mean for Harrison, case-wise, career-wise. But I assumed Kingston's big outside law firm would come to bat in a big way. That the proceedings would no longer be about me and Harrison.

But were they about us, anyway?

Not really.

Maybe a smidge.

Regardless, I'd made my decision.

We would accept the IRAA's deal, and we better not be late.

We slammed our car doors and marched toward the big shiny building.

...

Where the Kingston conference room was open and bright, the massive IRAA meeting room was the contrary. Black leathers, cherry woods, forest greens. In the corner, a copper bar cart held whiskeys the colors of topaz and honeycomb.

The crowd here was also a contrast to the youthful energy of Erin and Harrison. Lots of white hair and ill-fitting suits. So, I was surprised—seated around the long table with seven men who looked over sixty—when an elegant woman waltzed in, shaking our hands with warmth. She was tall and sleek with blunt bangs and a chin-length bob. Her sleeveless gray dress showed boxer biceps and a slim waist.

"Constance Zane," she said. "President of the IRAA."

I glanced at Peyton with eyes that shouted, *You didn't tell me the president was a pretty, cool-looking woman who couldn't possibly be older than forty-five.*

Peyton shrugged back, *I know, cool, right?*

Constance glided into the seat at the head of the table, next to us. Her thin layered necklaces glittered on-trend, but they clearly weren't faux gold, like mine.

I touched my neckline self-consciously.

On the table in front of us were thick piles of legal documents. I patted them, overwhelmed. They were stacked neat as place settings.

What were we signing away, exactly?

Constance explained the terms of the deal, her voice pleasant, booming, and smooth. The men around the room would apparently take the case from here. Lawyers, directors, entertainment executives. Many of them had known Wade Kingston personally—and agreed that he never intended to build the Godzilla of entertainment. At his heart, Wade Kingston was good, they said. The results of his power were not, they said.

I nodded as Constance spoke.

Her message was clear, her eyeliner dark.

I thought of Harrison's voice in my ear.

Hot, and cold.

Bitter, and sweet.

Enemy, and secret dreamboat.

Time halted then, and I wasn't here. I was on the couch, next to my dad, twenty years ago, this time of year. Every Thanksgiving, since I could remember, we'd watched *It's a Wonderful Life* together.

"*Every time a bell rings, an angel gets his wings.*"

And every time, I would cry, even as a young girl.

My mind flashed to a scene I'd never forgotten—with George Bailey, his board of directors for the Bailey Building & Loan, and the villainous Mr. Potter. George Bailey represented goodwill and community. Mr. Potter, money and greed.

Always giving more than he takes, George is given a golden opportunity: to sign control of his dad's company over to mean Mr. Potter, for a mind-blowing salary.

George attends the meeting to strike the deal. He smokes a fancy cigar. But after he shakes Mr. Potter's hand, he looks down, rubbing his fingers.

Disgusted.

He'd sealed a devil's deal.

But it wasn't too late.

My heart raced now, and I cleared my throat, interrupting Constance. Unlike the little mermaid, I still had my voice, and you bet I was going to use it.

Before overthinking it, I stood up.

Peyton yanked hard on my pant leg.

I cleared my throat. "I am so ... thankful to all of you for this unbelievable offer," I started, sounding more serene than I felt. "For the brief you wrote—for having us here, for your interest in our humble case."

I looked to Constance, whose black eyes were bugging. Her face twitched, like she'd been slapped. I believed she and her team were amazing. They meant well, were doing good work. But handing my case to them felt all wrong.

"I can't do this," I finished. "I already have the best lawyer I could ask for, and—I want to fight this case on our own. I really can't thank you enough, everyone. We promise to make you proud."

The white heads and spectacles surrounding me started to whisper.

I looked down to Peyton, who closed her eyes. I knew she wanted to die in her skin right now. She squeezed the bridge of her nose. I had to believe she'd forgive me. Someday. Not now.

Shaking with nerves, but filled with peace, I looked up to the man directly across the table from me. Wispy white hair, bulblike nose, and sweet eyes.

He looked, in fact, I thought, a little like Clarence from *It's a Wonderful Life*, the angel who saves George Bailey by jumping off the bridge before he does, then changes everything with the famous dream sequence.

I swear to you, there at the table, the angel man winked at me, smiling.

Peyton would later roll her eyes.

Great, you're seeing things now? His cataracts were probably flaring. Next you're going to say you actually DO believe in real magic.

I knew she was momentarily exasperated that I would walk away from the deal, especially without warning her. I knew my timing was poor. But I had to follow my gut. I knew that we'd work it out, she and I, like we always did. I knew we'd keep fighting, and fair.

But I saw it.

I tell you, *he winked at me.*

...

Chapter Nineteen

SCOTTIE

I needed a change of outlook and scenery. With less than two weeks until Christmas and four weeks until the trial, I was starting to shake in my UGGs.

Peyton and I had never once been in a real fight. I knew this was rare for BFFs, but we were special. Small tiffs? Of course. Miscommunications? Duh. But in the past twenty-four years, neither one of us had ever been truly *angry* with the other for more than twenty-four hours.

That is, until now.

My behavior at the IRAA meeting was "appalling, unprofessional, and just plain stupid," according to Peyton.

"I'm *so sorry*, P." I'd trailed her afterward in the parking lot, both of our heels clacking on the asphalt like bullets. "I had to follow my heart."

Fuming, she had whipped around and pointed her car key at me, briefcase looped around one elbow, trembling. "Maybe if you tried using your *mind* instead, for just once in our lives, Scot, *we wouldn't be in this mess.*"

I gulped.

That stung.

"I just—" Her shoulders drooped heavily into what looked like sadness. "This is *really* how you repay me? For my hours of work—do you have any idea how many hours?—and for everything I've done for you? You blindsided me in there." She jerked her head toward the building. "Not to mention, we would have been *set. For. Life.* What part of that doesn't sound like something worth fighting for?" She'd exhaled. "I think I'm actually still in shock."

Desperate and sick at seeing her disappointed in me, I'd lunged forward to hug my best friend—but she warded me off with both hands. "No," she said, voice harsh. "I'll drop you off at home, but I'm going to need a minute."

And by *minute* she meant three days.

Without responding to me even once.

This had to be a record for us.

Finally, just when I was sure she had dropped my case, and, well, dropped me too, my phone had beeped with a terse text:

> Hey. I've decided to keep representing you. For my career, to be clear. I'm still mad, but I'm not quitting. Talk soon.

Once more: a chance.

I'd grinned, now more determined than ever to make Peyton proud. We were going to win this thing, come Harrison or high water. I could have no more missteps, though. Peyton was still my lawyer, and I would not blow this. *She* was something worth fighting for, if I'd ever known it.

I tried to not let it bother me that Harrison had also ignored two of my texts now. One the night of the art exhibit (a simple thanks) and the other asking his favorite brand of running shoes (a simple question).

I hadn't seen him in weeks now.

In person, that is.

I'd seen him in the media plenty—suddenly and unrelentingly.

More handsome in every shot, dang it.

Old pictures of Harrison as a Padre, in his tight baseball pants. His professional headshot, in a black suit. Brent and Harrison, side by side, striding out of the Kingston offices. Batman and Robin in Hugo Boss.

Right after Thanksgiving, the Kingston PR team had apparently decided it was time to reveal the name of their in-house lawyer. Which could've been a throwaway detail without the inherent star quality of Harrison Hayes. The headlines bordered on the hilarious:

» **Kingston Appoints Rising Legal Star in Holiday Case**
» **Former Baseball Pro Bats for Kingston**
» **Happy Holidays to Harrison Hayes**

I wanted to laugh and cry at the absurdity of it all.

This was my one true life.

Harrison appeared to be extremely busy—and as determined as we were to win. I chose to conclude he was trying to "do the right thing" by not communicating with me. He was officially not supposed to speak to me without my attorney present, I'd learned.

And my attorney didn't exactly enjoy him—not that I was her favorite person, either, right now.

So here we were.

When I'd finally told Peyton about our supermarket rendezvous and the almost-kiss—after she and I were speaking again, but before we'd be back to normal anytime soon—she chastised me, naturally.

"Wow. He should not have *spilled his heart* to you," she seethed, eyes rolling. "That was, like, *so* out of line. Harrison is an officer in the court of law, with an obligation to defend his company. Not to mention that was manipulative, trying to make you go soft for him."

"He was *not* manipulating me," I argued, believing it. "It felt natural. Genuine. You've got to trust me." *Right.* "I simply asked him about the Marissa situation, and he explained it. We were just ... eating."

"Eating it *up,* is what you were doing. Do you hear yourself? You are not trying to date this guy, Scot. We're trying to shed his blood."

"Do we have to use such violent language?"

"Yes. We do. Saddle up. And you are officially forbidden from speaking to him without me present. Not one more word. Got it?"

"Got it."

Maybe this new best-friend tension between us would give us an edge.

We could hope.

Craving a fresh location for the rest of my research, I sat now in the Orange County Law Library, located across the quad from the courthouse in Santa Ana, where we'd begin trial next month. Four stately buildings faced one another across the cool-green grassy square, usually punctuated with students, picnickers, and professionals. The courtyard was anchored by a circular fountain, round like a pendant and just as pretty. The buildings were old-fashioned with red-brick facades, ornate arches, and marble steps.

In the study hall where I sat now, bookshelves lined the cavernous room. Tables stretched long, where people like me hunkered down. Stained glass windows frosted the towering walls. The slightest whispers echoed and bounced off the towering ceiling. You could hear an earring stud drop.

I needed the quiet, though. In preparation for trial, I was polishing up my testimony and brushing up on past Kingston lawsuits. I'd learned more every day just how unlikely it was that we had made it this far. In Orange County especially, cases like mine against Kingston tended to die on the flower stem, never blooming. We had a chance here—a formidable chance—and this was more than a million plaintiffs had previously been able to say.

My claims were seeing the sun.

The high wall clock chimed four above me. My vision was starting to blur. I grabbed the back of my hard wood seat, spinning to crack my back. The reverberating vertebrae snaps confirmed I'd been here too long.

I was reaching down to yank my bag from the floor when my gaze caught distractedly on a guy down the corridor, facing me.

Watching me.

Weird.

I squinted.

He wore a navy peacoat, slim jeans, and brown loafers. I liked his style. He was strong and tall, but nowhere near Harrison's height. Sandy hair. Scruffy face, unlike Harrison's clean one.

My eyes popped.

As the man lumbered toward me, my heart surged into my throat.

I'd know that swagger anywhere.

Trey.

What. On. Earth.

Was he doing here?

How did he find me?

I looked to my left, then my right—disbelieving suddenly that I was awake. I pinched my forearm to make sure I was indeed conscious. Maybe Peyton was right; I really was seeing things now. Maybe it hadn't even been Harrison at Whole Foods that night.

Maybe it was all a dream.

Ouch!

My own pinch left a mark on my skin.

Trey was standing in front of me now.

I looked up at him, frozen.

My heart hammered. My stomach roiled. Hot tears slid down my cheeks before I could feel them coming.

I was so shocked and livid to see him, but started to thaw unconsciously at the familiar feel of his presence. He'd always warmed me. He was cozy, like apple pie. Blankets and movie nights. Love.

Or what I used to think love might be.

Our San Francisco life flashed before me. Runs through the city, late-night dinners, our zesty group of friends. I missed them all so much. They'd been my forever, that life. My heart, and my home.

I found myself wanting to hug Trey, hard, to feel wrapped up in him one more time.

But also wanting to deck him.

"What" I swiped under my eyes "are you doing here?"

He rocked heel to toe, front and back, like he always did when he was nervous. He looked great and I hated him for it. He looked healthy, handsome, and whole. He clearly had arisen from the holy hell of a hole he had dug for himself.

"I emailed you," he said quietly. "And texted. And … called."

"Yes." I folded my arms. "I know."

"And you couldn't have responded to … any of them?"

I swallowed the ball in my throat. "No, Trey," I hissed, looking around. People were watching. "Did it ever occur to you that maybe I needed some space?"

He grimaced, straightening. "Well, did it ever occur to you that … maybe I'd want to *know* before you sued one of the biggest companies in the world?"

He didn't.

"And what makes you think that's your business?" I shot back, too loudly.

His voice fell. "We had a life together."

"Yeah—and you did an unbelievable job of destroying that life, in front of everyone that we loved."

I was borderline yelling now, and the librarian stood at her desk. She lobbed me a warning glance over her cat-eye glasses. I motioned to the door. *Let's take this outside.* I packed up my bag in a hurricane.

Trey trailed me out the front door, down the steps two at a time, following me to the fountain. I took a seat on its concrete edge, and he sank down next to me. The rushing water might at least muffle our shouts.

I noticed a couple canoodling on a quilt, eating from one of those trendy charcuterie boxes. Probably speaking in baby talk, hunched toward each other. I wanted to hurl a book at them. *That cheese might last longer than your true love! FYI!*

I sighed, leaning forward, letting the weight of my head fall between my knees. My hair tumbled darkly around my weakening shoulders.

Trey touched my back, but I didn't flinch. I feared, for a second, that I might be out of fight. Or maybe I just needed a nap. A nap from all this—

From my gosh darn one true life.

Didn't Trey know what he stirred in me? Rage, frustration, embarrassment. I thought of a meme I'd once saved: *"Don't look in the rearview mirror. You're not going that way."* Right? What was the point of this melodramatic return of his?

I was moving on. I was in a big lawsuit! I had a tiny crush on a guy who wouldn't text me back!

Maybe I should stop listing off my achievements!

"Scottie," Trey said softly. "Can I say something? Can you just ... hear me out—in the flesh—and you never have to see me again?"

I remained hunched over, cloaked in my hair, but I nodded.

"Can I at least—see your face while I say it?" He paused. "You look like the girl from *The Ring*."

I loved *The Ring*—and he knew it. I couldn't help but giggle at that.

I breathed and sat up, knowing mascara striped my face like a zebra. But it was nothing he hadn't seen. I stared at him helplessly, not caring that I looked straight cold-blooded out of a horror movie.

Trey buried his fists in his peacoat, rocking. "First—I do want to say that ... I'm proud of you. I mean, wow. I'm not going to say that I ever would have seen this coming, in a million years. You've never struck me as someone litigious. But everyone's talking about you, and your case. Like, everywhere, Scot. Our friends, but—"

My heart lurched at the compliment—*he was proud of me?*—but then soured quickly at the thought of all our friends hanging out.

Without me.

I looked away.

"Sorry—" he stammered. "Everyone ... misses you, by the way. I just meant that you're really, *everywhere*. It's pretty amazing. I'm rooting for you."

"Are you really?" I asked. I had continued to resist the reality that *everyone, everywhere* knew about me and my lawsuit. But Trey's cheers? I guessed I could take them. It was the least he could give.

"Of course I am." Trey sucked in a breath. "The next thing I want to say, and you'd know this if you'd read any of my messages." He paused. "Did you really not read any of them?"

"There were *a lot* of messages, Trey."

He blushed. "I know. I just—wanted to tell you that … I've only spoken to Jade once since the wedding. And that was to tell her that she and I are over, forever. That our relationship was the biggest mistake of my life and that it should never, ever have happened."

I winced, feeling a stab of sorrow for Jade. No woman wants to be told she was a mistake. Not ever. Not even as the other woman.

Maybe especially as her.

"Trey—" I interjected.

He held up a hand. "Can I finish, please? I've been wanting to get this off my chest for four months."

I nodded, shivering in the cold.

Trey peeled off his coat.

"No, please don't—"

He draped it over my shoulders anyway, and, fine, the curtain of heat felt like heaven. Turning to me, Trey grabbed my hands. "I will carry this regret for the rest of my life. But I can't go on without saying that if there's any chance—the wildest chance—of getting you back, I'll do anything. *Anything*. I'll move down here, move out of state, start with a first date. I'll propose right now. I want you back, Scottie. I do."

I do.

I should've known this was coming.

I groaned, lifting my face to the blanket of sky.

Why here, why now, and *why did you have to do what you did, Trey?*

I thumbed the tops of his hands, gazing into his face.

The face five minutes from being my husband four months ago.

Pancake breakfasts, three kids and a dog, wrinkling into the decades together. Our future—I saw it all. His sharp cheekbones and crooked smile. His charmingly imperfect teeth and soft hands.

So close.

But so far away.

It was never going to happen.

Something palpable had shifted in Trey since the wedding; I physically sensed it. He was steadier, somehow, more grounded, and making excellent eye contact.

I realized only now that his shifty energy in our final year together had likely been a sign of the cheating. I'd tallied it up to wedding nerves, but obviously, I'd been wrong.

He did seem honestly sorry tonight. *He did.* Beholding him now, I believed in my heart it was possible that he had changed, or begun to.

I also knew, without a doubt, that I could never trust him again.

I didn't feel romantically toward him anymore, I also recognized in this moment. There was no longing, no butterflies.

I realized something else profound, too.

The anger at Trey was physically leaving my body, like a cold that had lingered for far too long, now escaping in a small sneeze.

I was going to be okay.

I no longer loved Trey, but I didn't have to hate him, either.

For years, the smell of Trey's cologne or the fit of his jeans would set my whole body on fire. Here in front of me, though, I simply saw a guy in my rearview fading farther away by the second.

I saw a broken person who cared enough to come here, apologize.

I saw a man I could forgive.

Perhaps.

Before I could stop myself, I threw my arms around him, and cried.

He cradled me for a long time before I finally let him go. With all of it, every last bit. The wedding, the pain, the betrayal, the move, the end. I couldn't carry it anymore.

"I can't," I whispered into his neck. "I can't, Trey. But thank you—for coming here. I think … I think I needed to see you."

His mouth arched down, and his blue eyes glistened with pain. He tucked back a piece of my hair. He didn't need to say what his whole face shouted out loud for him: *I wish I could take it all back.*

When my eyes were dry, and Trey's coat back on, we stood up for one last hug. We exhaled in heavy unison.

"Do I look hideous right now?" I asked as he held my shoulders.

"Disgusting." He shook me playfully.

I punched him. "Stop."

"You know, you'll always be the best girl in the world," he

said sadly, rubbing the end of my nose with a knuckle. "I'm so sorry I hurt you." He began to walk backward, saluting me. "Now go win that lawsuit, okay?"

I watched my ex-fiancé fade away like a mirage into the moonlight.

...

I felt lighter as night fell harder. I'd never been here, on the civic center grounds, past sunset. Street lanterns lit up the quad. Couples strolled to their cars, hands entwined. Students returned to their apartments. I sat on my bench, inhaling the scene, replaying my conversation with Trey.

You rehearse those meetings in your head, like movie previews. The run-ins. The sightings, at last. What you'll finally say to the person who shattered your heart. The ex, the estranged parent, the bad friend.

You can't wait to *let them have it.*

Insults rehearsed. Faculties sharp. Confidence at its prime.

You'll yell, maybe scream. You'll get every word right. You'll cut them right to the vein.

Some of it might be essential. Life-changing, empowering.

But it also might not go that way.

You might shockingly feel new softness where you once knew only knifepoint. You might forget to be mad. You might melt into your enemy's arms, in your final fall to forgiveness. You might be released, once and for all. You might, indeed, let them have what they needed the most.

My breath pillowed into a mist.

"Scottie?"

I jumped, unsure from where the voice came. I looked around skittishly. I thought I was just about the only human left in the quad.

But, alas, another figure emerged from behind the fountain. I was like *The Bachelorette* tonight. Handsome stalker edition, fountain and all.

Harrison waved at me, grinning.

What?

I held myself back from hopping up into his arms, and into that broadening smile.

What a bizarre situation.

I had no clue where we stood.

In the past four weeks, we'd been seeing a lot of each other in the press, as official, public archenemies, but we hadn't spoken at all. I waved back in my greatest effort at nonchalance. "What are you doing here?"

"I had to grab some documents from the courthouse." He nodded sideways. "What about you? It's late."

"Not that late." I shrugged. "It gets dark so early now. I was doing some work for the case. In the library."

"Gosh, I love that library." He stepped cautiously closer to me. "It was built in 1901."

"Wow. Old. Almost as old as you." I gave him a tiny smile.

He chuckled, and I thought I saw relief in his eyes. "Basically."

Silence hung.

I didn't know what to say.

"Hey," he said lightly, pulling his phone from his pocket. "I am not supposed to be talking to you, you know."

I shrugged. "Yes. I do know. But you can *acknowledge* me, right?"

He risked another step, and another. He held up his phone. "Can I see your phone?"

I frowned. "Or you can finally text me back from the one in your hand."

"Ah. I'm—sorry about that." He shoved a hand into his hair. "Not responding. I can't risk a paper trail. I could get slaughtered for talking to you at this point."

Everyone with the violent words.

"Better get running, then." My voice was bitter and dry, but I was okay with it. "We both know you're fast."

"Just give me your phone, okay?"

"This sounds wretchedly unadvisable," I said, procuring the thing from my bag and tossing it to him.

I watched as he opened Spotify. He swiped and tapped on our two screens like a court reporter.

My eyebrows scrunched. "What are you doing?"

"I'm AirDropping you something. No paper trail. See?"

"Sneaky!"

"I know." He put my phone back in my palm. "There. I made you a playlist. For the trial."

"You ... what?"

"I couldn't help but notice, the day I first met you, that you were running to a playlist called"—his mouth curled into his dreamy half smile—"Heartbreak Hits. And, well, I think you can do better. You're going to need more umph than that if you *really* want to face off with me."

I was pretty sure that I wanted to do more than that.

Again, though, I didn't know what to say.

"Well, thanks!" I mustered. "No one's—no one's ever made me a playlist before."

"You can't be serious."

I shook my head no.

"Burned you a CD? Mixed you a tape?"

"Not once."

"Crying shame. Now you have one. Your name is, unfortunately—fortunately?—in my face all day, every day. Morning, afternoon, and night, so—you'll see what I mean. I'll see you in court. Okay?"

I nodded. "Okay."

...

Threading my way through traffic on the way home, I cackled and choked on surprising bursts of emotion. Harrison had made me an entire playlist of songs that had my name in the title or lyrics. Twenty-eight of them. *Jolly Holiday*, he'd named it. Songs by Billie Holiday, too, and a handful of Kingston hits, ones I assumed were his favorites.

"Love is Never Lost" was the first song, as if he knew. Next came "Jolly Holiday," followed by the most random collection of melodies one could imagine.

"Holiday" by Madonna.

"Holiday" by Green Day.

"Holidae Inn" by Chingy.

"Happy Holiday" by Andy Williams.

"Merry Christmas, Happy Holidays" by *NSYNC.

And finally, "Scotland the Brave."

When I arrived home, I went to text Peyton and check in about the week, businesslike. But when I opened my Messages app, I saw a text already typed into the white box.

No recipient chosen.

No paper trail.

It was a drafted text, cursor still blinking at the end of the message:

> You looked beautiful tonight. Even though it looks like you might've been crying. I hope you're okay. I look forward to seeing you in court every day. More than you know. HAPPY HOLIDAYS! Harrison

. . .

Chapter Twenty

HARRISON

It was eight o'clock on a cold winter morning. We had one week until trial. Let the countdown begin.

In my seven years of practicing law, today was my first-ever jury selection, also known as *voir dire*. I was excited. I hadn't done this since law school, and I was thankful for my shark at the helm. Brent Callahan knew how to pick them, apparently, and I couldn't wait to watch him in action. The Kingston attorneys compared him to a conductor directing an orchestra. Pointing, picking, and peppering the souls in the stands. Composing his music. His squad. You could even say his disciples.

At one table facing the front of the room sat me and Brent. Peyton overtook the far table, all by herself. I'd greeted her earlier with my charms.

"Ms. McKenzie, you look *ravishing* today." I really did like her pink skirt suit and respected the audacious choice. "Nice to see you."

She smiled tightly. "You too, Hayes. Good luck, boys."

We knew she didn't mean it.

She looked good but seemed grumpy.

Judge Craig Davidoff presided over us in a high-backed brown leather chair, flanked by the state and national flags. Behind him, walnut wood stretched floor to the ceiling in wainscoting. Custom wood millwork was everywhere. The ceilings were lofty and painted like the Sistine Chapel. The blue-and-gold pattern in big squares felt almost saintly. This was the oldest courtroom in Orange County.

I felt lucky to be here.

Today, twenty-four members of the community would soon arrive: the potential jurors. We'd make our final cuts, down to twelve, taking turns with Peyton, asking questions as we whittled down to our top picks. Brent would probe into their backgrounds, beliefs, and biases. We'd find out if they held preexisting knowledge of the case—and if so, whether this knowledge would impede their ability to serve as unbiased jurors.

In filed our candidates suddenly from the side door. I watched obsessively as they took their seats, eyeing them for obvious frontrunners.

The pretty, bright-eyed blonde twentysomething in her French braid.

The grandma type in her crocheted shawl and low bun.

The Hispanic man with big muscles, kind eyes, and tattoos.

I looked for every person who might hold an air of the magical. The least cynical of the bunch. The ones soft enough to make bucket lists, and hard enough to stand for tradition.

I turned to Brent. "What's our ideal juror?" I whispered. "What are you looking for, more than anything?"

I had my take. I wanted his.

His pencil scratched numbers into a paper chart he'd sketched of the jury box. "We want Kingston aficionados. Hearts of gold. Anyone who hates cancel culture."

I laughed.

"The mercy lovers." He stabbed the pencil behind his ear. "Thankfully, almost everyone up there will have an opinion of Kingston. We just need to strike the ones who have a chip against the machine. We also need the romantics."

"Not the ones jaded by love."

"Exactly. Mr. Tinder up there?" He gestured to a beefed-up guy in a tight white tee, hair sculpted into spikes. His huge hands were practically twitching without his phone.

"Oh man."

"I checked his socials. He's probably dating as many women as we need jurors. Hard pass. We need commitment. Quality. Kingston."

"Gotcha."

Judge Davidoff pounded his gavel. "Mr. Callahan," he bellowed. "You may begin."

Brent stood. "Thank you, Your Honor."

He scoured his chart one more time before approaching the jurors.

"Thank you for being here today, ladies and gentlemen. We'll make this painless and swift. Now—who here has ever seen a Kingston movie? Show of hands?"

Twenty-three of the twenty-four shot a palm in the air. Brent zeroed in on the middle-aged redhead with gray in her part and both hands down in her lap. She was probably Brent's age, without the expensive face creams. Her dress could have come from *Little House on the Prairie*.

"Ma'am." Brent addressed her. "You've never seen a movie produced by the Kingston Company?"

"No, sir." She had a pleasant, makeup-free face. Her voice was soft, like a song. "We don't have a television. Or Internet."

"And why is that?"

"It goes against our beliefs."

"Which are what, exactly?"

"I'm part of the Graceweavers, sir. We're a group of people who live together, as one. We earn our keep by way of our quilt shop. We don't consume modern media or entertainment. We strive to keep our minds and hearts pure."

With that get-up and dialect, she could have stepped out of Frontier Country at Kingston Court. But nope. She was from that local cult I'd only heard whispers about. The members apparently lived on the same street, living off profits from their huge craft shop. I wasn't sure their set-up was legal—rumor had it they shared more than craft supplies, namely, *spouses*—but we couldn't have her type on this case.

Anti-entertainment.

Not happening.

I crossed out Juror #14 on Brent's chart.

"Thank you, ma'am." He paced the marble floor. "So, to rephrase. Is everyone here familiar with our defendant, the Kingston Company?"

Laughs echoed against the wood walls.

"I'll take that as a yes." He looked respectfully to Judge Davidoff.

Translation: Everyone breathing knows Kingston, sir, so let's just all do our best.

"Next question, show of hands. Has anyone here ever been left at the altar? Abandoned on your own wedding day?"

To my surprise, my tattooed man raised a hand.

Dang it.

I slashed Juror #4.

"Thank you, sir. And I'm sorry. Her loss."

More laughs. Brent was good. My favorite law school professor always said the best trial attorneys were natural-born entertainers.

Brent walked up to my young, braided blonde. "Miss, what's your name?"

"Elizabeth Stapleton, sir." She was wearing a lavender yoga set, holding her knees.

"How old are you?"

"Nineteen, sir."

"What's your favorite movie?"

She hesitated. "*Anastasia.* The animated film."

Brent flashed me a thumbs-up behind his back. It wasn't Kingston. But it was close. Magic, royals, glitter, darkness, and family. Even talking animals. It was the perfect answer. We wanted her on our team.

"Do you believe in love, Miss Stapleton?"

Her eyes darted side to side.

"It's not a trick question. How about this? Do you believe you'll find love someday? Get married? Live happily ever after?"

She nodded, relaxing. "I do."

Now I got *two* thumbs-ups.

I circled Juror #7.

We continued like this for hours, until my butt fell asleep. But I was high on the rush, watching our jury take shape. Brent kept everyone laughing, raising their hands, giving us helpful answers.

At the end of the morning, Brent confirmed that we'd like to excuse Jurors #1 (Tinder Boy), #14 (Graceweaver), and #4 (Runaway Bride's Ex). Peyton didn't slash our top picks, so we were pumping our fists. She excused Jurors #3, #12, and #22: an author of fantasy children's fiction, a man with a Rickey Rat figurine collection, and a woman with a daughter named Cinderella, not kidding.

Brent and I convened afterward in the café on the property, between the courthouse and city office building.

"That was amazing," I said. "I'm feeling so great about this."

"You should. You've been an asset to this case, Hayes. Incredible work. You have a bright future ahead of you."

He didn't say the unspoken, sitting there at our small iron table.

Incredible work since the photos with Scottie.

I had been a good boy.

It was water under the drawbridge. Our witness list was stacked high. We were ready to slay.

"I also have news," Brent went on. "Big news."

I swirled my latte. "Yeah?"

"I tracked down an essential witness. One I didn't think we could get." He toasted his Arnold Palmer in the air, grinning like a cartoon feline. "The witness of all witnesses. It wasn't easy, but I made some calls."

Wade Kingston?

Had he really done it?

My heart galloped.

My gaping jaw asked the question for me.

Who?

"Yep. I found Scottie's mom."

...

Part Three

Chapter Twenty-One

SCOTTIE

Kingston Fans Rally on First Day of Holiday Trial

Opening statements begin Monday in the trial of 28-year-old Scotland "Scottie" Holiday against the Kingston Company headquartered in Anaheim, Calif. Represented by litigator Peyton McKenzie of Cashion & Baker, the Orange County native filed complaints in October against the media giant. Holiday holds that Kingston failed to deliver on its brand promise of fairy-tale idealism. She was left at the altar of her Napa County wedding last summer by Bay Area businessman Trey Kelley, 34.

Since the court accepted her case, Holiday's lawsuit has struck a chord with Kingston enthusiasts and haters alike. Early this morning at the steps of Orange County's historical courthouse, devout Kingston employees—known widely as "Kingstonites"—along with fans, gathered in costume to march on behalf of the multibillion-dollar conglomerate. The trial is expected to last through the end of the week.

...

Peyton and I stood side by side in front of the bathroom mirror. My palms were perspiring. *Every* part of me was perspiring. This might as well be a sauna. Wouldn't that be nice? If it were the spa instead of the courthouse?

I sucked in a breath.

We were ready.

My lawyer looked unbelievably chic in her brown-and-white tweed cropped jacket and matching skirt. She wore nude pumps and nude lips, hair a straight sheet of blonde.

I wore a sage-green satin blouse that made my eyes pop like champagne. My dark hair was spun into waves.

Pride and joy swelled in my stomach. The only thing that could have made this day better would've been knowing Peyton wasn't mad at me. I refrained from grabbing her hand, but I was silently squeezing it with my heart.

Thank you. I love you. I'm sorry.

We weren't saying much to each other yet, but still. We bowed our heads in shared silence, our battle awaiting us down the hall.

Dear God …

Please let us win.

...

The gallery was packed full of spectators, not an empty seat in the pews. Whispers hummed. Papers shuffled. The gavel smacked.

Whack, whack, whack.

Judge Craig Davidoff stood up between the two flags,

overhead lights reflecting on his bare head. His round silver glasses teetered on the end of his nose. "Good morning, ladies and gentlemen. Calling the case of Scotland Holiday v. The Kingston Company. Are both sides ready?"

Harrison and Peyton rose. Even more than giving a rock-star testimony, my biggest challenge this week would be to not stare at Harrison like a fool.

I indulged one look.

Black suits did him all the favors.

Scratch that.

Harrison was doing the favors, for every woman present with eyes.

But where the heck was Brent Callahan?

Was he late? Well, that would be awesome for us. I swept the room, behind my right shoulder.

No sight of Brent, but I smiled at the faces I knew. My dad in his one gray suit, his thick brown hair freshly cut. Colby, in a three-quarter-length-sleeved black dress, hugging her muscly length. The rest of my bridesmaids, except for Jade. We'd found tidy closure in a phone call only last week. She'd cried, a lot. She seemed more upset than I was. Heartbroken, still, over Trey. It felt nice to release her, too. Tender, and awful. But good.

"Ready for Scotland Holiday, Your Honor." Peyton gave a taut bow.

"Ready for the Kingston Company, Your Honor." Harrison did the same.

Judge Davidoff bestowed each of them a long once-over, then asked the clerk to swear in the jury.

A gruff and bulkily suited woman emerged on behalf of the court. "Will the jury please stand and raise your right hand?"

They obeyed in unison.

"Do each of you swear that you will fairly try the case before this court, and that you will return a true verdict—so help you God? Please say 'I do.'"

"I do."

So, help them, God.

"You may be seated." Judge Davidoff perused the audience, his presence equally quiet and thunderous as a bass. "I ask everyone to give your attention to the attorneys, who will present their opening statements."

You got this, P.

I believe in you.

I still believe in us.

Peyton stood up with glamorous dignity, letting her eyes stroke the room. She walked toward the jury, nodding first to Judge Davidoff.

"Your Honor—and ladies and gentlemen of the jury." Her high heels clicked on the marble. "From the time women are little girls, they are pummeled with stories. Stories that build them. Shape them. And guide them. Whether they realize it or not. We are all the product of our greatest influence. Humans are made by the messaging they receive. Namely, by the stories they hear. Of beautiful stories, and hopeful stories. Cautionary tales, and fear-inducing anecdotes. Don't take candy from strangers—or you'll be snatched. Buy this shampoo—and you'll have this hair."

Peyton paused, pointing to a young blonde juror with *fantastic*, hot-roller hair. The girl grinned, and the female jurors laughed.

"We hear a million little stories—every single day of our lives," Peyton continued. "Instructions. Suggestions. Things to buy. Decisions to make. Some of these are paid advertisements. Others—we know—are fantasy. But what about the stories that happen to fall in between?"

She let that fall.

"What about the stories *spoken* to us as truths, but that secretly pack the poison of, say, a red apple? *Make a wish*! And it will come true. *Stray off the path*—but you will be rescued. *Fall in love*—and you will live happily ever after."

She stopped in all the right places as the faces soaked in her words.

"Do these *stories* sound familiar to you, jurors? Of course, they do, because these stories are the oxygen we have been breathing together for decades—ever since a man named Wade Elliot Kingston from Guthrie, Oklahoma, began to sketch rodents and castles as a young kid. What Mr. Kingston never could have foreseen, however—and what I doubt he ever intended—was that his *stories*, his *worlds*, his *fantasies*—would become assumed *realities* of the world."

She breathed, looking now to the audience. "Today, to remind you, everyone, the Kingston Company is a massive media enterprise worth $100 billion. Kingston owns fifteen networks, seven production companies, and twelve theme parks at six different resorts. To paraphrase: if you encounter a message—whether about shampoo or princesses—it's likely coming from Kingston."

Peyton returned to the jurors, engaging them, one by one. "Over the course of this trial, you will hear a story," she bellowed. "A real, living, breathing, powerful story—of our plaintiff, Scottie Holiday. Like so many girls before her, Scottie grew up with stars in her eyes and Kingston songs in her ears. Scottie believed in what Kingston was selling—why wouldn't she? She was a child—until these beliefs exploded in her two hands.

"Ladies and gentlemen, you will come to understand how a lifetime of infiltration by Kingston's messaging has left Scottie in a pile of heartache, destruction, and loss. Our case will prove that the Kingston Company not only failed Scottie with sensational deliveries of false advertising, but also that her quantifiable damages deserve restitution. As we share our story, may you consider the little girl here—"

She gestured to me again.

I saw her eyes sparkle.

Yes.

"—who simply believed in fairy tales. And now, who lives her personal nightmare. By holding Kingston responsible for this grave injustice, we will not only do right by Scottie, but by the youths of our future who might dare to dream in the realm of reality. Thank you."

I restrained from slapping my hands together like cymbals as she took her seat. *Perfect,* I said to her with my eyes. Her mouth quirked in a pleased smile. All twelve jurors were arched in their seats, enraptured.

That was Peyton. Beauty and fire. Rising up to defend me even though I'd betrayed her.

Harrison rose. He strode to the jury box, walked the length of it, making eye contact, smiling, nodding, connecting silently with every soul possible, before he even uttered a word.

Big shot Brent nowhere in sight.

It didn't matter, though.

Harrison held a vice grip on our attention.

The room's female gazes stuck to him like globs of bubblegum. Kingston could not have a better front man in here. He could fill in for any Prince Charming at the wave of a wand.

I recalled the addictive scent of him.

Spicy wood and fresh showers.

"Good morning," he began. "Your Honor, members of the jury. Thank you for being here."

Today his shoulders were broader. His smile was sexier. I hadn't thought either were possible.

"As my opposing counsel graciously pointed out, ladies and gentlemen: Story, we agree, is everything. The fabric of humanity, from the beginning of time." He paused. "We *believe* stories. We *live* stories. We are the collection of our own experiences—good, bad, pleasant, terrible, life-changing—each of us comprising a story, a sentence, a paragraph. Maybe more than a chapter or two we'd like to rip out or burn."

Laughs bubbled across the room.

"Over the course of this case, you will hear a '*story*'"—he went hard with the air quotes—"of how the Kingston Company destroyed a twenty-eight-year-old woman's life." He glanced at me, but not in the eye. "We made Ms. Holiday believe in fairy tales, outrageously, unfairly, and even—argued here now—*illegally*. Our plaintiff believed in the magic of Kingston, until she didn't. She accepted a man's proposal, and he turned out to be a frog."

More chuckles.

Fine, you hottie, you're good at this.

"Ms. Holiday feels blindsided, tricked, and wholly betrayed by the Kingston stories and characters that are—yes—to many, as real as oxygen."

Great! We agree. Can we go now?

"But if we start now," he continued, "with *rewarding* disappointment when expectations don't live up to art forms—where then, I ask you, does it stop? Picture, all of you, a world without entertainment. Without art. Without dreams. Really: imagine it."

He fell silent, encouraging this notion to marinate. "And now, consider this. Who among us also felt lost, confused, isolated, aimless, *abandoned*, even, as a child—but gleaned inspiration from some source beyond ourselves? Experienced a stirring we can't put to words, but know we felt in our hearts?

"Impossibly, indescribably, art has the capacity to move us— when we can't find our own way, our own feelings. Maybe you have experienced this. Maybe from a song. Maybe a painting. Maybe from Kingston's work.

"We won't argue, jury, that Ms. Holiday's experience with our brand is anything but unfortunate. But if we begin to discount historical masterpieces—in our case, largely, animated films inspired by folklore dating back to fifteenth-century Europe—*what then?* And further, if we strip entertainment of joy and enchantment, where might that leave us, in five years? In fifty? Five hundred?"

He paced the floor, keeping his tempo.

"And what about Kingston's nuanced lessons of what it means to be human? For every princess scooped up by a prince, there is a meaningful backstory. Resilience in the face of despair. Kindness in response to cruelty. Friendship in unlikely places.

"Kingston might be best known, on the surface, for telling a fairy tale. But even the most discerning critics must reckon with what Wade Kingston tapped into, deep within the human psyche. Wade Kingston's work has pioneered forms of expression, lifted spirits in war and tragedy, forced us to keep believing.

"Imagination. Innovation. Conquering fear. The power of possibility, and the sanctity of our dreams. The defense will rise to prove all of this."

He looked straight at me now, eyes ablaze with excitement. "And finally, we will illuminate that the blame for Ms. Holiday's current *'condition'* does not fall to Wade Elliot Kingston, his company, or any of his creations. Unfortunately—and unfairly, yes—this young woman has faced troubles all her life. She might very well be jobless, homeless, and stuck in her own despair, had she never encountered our films."

Wait.

Homeless?

I thought you said I was independent and strong.

Frowning, I folded my arms.

"I look forward to the upcoming week," Harrison finished. "Thank you all."

The crowd murmured.

Bang, bang.

"Thank you both." Judge Davidoff slipped off his spectacles. "We'll take a brief recess and return in fifteen minutes for the case of the plaintiff."

...

Chapter Twenty-Two

SCOTTIE

"I'd like to call Dr. Sarah Perrish to the witness stand."

Peyton beckoned my former therapist to the front of the room, where the good doctor slapped her hand on the Bible, taking the oath. *The whole truth and nothing besides.*

Down from San Francisco, just for the day, Dr. Perrish wore a gray sheath dress and pearls, her nose upturned, eyes wide, brows full. *Brooke Shields,* I'd thought instantly from her therapy couch. A square face, honest and strong. You somehow noticed her beauty secondarily, once you'd taken in her authority.

Then you wondered, *Is she the prettiest lady I've ever seen?*

"Please state your first and last name, for the record," Peyton instructed, once our witness sat down. Peyton gripped a folder under one arm.

"Sarah Perrish," she stated. "Doctor of clinical psychology."

"And where do you live, Dr. Perrish?"

"I live in San Francisco, in the neighborhood of Nob Hill." Her voice was medicine, smooth.

Dear Lord, I missed her.

"In what capacity are you acquainted with the plaintiff?"

Dr. Perrish looked to me warmly. "I was Scottie's therapist, following the breakup of her engagement."

"How often did she come to see you for appointments?"

"Twice a week at first," Dr. Perrish confirmed. "Later, once a week, in the time just before she moved home to Orange County."

"Would you say," Peyton asked measuredly, "that this is typical for a patient? Twice-weekly therapy?"

"The frequency of appointments depends entirely on the individual," she responded. "I tailor my treatment plans to well-being, objectives, and progress. But it's less typical, yes, for my patients. I see patients more than once in a week—as a starting point—if they have endured a certain level of trauma or find themselves navigating distress beyond their own faculties."

"Is that how you would describe Ms. Holiday's 'state of being,' then, Dr. Perrish?" Peyton opened her folder. "Recovering from a trauma, navigating distress beyond her own faculties?"

"Yes, without a doubt," Dr. Perrish stated into the microphone. "Trauma is defined as a 'deeply distressing or disturbing experience.' I think getting left at the altar by the man of your dreams more than qualifies."

The jury tittered with amusement.

"Speaking of the wedding, Doctor. What were the specific words Ms. Holiday used, in describing her wedding to you, the wedding that ended in tragedy?"

"She called it a *fairy-tale wedding*. Whenever she was describing it. I can count numerous times when she used this specific description—and repetition of exact phrases is always telling, in psychological evaluation."

"And where do you suppose she originally learned that phrase? *Fairy-tale wedding*?"

Dr. Perrish looked to the jury. "I know for a fact that she learned it from Kingston."

"Did she ever mention Kingston to you in her therapy sessions?"

She nodded, confirming. I was forever indebted to this therapist's furious note-taking. It had been a quick mention, briefer than breath, but I remembered saying it.

"Ms. Holiday did mention Kingston," Dr. Perrish said, "in describing her childhood. Following her mother's abandonment, specifically. She spent a lot of time alone, I learned, and she really took to the princesses."

I couldn't look at my dad.

"Dr. Perrish, is it your professional opinion that this time spent, ingesting Kingston content, following clear and present upheaval, could have shaped dreams and expectations in her formative years?"

"Absolutely."

"And finally, in further validation of my client's emotional damages, can you please describe Ms. Holiday's condition—in your words—on the first day she came to your office?"

Dr. Perrish cocked her head at me, eyes full of empathy. "She was anxious, depressed, uncertain, despondent, angry. Not sure where to place her fury, or her feelings of brokenness. She was mentally and emotionally unwell. I was glad she came to see me."

"And physically? How did she seem, at that time?"

"I'm not a medical doctor," Dr. Perrish allowed. "But it is my professional opinion that Ms. Holiday was, categorically, not in a healthy place. She was having severe trouble sleeping, dropped weight over the course of our time together, and continued to go on lengthy runs when she needed to rest. We also talked about cutting back on caffeine."

I gulped. *Oops.*

But my jeans were fitting correctly again.

It had been a dark time.

"And although you never personally knew Ms. Holiday prior to this recent, enormous personal upset—what is your professional assessment of the adult woman she seemed to be prior to her failed wedding?"

Dr. Perrish's mouth tugged up in a grin for the jury. "I gather that Ms. Holiday was a confident, upbeat, brilliant girl, who took people—who took *everyone*"—she shot at look at the defense table—"at their promise."

"I have no further questions, Your Honor."

Judge Davidoff motioned to Harrison. "Does the defense have any questions?"

"Not at this time, Your Honor."

"Then the witness is excused."

Next came our expert witness and scholar, renowned in academia for her Kingston work: Dr. Jennifer Bakerman, Ivy League professor and sociologist. Dr. Bakerman was a force of conviction in her black suit, milky skin, and high cheekbones. She was even a little villainous, with a gaze piercing enough to make you hinge forward. She was willing to confirm everything we possibly needed, and more, with even more class and more persuasion than we could imagine.

She commanded the room like a sergeant with her cogent testimony.

Kingston overtook classic fairy tales—oral stories traded by European village people as early as the fourteenth century—and regurgitated them for mass consumption. They brought a dangerous modern spin, marked by single-minded cultural norms and social ideas. As a film genre today, Kingston, in fact, presents a conflicting set of morals that we must navigate for our children.

Kingston says courage and kindness are important, yes—but not nearly as important as beauty.

Kingston says marriage is the pinnacle of achievement, not one of many possible outcomes.

Kingston says, if nobody's listening, be willing to give up your voice.

(We won't even touch the company's decades-long problems with diversity and representation.)

Dr. Bakerman cited several A-list female celebrities who have proclaimed they don't let their daughters watch Kingston's cartoon fairy tales.

In short, Dr. Bakerman slayed it—and I couldn't help nodding to the caliber of women here willing to testify on my behalf.

Colby took the stand as my former roommate, sharing her front-row view of my spiral. My dad did, as well, while my heart clenched into a ball. No one from the IRAA was willing to testify, after my walkout, but we still had their airtight amicus brief as evidence.

I stretched as Judge Davidoff confirmed it was lunchtime.

I'd never been so ready for recess.

...

We'd agreed to save me for last. The knockout witness, exclamation point, grand finale. *Keep everybody on edge.* Make the jury wait for it.

I was so glad we did.

Poised like a ballerina, prepped to perform, I sailed through Peyton's questioning of me with likeability and precision. At least—I thought so. I sat tall inside the witness stand but was careful to stay relaxed.

We'd rehearsed, and rehearsed, and *rehearsed.*

Peyton's advice ping-ponged around in my head, coaching my every move silently as I talked.

I remembered that body language and eye contact mean everything to a jury in determining the credibility of a witness.

I doled out my gazes generously, but strategically, to Peyton, the jury, and the audience members.

I smiled, but not too much.

"Ms. Holiday, then, to wrap this up." Peyton stopped in her pumps now between me and the jury. "Do you believe you would have fallen for these particular men in your past—from junior high to your ex-fiancé—without the conscious or unconscious influence of the Kingston Company?"

"No, I do not. I believe the similarities of my former romantic partners to Kingston heroes are legitimate—and not a coincidence."

"And you believe Kingston was a formative influence in shaping your decision-making abilities, particularly when it comes to love?"

I leaned into the microphone. "Yes, absolutely."

"Finally, then." Peyton sidled one step closer to me. "You agree that the Kingston Company acted negligently and outrageously in portraying an outcome you assumed would be yours—and you are here, today, simply to seek repayment for the losses incurred as a result of this grossly false advertising?"

"Yes. Exactly."

"No further questions, Your Honor." Peyton waltzed triumphantly to our table.

Judge Davidoff's voice echoed. "Does the defense have any questions?"

I froze, heart skittering under my blouse.

"Yes, Your Honor. I do." Harrison breezed out of his seat, approaching me. He waited a few beats, his stare on me like a spotlight. "Ms. Holiday, if we may, let's go back to your childhood, where all of this—supposedly—began."

I nodded.

His rich brown eyes would *not* melt me like chocolate sauce.

"What did you want to be when you grew up, Ms. Holiday? Professionally?"

"A dentist," I said definitively.

"And what *did* you become, when you grew up?"

"A dentist," I repeated, more loudly.

"Would you call this a *dream* you had, Ms. Holiday—something you *wished* for?"

Oh please.

Not this line of argument again.

"Objection!" Peyton interjected. "Leading the witness."

"I'll repeat the question." Harrison pulled on his tie. "Ms. Holiday, would you call becoming a dentist a *dream* you had, when you were young?"

I looked to Peyton, but her tight nod was unhelpful.

I hesitated. "Yes. I suppose I would. Call it a dream."

"A dream that came true."

"Yes—until it was taken from me."

"What do you mean by that, exactly—*taken* from you? Isn't it true that you quit?"

"Yes, I had to," I explained. "As Dr. Perrish confirmed, I was unable to sustain my existing life in San Francisco and remain healthy—emotionally, and physically. Lots of people take time off in the wake of a devastating event. I miss my profession, every day."

"But clearly you don't miss dentistry *that* much," he chided, eyes panning the jury. "Since you decided to put your time and energy into *all this*"—he gestured theatrically—"instead of finding a new job."

"*Objection!*" Peyton rose, her cheeks fiery hot. "Badgering the witness!"

"Sustained," Judge Davidoff agreed, raising a brow at Harrison. "Find the point, Counselor."

Harrison smirked. "Ms. Holiday. You said that becoming a dentist was a *dream* you held. And it came true." He waited a beat. "Would you, then, agree that dreams *can* come true?"

I sighed frustratedly, hating to answer. "Yes. I suppose they can."

"Even for those individuals *not* dealt a winning hand—arguably, like yourself, without a mother, and with emotional challenges."

I nodded. "Yes."

"Like the world-famous Kingston song, 'When You Dream Upon the Dawn.'"

My throat burned. No objection from Peyton. "Yes. I suppose. Like that."

The jury rustled.

Harrison traveled the length of them again, before turning back to me. "Ms. Holiday, I'm going to ask you the question that everyone here—everyone, *everywhere*—must be dying to know." He paused for effect. "You're twenty-eight years old. You're young, you're bright, and you're beautiful."

Did he say I was beautiful?

I rolled my eyes in rejection of the offhanded compliment. His dimples had never been so annoying. Was he allowed to flatter the witness? Any other time I would've thrilled at his words, but now I just felt confused.

"You arguably still have the world at your fingertips," he continued. "What I want to know is, after *all* this"—he presented his hands again—"regardless of your case outcome, do you still believe you might one day find your happily ever after?"

"*Objection!*" Peyton planted her fists on the table. "Badgering my witness!"

"Sustained." Judge Davidoff eyed Harrison warningly. "Rephrase the question, please."

Harrison stood squarely in front of me now, eyes up.

For one small moment, a fleeting moment, the people, and the hum, all round me fogged into a blur.

The jury, the crowd, even Peyton.

I looked at Harrison, and only Harrison, wonderingly.

I heard the Holiday playlist he'd made me. I thought of his sixteenth birthday forgotten, of his shoulder shattering into pieces and subsequently, also, his life. Yet here he was, defending Kingston, while I blamed them for, well, everything.

How had we ended up on such bipolar opposite ends of the aisle?

How had this massive punk of a man climbed so far inside my skin?

"Ms. Holiday, answer the question—yes or no." Harrison cleared his throat, looking harder into my eyes than he ever had before, and I felt them everywhere. In my eyes, in my throat, in my stomach.

"Do you believe you will find love again?" he pressed. "Do you still believe—in a love that could make you happy?"

The blur had cleared, and the room might as well have.

It was just us two now.

Scottie vs. Harrison.

Harrison vs. Scottie.

He didn't say *perfect* love. He didn't say *happily ever after*. He didn't even say the big D word.

Dream.

My eyes burned. I wanted to lie. I wanted to die. I wanted to give him the answer I felt when I filed this suit in the first place.

Instead, I told him the truth.

"Yes. I suppose I do still believe in love." My answer surprised even me, and Peyton might officially murder me now. But I had sworn under oath. And I suddenly felt so impossibly thankful that I'd never said *till death do us part* before.

Because I did believe, and the realization barreled me like a wave.

But I didn't believe because of the men in my past.

I believed because of the one standing in front of me.

"I have no further questions, Your Honor."

...

Chapter Twenty-Three

HARRISON

Was it possible to *hear* another person sweating? I wondered. Was that whole room of strangers aware that my undershirt had soaked through my black Armani suit?

I'd never been so wrecked with nerves.

Scottie's stupid green shirt and ridiculous eyes were not helping.

Does she feel it, too?

I was practically shaking with what her admission just meant for our case—Scottie still believing in love—but this wasn't over yet.

Not even close.

Thank God for a half-hour break.

I sneaked out the courthouse back door, desperate to keep away from the pack of reporters. They probably wouldn't move from the front steps all week.

I wound my way to the café for a decaf coffee, needing something to guzzle but not more caffeine. I grabbed it and found a bench at the back of the building, in the shade of a giant sycamore. I luxuriated in the second to breathe.

If only the reporters—the world—knew the truth.

The wild, unthinkable truth of Wade Kingston.

I wasn't sure I believed it myself.

Two weeks ago, Abel Iverson had called me into his office. This only ever happened two times a year: my reviews. And one review had just happened two months ago. So, logically, I prepared for the worst. Brent Callahan must have ratted me out about Scottie and the untimely pictures of us. Or Cooper—gosh, what a perk of this case, hardly having to see him—had finally unearthed some stupid reason to fire me.

I had no clue what to expect.

That day had been another sweaty one.

Back in one of Abel's white chairs I sat, waiting for the head of legal to arrive at the helm of his gargantuan desk. When he did come, though, he didn't look angry—or sorry. He looked *thrilled*, in fact, buzzing with energy, maybe even a secret. Before sitting, he greeted me with the warmest handshake conceivable. An embrace would not have surprised me.

"I should probably have you sign in blood for what I'm about to tell you." Once in his seat, he nudged his mouse, computer firing. "But I'm going to trust you. This stays in the vault. It's doubtful anyone would believe you, anyway."

I nodded unsurely.

Thanks?

He continued. "Brent Callahan is being taken off the case."

I jerked. "The Holiday case?"

He chuckled. "You know of another big case sucking all of our time and resources?"

No, I supposed I didn't, but—we were fourteen days from trial. "But—Brent *is* the case," I pointed out. "Without him, we simply don't have one. Because we don't have an attorney."

"That's not what I understand."

"What do you mean?"

"Brent—even Cooper—have been raving about your performance," he said. "Your dedication, hours, and creative approach. Everyone is impressed by you. Even the media, obviously."

I stared at him dumbly.

Where was this going?

"I got a call, Hayes."

"What kind of call?"

He sighed heavily. "A call I have only received one other time, in my fifteen years at the company." Now he was serious, jaw set.

"From Bill?" Our CEO.

I secreted more sweat, if that was possible.

"No, young man. From—him." He pulled a framed snapshot from his bottom desk drawer and shoved it to me. "I don't like clutter on my desk, but here. I always have this on hand. It's ... significant."

I looked down at the photograph of him and Wade Kingston, smiling proudly on either side of George H. W. Bush, at some gala.

I admitted, I loved the Bush family.

Had a president called for me?

What was happening?

I slapped my knee, cackling now.

Oh, this Abel Iverson, he was a *jokester*.

But he did not laugh in return. His mouth was a tight, earnest line. So I chilled out and shifted, sitting up board-like in my seat.

"Wade Kingston phoned." Abel scratched his white head.

"Yes—he's alive. Yes—he's *involved*. Nobody, *nobody* knows. Except for Kingston's top executives. And Wade instructed in no unclear teams that Brent should be removed from the case. And that, ah, you need to handle it from here."

This had to be a joke.

Just the prank of the year.

But Abel's stony face confirmed this wasn't funny.

"So ... Wade Kingston is *alive*," I parroted, voice level, willing myself not to crack up. "And—active in the ... company."

Abel nodded. "Not wildly so—but yes. I'm not going to tell you where he is. Because that stays in *my* vault. But, again, yes. Wade Kingston is very much alive and involved at the highest level, when and if he chooses to be."

I stared, dumbstruck, looking around for the cameras.

You got me, guys!

I almost tossed up my hands.

But, all right, then—

Let's assume this was true.

Why in heaven's name would Wade Kingston give Brent the boot—and choose to trust *me*? A rookie attorney with nary a case to speak of?

Reading my incredulity, Abel prattled on. "When Wade started Kingston and opened his theme parks, he never predicted the number of lawsuits he'd face. Hundreds. Thousands. Immediately. It became quickly apparent that he would need to be lawyered up."

"Of course."

"Well, as with everything, Wade had a strong opinion about

this, from day one. He didn't want a storm troop of suits from LA. He wanted someone with heart, who he felt embodied the soul and bootstraps of Kingston."

I blinked.

"So, he convinced a young, vibrant, thirty-one-year-old attorney to leave big law and set up his own practice, with the promise Kingston would give him all their legal business. This attorney was funny, handsome, and friendly—a fantastic storyteller and loyal friend. His small team handled Kingston's lawsuits for years."

"Until Wade disappeared."

"Exactly. Wade lets the current board of executives handle everything—it is extremely rare that he interferes. He is ... *content to live his life*, we'll say. But along with the rest of the world, Wade caught wind of the Scotland Holiday case, and feels very strongly that you are the man for the job. I think—" He paused. "You remind him of that first attorney. Maybe also, a bit, of himself."

I leaned back, letting this update work through my shell-shocked system.

I knew Abel Iverson didn't have this kind of extra time on his hands, to regale a young attorney with fantasy hour.

The longer I sat here, the more I knew it was likely ...

True?

And so, I started to nod, shifting my mental gears toward how in God's name I was going to handle this case on my own.

A lawsuit this size as my first?

Unthinkable.

But if Wade Kingston thought I was the *man for the job*—it would be days before I could take the thought seriously—then come hell or Holiday, I'd swing for the moon.

I pushed through my incredulity to talk through logistics and accept the challenge of my young lifetime.

Abel would take care of the press, he said, explaining that Wade Kingston taught him something important: the power in not giving a reason that is not due.

On my way out, head spinning, my eye caught again on that tiny glass swan on Abel's bookcase. "Mr. Iverson. Can I ask, does that swan ... have some significance? I can't help but notice it whenever I'm in here."

He glanced at it, eyes clouding over. "Yes." He folded his hands on his desk. "Reminds me of the other time Wade Kingston phoned me."

"Which was—"

His chest heaved. "To say he was sorry ... that my wife left me." He paused. "It's from the Kingston glass shop, on Grand Street. I bought it for her on our first date. Wade knew us ... as a couple. We used to be very good friends, us four. My wife left the swan when she left me. I keep it as a memento of ... something I'll never get back."

I swallowed, nodding my thanks for the explanation.

I started to back out of his office, but Abel had one more thing to say.

"I haven't always held onto what I had," he said. "Love is—mercurial. But it's also everything. Wade has always known that. Better than anyone."

I gulped.

I said nothing.

He turned back to his computer, and I noticed his eyes were wet.

...

And now, here I was, ready to examine my first witness for the defense: Princess Ashley Everdale of Cardiox Gym. She had wowed me in her deposition responses, so I knew this would be a slam dunk.

"Can you please state your full name, for the record?"

"Ashley Everdale."

"And where do you live, Ms. Everdale?"

"In Newport Beach, California." She wore a hot-pink plaid dress with three-quarter-length sleeves. Flawless for the occasion. It's not every day a real princess takes the witness stand.

"If you don't mind, let's jump right into your *impressive* history as a Kingston employee. When did you work for the company, and in what capacity?" I looked from her friendly face to the jury, and back again.

"I was a princess at Kingston Court for ten years. I was hired as Cinderella and later worked as Rapunzel, too." She looked virtuous, hands folded, smile bright.

"And how would you describe the job? Did you have a positive experience as an employee of Kingston—or a *Kingstonite*, as we say?"

"My years with Kingston were some of the best of my life," she effused. "The company holds to its values of optimism, kindness, community, and innovation. These qualities live in color at every level of the company. It was my honor to represent two of their most iconic princesses."

She shared the best tokens from our date: the children's last wishes to meet her, the friendships she made for a lifetime. She gave additional information as well: anecdotes from the park grounds, where kindness and magic unified people from every far walk of life, plus inspiring tales from the international parks.

I looked to the jury when she finished speaking. Unsurprisingly, they were starry-eyed.

Yes!

"No further questions, Your Honor," I said, returning to the defense table.

Judge Davidoff nodded. "Does the plaintiff have any questions?"

I looked to Peyton, who pulled a face that said, *I thought you would never ask.*

Uh oh.

She stood. "I do, Your Honor. Thank you."

She marched up to Ashley.

When face-to-face, the two blondes were practically mirror images. "Ms. Everdale, my first question about being a Kingston princess is simple. While dressed up in your gown, hair done, crown on, makeup lacquered—when you're on the clock—are you ever allowed to break character?"

She shook her head. "No. Of course not. We liken it to being on set for a film, or TV—but the camera is always rolling."

"What would happen, then, if you did break character? If

you did something, say, entirely *un-Cinderella*—like breakdance down Grand Street? Or smoke a cigarette? Or tell someone you weren't the real princess, but that you were actually a college student at UCI who worked as a princess on your days off?"

Ashley narrowed her eyes. "Like any job with *rules of conduct*, I would probably get a slap on the wrist, and then fired, if the behavior persisted."

"Fair enough. What if, then, for example, a young girl came up to you—crying—because someone said you weren't real? That there was no such thing as Cinderella?"

Ashley's face darkened.

"Objection!" I called. "Irrelevant."

Judge Davidoff coughed. "Overruled."

I wasn't liking this.

Ashley looked to me, her pretty face apologetic. She didn't answer Peyton's question.

Peyton tried again. "Ms. Everdale, isn't it true, that in your"—she opened her folder—"*fifth* year with Kingston, as Cinderella, a little girl came up to you *crying* because she was told you weren't real?"

Ashley squirmed. "Yes," she said finally. "That happened."

"And what did you say to her?"

"I told her that … a dream is a wish her heart makes. And that if she wished I was Cinderella, then of course, I was Cinderella."

"Is that all?"

Ashley looked to me again, and I nodded to keep telling the truth. "I told her that little girls who believe in magic grow up to be princesses themselves. And little girls who don't believe in magic—I don't know. I left it kind of open-ended. We were allowed to do that, though. Get creative with our script."

"But to be clear." Peyton's tone sharpened. "You lied to a *crying child* about your identity when she pointedly asked who you were ... and then, in the midst of this *tearful, confusing* moment, also told her that she will become a princess, too, if she simply believes."

Ashley's blue eyes went big as teacup saucers. "When you put it that way," she muttered.

"I'm sorry, Ms. Everdale, can you speak a little louder, for the jury?"

"Yes," she cried. "Yes. It was part of my job to"—she waved her hands around—"keep the magic going. Is that so *evil*?"

"Your words. Not mine." Peyton folded her arms. "But I can see you're getting upset. We can—shift gears. I have only a few more questions, on another topic."

Ashley shrugged in relief, and I felt horrible.

My princess was getting annihilated.

Peyton peered at me, and I shot her my best BE NICE look. She was on fire today. Almost like she was mad.

"When you were a princess," Peyton continued, "on a scale from one to ten, one being the lowest, ten being the highest, how important was your physical appearance to the job?"

"Obviously, a ten," Ashley said. "Like I said. As with any theatrical role."

"Sure, sure. So, it is my understanding that every few months, the princesses are paraded—in full costume—into a private stage area, in front of Kingston leadership and executives, to make sure you still look the part. Is that correct?"

"Yes, that is correct. It's in the manual, before you get hired. Standards of excellence."

"What, might I ask, then, would happen if you say—gained weight? Or got acne? Or, simply, had an accident, broke a bone?"

Ashley looked mad again. "As part of the *job,* we are required to *look* a certain way."

"So, let's keep it simple, then. You gain fifteen pounds, and your ball gown doesn't fit anymore. What happens?"

Ashley looked to me, and I wanted to slam my head on the table.

"The dresses only go up to size 8," she said quietly. "So ... up to that, you'd be fine. But if you gain past a size 8, you would be—in trouble. Or switched to a character with more—curves."

"Such as?"

She shrugged. "The fairy godmother, maybe."

"But no Kingston *princesses* have—your words, not mine—*curves.* Is that correct?"

She huffed. "No princesses are bigger than a size 8. Take that as you will."

"Even though"—Peyton looked to the jury—"the average woman in the US falls between a size 16 and 18."

I stood, fuming. "Objection, *irrelevant!*" Pointless details were flying all over the place. "Kingston princesses are aged sixteen to eighteen in our films. No one ever said they were supposed to be fully developed women—"

The jury murmured, and Ashley looked ready to cry.

Bang, bang, bang!

"Order, order!" Judge Davidoff yelled. "Sustained, Counselor. Strike her comment from the record. Ms. McKenzie, do you have any more *peaceable* questions for the witness?"

Peyton smiled connivingly at my princess. "I think I've made my point. No more questions, Your Honor."

Judge Davidoff banged the gavel again. "Counselors, please approach the bench."

Peyton and I stood shoulder-to-shoulder in front of him, like two kids in the principal's office.

"We are now going to break for the day," he said. "Is there anything final you'd like to say?"

"Yes, Your Honor," I blurted.

I hadn't been planning to do it. I really hadn't. But Peyton was playing dirty, and I needed this win more than anyone knew. I would handle the fallout later.

"I have a surprise witness I'd like to call tomorrow," I said. "She can be here by 11 a.m."

"*Excuse me?*" Peyton pivoted to glower at me. "You have a surprise *what now?* When I've had zero time to prepare for cross?"

I implored the judge with my eyes. "It's—important, Your Honor. Very important."

He rubbed his temples, considering. "Eleven in the morning gives you plenty of time, Ms. McKenzie. I'll allow it. Please meet me after in my chambers, though, both of you."

Peyton rejoined Scottie, who looked, well, beautiful—but also bewildered and unsure how to digest this.

I felt a pang of guilt.

Just you wait for tomorrow.
Even if it broke my own heart.

...

Chapter Twenty-Four

SCOTTIE

My head swam. The wood walls closed in around me. This might as well be county prison. I blinked, unmoving, eyes forward, crossing my high-heeled ankles under my chair.

I couldn't look at Harrison.

Whatever I thought I'd seen in him—sweetness, gentleness, soul—none of it was the truth.

He was a walking lie.

Just like everything else.

Lies, lies, lies, lies, lies.

I wished angrily that I could speed back time and recant my testimony from yesterday. I didn't believe in love.

I wasn't sure I believed in anything, anymore.

My head still throbbed from last night's tears, but I felt better today. There wasn't much left to emote. I was drained, in every sense.

Peyton squeezed my hand under the table, saying so much without words.

You're my best friend. I love you so much. Forget about everything else.

Forgiven.

Your mom might've left, but I won't.

The gavel smacked.

"Welcome back, ladies and gentlemen." Judge Davidoff looked rejuvenated, like he'd needed today's late start. At least one of us was ready for this. "We're here again for the case of Scotland Holiday v. The Kingston Company. Is the defendant ready to continue presenting his case?"

In my peripheral, I sensed the giant ascend from his chair.

God, I know it's wrong, but...

I hated him. Consuming and murderous, red-hot, pure hatred.

He'd invited my mom here today.

He. Found. Her.

My mom.

"Yes, Your Honor. Ready for the Kingston Company," echoed Harrison's voice.

"Go ahead, then." Judge Davidoff leaned back, folding his hands on his belly.

Harrison coughed. "I'd like to call Dolly Ruth Holiday to the witness stand."

My throat filled with love, and sorrow, and rage.

But I had to look. I couldn't *not* look. I'd waited twenty-two years for this.

Slowly I spun my gaze to the right, as a woman, lithe and graceful, made her way to the witness stand.

So familiar, and a stranger.

Her hair was dark, pouring in a waterfall down her back. I touched my own waves, a reflection of hers.

Her black dress was simple. Her posture, tall. From her profile, I could see she was solemn.

She had my same tiny and upturned nose.

As she placed her hand on the Bible, she squeezed her eyes, whispering, and I would've killed to hear what she was saying. To either God, or herself.

When my mother sat down, and faced the audience, waves of anxiety rippled from my head to my toes—but then, slowly, they calmed like a prayer.

Maybe God heard my mom's cry, or mine.

Mama.

Is it really you?

She smiled at me, and my heart cracked in half. It was the smile that had stayed in the glow of my memory since the singular day that she left. The size and its light were the same—but it was still not the smile I knew.

Her teeth were gray, the top four twisting chaotically into each other. A few on the bottom were missing.

Her olive skin was luminous, though. Light makeup blushed her sharp features, and she didn't need anything more. Her eyes were sea foam, like mine.

Peyton's hand crushed mine harder, cracking the trance.

I'd never let Peyton go, either.

Don't cry, don't cry, don't cry.

This was court.

Ahem.

"What's your full name, for the record?" boomed Harrison.

My mom's eyes sparkled; she looked so calm. "Dolly Ruth Holiday, Sir."

"Where do you live, Ms. Holiday?"

"My residence is in Medford, Oregon. In a cabin, next to a river."

"Are you married?"

"No, not anymore. I ... was. Twice. To—" She nodded to Dad in the audience. "Paul Holiday. And later, to a man named George Duncan. He died ... three years ago, of a heart attack. He was a very good man."

"And you kept the name Holiday?"

Her eyes dropped to her lap before piercing me, like the sun. "Yes. I did. It was my way of keeping a piece ... of my past."

I swallowed.

Of me?

"Who, for the record, is Scottie Holiday, the plaintiff, in relation to you?" Harrison asked.

"Scottie Holiday, the plaintiff, is my daughter."

The jury rustled.

I was transfixed.

Harrison plowed ahead. "Ms. Holiday, is it true that you left Scottie and her father, Paul? And never returned?"

"Yes. That's true."

"Why did you leave?"

She bowed her head, looking ashamed. "I didn't want to put them through my ups and downs anymore. I was an addict. I was—*bipolar*, I'd later learn. I was ... not faithful. To Paul. Or to Scottie. They both deserved so much better." Her voice caught. "They deserved ... everything."

"Where did you go, Ms. Holiday? Back then?"

My jaw dropped. *Could it be so easy?* My mom on the stand, sworn to truth, hammered with every question I'd mulled for two decades?

"I went up to Portland," my mom said. "I hitchhiked. I had some family there. I intended to get clean, find my way, but—I had a rough go. A rough decade, really. Drugs, alcohol. More ... men. Not good ones. I—" She looked down again. "I lived ... on the streets, for a while."

My stomach twisted.

I wanted to hold her and punch her at the same time.

Harrison glided back and forth down the jury box. "You were homeless, then?"

She cleared her throat. "Yes. I experienced a season of homelessness."

"And how did you end up in Medford, specifically?"

My mom brightened subtly. "I finally met a good man. Through ... a church. He helped me. We fell in love. We wanted a smaller town, a piece of land, so ... we moved. He bought us our cabin there, in Medford, by the water."

Harrison paced, jury still.

"Ms. Holiday, is it true that during Scottie's upbringing, you would leave her alone at the house, without any supervision? Under the age of six?"

She shrank in her seat, eyes down. "Yes. It's true. It was a different time, but ... it's true. And I regret it."

"And when you were home, you were—'exceptionally loving and kind. Doting, and warm.' The plaintiff's words. Is that true?"

She perked up a little. "Scottie said that?"

If you can answer me, please," he said flatly. "Does that match your memory?"

"I'd like to think so." She sighed. "I have a backache, every day, from the regrets I carry."

"Would you then, Ms. Holiday, describe Scottie's upbringing as—*neglectful*?"

She hesitated. "I never … hurt her. Physically. Just so everyone knows. Feels like I need to say that. But … neglectful? Yes. My actions were inexcusable. I did not act as a mother. I was … negligent, yes."

"Negligent. Hmm." Harrison looked at Judge Davidoff, then to Peyton. "The Kingston Company is defending, today, against negligence."

"Objection," Peyton shot. "Irrelevant."

"Overruled," Judge Davidoff clucked. "Continue, Counselor."

"Would you say, Ms. Holiday, that your actions—your mothering, or lack thereof—could have caused your daughter, the plaintiff, emotional damages?"

"What do you mean by that … specifically?"

"Do you think your abandonment of Scottie could have *damaged* her, Ms. Holiday? Impacted her decision-making abilities? Her views of love? Her long-term well-being, into adulthood? Perhaps caused her to seek love in the wrong places—and suffer exceptionally when it didn't work out?"

"Objection, leading the witness!" Peyton cried, rising up.

"Overruled, again, Ms. McKenzie," Judge Davidoff shot.

Hot tears seared the backs of my eyes.

Harrison had brought me my mother.

But now he was taking my case from me.

My mom pierced me with her jade eyes. "Yes." She nodded sadly, looking surrendered. "I have no doubt that my actions have caused my daughter irreparable damage."

"Ms. Holiday, I must also ask," Harrison continued, insatiable, "in all your years away—twenty-two, to be precise—did you ever try to get in contact with your daughter, or your ex-husband?"

Her olive complexion fell ashen. She froze, like she'd seen a corpse dancing. She stared at the audience, blankly.

Wait, no. She was staring at *someone*.

My dad.

My eyes flicked in horror between them. *How he must feel right now.* But he looked so calm. Serene, even, solid as stone.

Also not one bit surprised.

"Ms. Holiday," Harrison repeated. "Have you, or have you not, ever attempted to make contact with Scottie or Paul, since you left them?"

My mom gulped so hard I could feel it inside my own chest. She nodded at my dad, and then spoke. "Yes."

"Yes, you tried to reach them?"

"Yes," she repeated. "Many times. I contacted Paul, when I got to Portland—and many times the first ten years I was gone."

I exhaled.

No.

She was a liar.

Like everyone else.

Dad would not keep that from me.

I jerked my head back at him, but he just shrugged, mouthing the words, *I'm sorry.*

Bewildered, I looked to my mom, and Harrison at her side, who kept pressing. "What did Paul say when you called him, Ms. Holiday?"

"He said, repeatedly, that I had no right to see her. Every time. And he was right. He was done. He begged me to stay away. From him, but mostly, from her."

"And you listened?"

She started to nod but stopped. "I didn't listen until—" Her pause was prolonged, and then deeply uncomfortable.

"Until what, Ms. Holiday?"

She choked out the words. "Until he offered me money." She exhaled. "Money I needed. At the time. Paul paid me to stay away from Scottie. For good."

I thought my world had already stopped, until this moment crashed into me. Until my dad—my beloved dad—joined the ranks of people who'd picked up a dagger and thrown it into my back.

I couldn't look at him.

Or at my mom.

In this moment, I was an orphan.

Instead, I looked at my lap. I watched hot tears soak my hands.

"Did you ever—look Scottie up? Keep tabs on her?"

"Of course," I heard my mom say. "I'm so proud of her. Star student, pediatric dentist, and, of course, this case—she's incredible. I would give anything, and I do mean anything, to take my decisions back."

"So, you do," Harrison asked, voice quieter now, "take *full responsibility*, for any of your daughter's emotional distress which might have flared following her broken engagement? Triggered her abandonment issues? And might continue to flare, at any time in her life?"

"Yes. I take full responsibility. For Scottie's past, current, and future distress."

"I have no further questions, Your Honor."

Judge Davidoff's voice piped up from his lectern. "Does the plaintiff have any questions for the witness?"

Peyton stood next to me and confirmed what we had agreed upon. "We do not have any questions, Your Honor."

As the rest of the day droned on, every additional testimony crunched around me like ambient static. Harrison called a Kingston scholar for his side, and one of the company's top animators.

But I couldn't focus.

I didn't care.

I just wanted to talk to my mom.

But when Judge Davidoff slammed his gavel again, and said we'd reconvene for closing arguments in thirty minutes, I looked back, and she was gone.

...

"Ladies and gentlemen, I am so thankful to you for the time, attention, and perspective every one of you has brought to this case." Peyton placed her palms on the wood bar before the jury, leaning and pleading with effortless class. "Throughout this trial, you have heard two sides of a story. You have heard the side of a young girl, abandoned too soon, unfairly promised a fairy tale that left her shattered and lost. A girl without a job, a girl without a partner, a girl without a mother—until today, that is.

"And you have heard the side of a world-famous corporation. A shiny brand with bottomless pockets, countless fans, and, incidentally, films without healthy mother figures."

The jury chuckled unsurely.

"Tomorrow, you begin jury deliberation. And as you do, I want to remind you that civil cases, like this one, are not the same as criminal cases. Despite how *spicy* things might have gotten in here"—she waved a hand around—"there is no criminal here."

She smiled coyly, pacing. "Your job, ladies and gentlemen, with the evidence you've been presented, is to ask yourself: Is it *more likely than not* that Scottie Holiday was duped by fairy tales, and incurred damages due to false advertising? That's all it needs to be. *More likely than not.* Not a hundred percent. Not even eighty percent. Is it *more likely than not?*

"I implore you, as you consider, as you dig into yourselves and converse with one another about the facts on the table: Ask yourselves about justice. Ask yourselves about love. Ask yourselves about happily ever after. Ask yourselves what Scotland Dolly Holiday truly deserves. Thank you, again, for your time."

I smiled proudly as she sat down.

We did it, I mouthed.

Harrison stood, sashaying up to the jury. He paused in front of the young blonde with fantastic hair, who'd blinked maybe once this whole week. He nodded to the grandmotherly figure with the gray snake of a braid, and to a middle-aged man with glasses and a crisp collared shirt.

"Thank you, ladies and gentlemen, for your time and attention on this very important case. This trial, as we all know, has earned a place in the national spotlight, but more importantly, in our hearts. We know this lawsuit is about more than Scotland Dolly Holiday. We know it's about the invisible spirit of Kingston that moves and breathes. It's about fantasy. Wishing. Being. Believing. The invisible cries of our hearts.

"Your job, however, as the jury, is to look at the law, as it relates to Ms. Holiday. I don't doubt we were all moved, in some way, by the story that unfolded this week. But I ask you. Is Kingston responsible for the damages that have occurred? Is our work truly and inarguably classifiable as false advertising to Scotland Holiday—and to the billions who encounter our stories each day?

"Think about Kingston Court, for a second—of the people who walk, eat, laugh, wear matching T-shirts with fourteen family members, all gallivanting like kids. Eating corn dogs, and churros. You cannot deny, those people are *happy*. They're filled with joy. They are drawn to something indescribable—something magic—that only Kingston stirs in their hearts. Like they do to our movies, people come back, *and back*, for more. We give them something intangible. We give them, yes, a dream.

"Is Kingston Court real life? Maybe so. Maybe not. Whatever it is, though, I ask you: Would we want to take this away from people? Would we want to take away hope? Would we want to take away art? Would we want to take away the possibility ... of the impossible?

"I trust you will weigh the evidence and arrive at the right conclusion. Thank you, again, for your time."

...

Later that night, I hugged my knees on the couch in the living room silence, surrounded by the debris of our valiant battle these last couple months. Files, papers, and boxes, oh, how the boxes still towered high. Every building block was present here now—that is, except for Peyton. She and I were okay now, thank God, but I needed to be alone after that afternoon, and she understood completely.

In two days, we'd have our verdict.

Knock, knock.

Knuckles rapped on the wall, and I peered up with still-burning eyes.

Dad.

I should've known he'd be home soon.

"Can I join you?"

How could he just, well, *ask* me like that, precisely in the way he had *always* asked me, whenever he wanted to sit next to me on the couch? From my earliest memory, the feel of him next to me had been my constant comfort and my steady warmth, the assurance that I would never be left alone. The understanding that he'd never *lie to me*? That was a given. We didn't have any secrets. He was my person.

My person, the liar.

What a depressing life theme.

I huffed.

He sat next to me anyway.

I stayed snug in my cozy ball, compact in my worn-down sweats. Dad's flannel and jeans and faint smell of earth relaxed me, despite my best efforts. I rested a cheek on one of my knees, head away from him.

"Do you remember the first Sunday after she left?" he asked.

I exhaled, and my chest tightened.

Not precisely, no. I did not. I remembered the night *before* she left—but nothing after, not with clarity. Just a blur of abandonment for months afterward, fraught with emotion and tears. I remembered the nightmares, the questions, the Kingston movies. As I strained for memories of any specific Sunday, any specific calendar day at all, I found nothing.

Blank screen.

"You ended up in my room, on the floor," Dad continued. "I didn't hear you come in, but I woke up to you on the ground next to me around four a.m."

I nodded. I did that a lot. I'd usually wet the bed, too.

"You never talked in your sleep, but early that morning, you did."

Surprised, I shifted toward him slightly. I had no memory of ever—*ever*—talking in my sleep. "What did I say to you?"

He rested his arm on the back of the couch. "You didn't say anything to me," he said. "You were praying to God."

I felt a jolt in my heart.

I sensed God a lot, as a kid. I'd loved Sunday school so

much—the smiles, the songs, and the stories. I loved the image of God as a shepherd, the thought of someone so big and so mighty, powerful enough to reign over all, but gentle enough to chase after the one wayward sheep.

I used to talk to him often.

Somewhere along the way, I had stopped.

"You were whimpering, but your words were clear. You said, 'God, if you're real, please bring Mommy back. And don't ever let her leave me, ever again.'"

I swallowed, reimagining this little vignette.

It sounded about right to me.

"So ..." I said cautiously. "God was *trying* to answer my prayer. Mom *did* want to come back. And *you* chose to get in the way. By paying her off." I shot him a glance to see my words land sharply on his handsome face.

He scratched his chin, wincing. "Or." He paused. "Maybe I had seen her come back home—only to leave us—a hundred times, and I didn't want you pinning your belief in God on an addict, one who I knew would leave us one hundred more." He sighed. "She wasn't clean yet, Scot. It took years. She didn't get sober until I set her free, once and for all."

"Ha!" I yelled, hurt. "Is that what I was to her? To both of you? *Prison*? She got to go free, and you had to stay, what, unfree? Chained? To the kid?"

"Scot." Now he sounded hurt. "You know that's not true. That Sunday morning, hearing your prayer, I made my own promise to God."

"Which was ..."

"That I would protect you. That I would love you. That I would give every day of the rest of my life to seeking God's wisdom for you. It was the morning I didn't know *how* I would manage to raise you up by myself ... but I knew I could protect you. That, I could do. I knew I could be God's loving arms to you."

"She was *my mom*, though, Dad," I cried. "You didn't think I had a right to know she still wanted me?"

"She was sick, Scot. So sick. I just ... couldn't risk it. If she broke your heart again, the blame would be mine. No one else's. And I couldn't live with that. So I did what I thought was best. I truly thought I did the right thing."

"You lied to me!" I shouted. "You ... lied."

He nodded, leaning over to hug me. "I did. And I am *so sorry*, sweetie. I hope you can find a way to forgive me. I hope you can see that everything I did—everything I've *ever done*—has been out of my love for you. And not because I had to. Because I had the privilege of raising the best little girl in the world. Just ... *look at you* now. I am so unbelievably proud of you."

We sat there together, father and daughter, as I slowly and eventually buried my head in his shoulder.

I imagined, for a moment, if my prayer had come true. What if Mom *had* returned, and stayed forever? Well, wouldn't that have been my true fairy tale?

But what if she'd returned ... and left again?

Over and over and over?

Validation that not only she, but God, had forgotten me. Didn't care about me one bit.

I squeezed my eyes shut before I realized my soul was risking a prayer to God now.

Are you real? Did you hear me then? Have you been working on the answer for decades? Did you bring my mom back to court for me?

I brushed it away.

"That was when you got really into church," I remembered, eyes flying open. "Right away, after Mom left."

Dad nodded.

"And why you've been ... sad that I haven't ... gone back."

"I want your faith to be your own choice, always," he clarified. "But ... yes, of course I wish you would give God another chance. Join me at church sometime. I'll never forgive myself if you let yourself think God did this any of this to you. Or if you think I kept him from making your dreams come true. I love you, Scot. More than anything. There's nothing I wouldn't do for you."

His brown eyes were pleading, his scruff three days old.

Forget about leaving me behind; how could Mom have left *him*? His knowing heart, his quiet humility, this unmoving strength, after everything.

I couldn't stay mad.

I just couldn't.

I leaned over to hug him like the bear that he was. "Thank you," I whispered. "For saying that. I'm hurt, and confused, but ... I love you. Thank you, Dad. For doing your best. For everything you've ever done for me."

And God, I dared silently once again, my stomach knotting at thoughts of the trial, *if you're real, I'm asking you this. To please finish writing this story, because I really don't know how it ends.*

...

Chapter Twenty-Five

SCOTTIE

I'd never counted down to a Friday with such fanaticism. Climbing up the steps of the courthouse this morning had been a circus trick. Reporters teeming, phones snapping, pens scratching on pads like claws. I weaved my way through the mayhem.

Ms. Holiday, do you predict the jury will find in your favor today?

Ms. Holiday, what is your opinion of opposing counsel, Harrison Hayes?

Ms. Holiday, is it true this was the first time seeing your mother in more than twenty years?

I sat now next to Peyton, back at our trusty table, both of our knees bouncing with jitters. No matter the verdict, we'd battled.

Boy, had we fought with our lives.

In the last two days, my anger toward Harrison had still bubbled hot, but was now maybe more of a simmer than a boil. This was partly due to finding resolution with Dad. Despite my initial shock and rage, we now felt closer than ever. We'd continued to talk—and talk and talk—and I knew it was the whole truth.

He'd done his best to protect me.

Additionally, I'd sensed a seismic shift in my spirit since

finally seeing my mom. Since hearing her voice. I wasn't exactly *satisfied* by the reunion, if you could call it that. But I'd heard things I'd needed to hear, I realized, whether I liked them or not. I'd discovered information I hadn't even known I was searching for.

Judge Davidoff cracked his gavel down one final time. "Good morning, everyone. Welcome to the last day of the trial. Please, be seated."

The room obeyed, collective eagerness thick in the air.

The judge addressed the jury. "Have you reached a verdict?"

The nubile blonde stood. I'd learned her name was Elizabeth and that she taught yoga, which made abundant sense. "We have, Your Honor."

"And what do you say?"

"We, the jury, in the case of the Kingston Company versus Scotland Holiday, rule in favor of ..." She paused. "The defendant. As such, no damages will be awarded to the plaintiff."

The room hushed before erupting into applause—

Into roaring claps not meant for me.

My stomach plummeted in disappointment.

We lost.

We lost?

We gave all that we had—

And we lost.

I pivoted to Peyton—but she was smiling.

Why are you smiling?

She shrugged. "You can't win 'em all." She rolled her eyes to the decorative ceiling above us. "I mean, don't get me wrong.

I *wish* we were lounging on the private island we bought with our millions—but, we fought fair, Scot. We threw it *down*. I'm so proud of us. I really am."

I hurled my arms around her neck. "Forget the millions." I meant it. "I'm just glad I didn't lose you."

"*Stop!*" she shrieked. "You'll get my spray tan on your white shirt!"

Ah, the truest friend, till the end.

Then in my line of sight, across the aisle, I spotted Harrison in a slim-cut gray suit, peering back at me, flashing a tentative grin.

Disappointed as I was, I knew how monumental this was for him and his career. *He did this*, without Brent, without a boss, without anyone but himself.

I'm sorry, he mouthed.

His brown eyes. They said sorry, too.

But I looked away.

As if hosting the wedding reception I never had, I floated around the room, chatting with everyone who'd graciously come to support me, even more of a crowd than I'd realized. Friends from high school, friends from Dad's church—and one older gentleman in the back who I noticed barely before he dashed.

The rosy-cheeked man from the IRAA meeting—

Or at least I was pretty sure.

My Clarence?

He tipped his hat and winked at me before ducking out the back door.

Peyton would fight me on this detail for the rest of our lives.

Harrison was swarmed, so I kept my distance, not that I wanted to speak to him anyway.

Or did I?

Was this where we parted ways?

After I'd mingled until I could mingle no more, I found the front double doors of the building, where I saw Harrison bound down ahead of me, onto the steps.

I impulsively decided to follow him, but he was too fast for me—*darn it*—always so fast.

Perhaps it was for the best.

I watched as he squished through the press. I heard the questions bounce off him like popcorn.

Harrison Hayes, how does it feel to be a rising star of the law?

Harrison Hayes, what happened to Brent Callahan, and why did he leave the case?

Harrison Hayes, was this really your first courtroom trial?

Meanwhile, my own questions echoed against the walls of my heart.

Harrison Hayes, who are you, really?

Harrison Hayes, were you conflicted about calling the plaintiff's mom to the stand?

Harrison Hayes, do you think about me as much as I think about you?

...

The following Monday, my rental car wheels spun down a windy dirt road. I wove between fir trees toward the destination marked on my notepad. I had zero cell service bars and ten million nerves.

When I'd asked Dad for Mom's address, he'd supplied it without a pause. It stung anew that he'd always known her location. But he was, without any doubt, a man I could trust. And forgive.

Now, I was approaching the classic log cabin with smoke swirling out of its chimney. Nestled on a quiet river, the home was somehow both stately and small. Made of real logs and boasting a deep green door.

My heart clenched at the thought of my mom living here, all this time, all alone.

Then, I spotted her.

Down at the water's edge, she stood in a creamy white sheath dress, sleeves billowing in the wind. Completely unaware I was coming, face to the sun.

I parked on the dusty road and walked down to her slowly. When she finally turned at the sense of somebody, I threw her an awkward wave.

She didn't even pause for a breath.

My mom bolted.

She ran to me.

Faster than I had ever seen anyone run.

Including Harrison Hayes.

In the purest embrace, she threw her arms all around me.

She held my shoulders to study me. She cradled my face, and I looked bravely into her eyes. I could handle the pain.

But none came.

She was my mirror, miraculous: the smatter of freckles on prominent cheekbones, flanked by brunette locks falling and shining like silk.

We didn't speak a word.

We just held each other, until the tears fell like grace.

"I'm so sorry, Scottie," she whispered, scratching my back in that exact way I remembered. "I know I can't take it back. But I can spend the rest of my life being the mom you always deserved."

She couldn't possibly realize how long I had waited for this, just to know her heart was still beating.

Then again, maybe she did know.

Maybe she knew better than anyone.

"You're here now." I sniffed. "We're here."

I wiped my cheeks as she—my mother—looped her arm into mine shyly. I touched her hand in an indication that the gesture was okay with me.

She pulled me up the bank toward her charming home and asked if I liked roasted chicken. I said of course I did, silently wondering if someday, in time, she could teach me how to make it.

I decided right then that the plaintiff could rest.

Finally, she could rest.

That every remnant of regret, anger, bitterness—I chose then and there to leave it at the Oregon riverbed, where it could sink, sink, sink … and stay.

Baggage sorted.

Grudges dumped.

Emptied and light, free to fly.

I was no longer the motherless girl, wishing upon a star. No longer the young woman with a lawsuit, swinging her flashy sword. No longer sad because somebody sadder left her behind at the altar. Everything had led to this afternoon, to this version of me, right here.

No longer an orphan.

Now, home.

I'd won everything.

And I knew it.

My mom opened her cabin door, green, like our eyes.

I walked through it.

Forgiveness.

You imagine those moments.

You'll let them have it.

Instead, you let them have you.

...

Chapter Twenty-Six

HARRISON

I wasn't prepared for the fanfare that followed the case. Every podcast and news outlet wanted an interview. I enjoyed it, for a stretch—but then I needed a break. The last six weeks had been one nonstop ride. E-ticket, as they used to say.

Neither was I prepared for how difficult it would be to track down Scotland Dolly Holiday's phone number. I really had deleted her texts, and for all my voracious stalking of her as my plaintiff, I had no reliable method of reaching her. I'd found one number listed on her Internet records, but it was a 949 area code, so probably old, or a landline.

I tried it just in case.

No luck.

I resorted to Peyton, my bestie, calling her at Cashion & Baker.

"Please," I begged. "I'll do anything. Give me her number."

"Anything? Like go back in time and *not* call my best friend's absentee mom to the witness stand? Cool. Thanks!"

Click.

That was my first attempt, but she had another thing coming if she thought I'd give up so easily.

"Peyton," I implored again the next day. "What do you want? Within reason."

She huffed over the line. "Okay. How about the $7 million we turned down from the IRAA because we wanted to fight within *reason?*"

"We? I heard that was all Scottie's idea."

"We're a team. Maybe you've heard."

Click.

I groaned.

Finally, on a lucky Thursday, when Peyton finally realized that I wasn't quitting, she sighed dramatically into the phone. "*Fiiiiine.* But I'm not giving you—or anyone—her number. Everyone wants a piece of her these days, in case you haven't noticed. But I know where she'll be tonight. She likes to go there, to clear her head. She's been doing it since we were girls."

Cool air hung in a cloud layer over the lake as my navigation confirmed I'd arrived at my destination. I found a parking spot in a bordering lot. The dark lagoon water glittered beneath the fog. I knew from Peyton that this was close to Scottie's dad's house. It was artificial but beautiful, in a way not unlike Kingston Court, illuminated by spotlights and rimmed with night joggers. A wooden bridge over the water connected tennis courts to a playground.

All of it glowed, like Scottie's eyes.

I rubbed my hands together, scanning the shoreline—finally spotting her on a bench. She was holding a bagged loaf of bread, throwing snippets to ducks.

Not wanting to scare her, I approached from the side. I sat next to her, waiting until she noticed, which didn't take long.

She turned to me blankly, then frowned toward the water.

"What"—she tensed up—"are you doing here?"

I smiled anxiously and held up my hands. "I'm just here to see you. No ... agenda. No rules. Just—finally, wanted to see you. Now that it's over."

She raised her brows and glanced around as if for clues.

"And—" I gulped, persisting. "I wanted to apologize."

She snapped her head to me, eyes narrowed. "Apologize for what? You were just doing your job."

I scratched my head. Of course she wouldn't make this easy on me. "For—winning, I guess. But mostly for blindsiding you. With your mom. I know how ... unexpected that was. I really went for the jugular."

"Yes, you *sure* did." She exhaled sharply and still wouldn't look at me in the eye. A few moments passed, ducks squawking, moonlight rippling on the water. "You know, I was *so* angry at you. Fuming. Just—furious. Mad at you. Mad at Kingston. Mad at everyone."

I flinched. "Yeah, I got that impression. But ... rightfully so."

"I might've won if you hadn't found her, you know."

"Yes. I know." I hated how true it was.

She tossed a lump of bread to a mallard, who eagerly gobbled it up.

"Brent tracked her down, and I just—" I sighed. "I wanted to win more than anything. I'm sorry, Scottie." I inched closer to her, and our shoulders brushed. "It was—impulsive. While I was questioning her, I wanted to die. If it makes you feel any better. The victory was totally tainted."

I saw her mouth twitch.

"It does make me feel better." She sighed. "That you were suffering, too, I mean. I'm still—I don't know, shocked that we didn't win. Outraged sometimes." She breathed. "But ... I went to see her. My mom."

My heart lurched. I wasn't expecting that. "You did? In Oregon?"

She nodded. "It was ... exactly what I needed, actually. We're ... in touch now. In cautious touch. Gosh, it's surreal to say that. She was basically dead to me, you know? And now she's just—alive. And gentle. And ... good. So, *fine*, I guess it never would've happened if it wasn't for you, so—" She jabbed my elbow with hers. "Thanks? I mean, I guess. In a really, roundabout, reluctant, messed-up way, I guess I have to say thanks to you. *Punk.*"

"You're welcome." Our thighs were touching now. "So ... did you ... like my playlist?"

She perked up a little, her beautiful silhouette. "I loved it," she admitted. "I really did. It made up for not being able to talk to you for weeks, after we—I don't know. I just ..." She trailed off.

"What?"

Say it.

Say it!

You feel it, too.

She looked me in the eye, finally, and then—I thought—down at my lips.

Is she leaning in?

As soon as I wondered, she yanked away, quickly, eyes darting back to the water. "You're really hard to read," she said.

"Like a fairy tale?"

She slugged my good shoulder. "I just don't know what your deal is!" She snapped the words this time, clearly frustrated. "This whole time. From day one. Do you like me? Do you hate me? Are you sweet? Are you terrible? I know about Caleb, by the way, your mentee. So don't even *try* to pretend like you're a true villain." She squinted, pointing at me accusingly.

She really would make a good lawyer, I mused.

Maybe as good as me.

I could start with my speech right now—or opt to lead with the evidence.

I decided to go with the latter.

I reached into my pocket, retrieving the string, letting it dangle between us.

Scottie crinkled her nose and reached out her fingers, frowning. "What ... *is* that?"

I swayed it back and forth in front of her cute nose. "I'm hypnotizing you. Is it working?"

She grabbed it, feeling the length of it, finding the knot in the middle.

Her eyes finally ripened to moons. "Oh. My. *Gosh.*" She gasped. "Is this ... my shoelace?"

Her eyes said the rest: *You kept it.*

"Of course I kept it." I closed my hand over hers, balling it into her fist. "Now—I have something to say. Closing arguments, round two, if you will."

She pulled back, taking the shoelace, and crossed her arms.

"Oh yeah?"

"*Oh* yeah." I cleared my throat. I didn't know if these arguments would be as convincing—but I could pray for a miracle.

"Ms. Holiday—"

She stuck out her tongue and shook her head violently.

Start over.

No more Ms. Holiday.

I laughed. "Ahem. Scottie. As you have—gathered, I didn't grow up with the most consistent experiences of love, or human connection. I was alone. A lot. With my thoughts, and my baseball—"

"And Kingston movies," she interjected.

I laughed. "Exactly. I didn't ever feel ... totally safe, is the best way to put it. I still battle that, to be honest, wondering where and when it's completely fine to be truly myself." I looked down. "Who will stay? Who will go? You know? I let romantic love in, the one time, and it left me in pieces, literally, pieces of bone." I paused. "Okay, that sounded more dramatic than I intended. I was referring to my shoulder ..."

She waved a hand in a *go on* motion and appeared to be stifling a laugh.

"So—I quit thinking about love. Altogether. It wasn't an option. I always figured I'd deal with it, down the line. Once my law career was more established. Once I had more time. Once I—" My eyes dropped. "Once I felt worthy of it."

I brushed a blade of grass from my leg. "Then you showed up. First in your hot little chai-tea workout pants, and later, across the conference table from me. At first, I was—well, furious. That my dream girl was actually a ... well, a witch with a chip on her shoulder the size of Florida."

"Nice Kingston reference."

"Thanks." I grinned. "But then, I had to form a case against you, and everything changed. I saw that you *had* a case. A real one. A brilliant one. Evidence, witnesses, and most of all—heart. You believed in what you deserved, and there's no way I was going to beat you if I didn't find that belief, myself. Brent helped with that, too."

She chewed the inside of her cheek.

"I won the case, Scottie, because I had to rise to your level. I had to dive into myself—which I *really* hate doing, by the way, so thanks for that. But I had to ask myself: Why do I work at Kingston? How—and why—is this company such a force? What are we giving to people? Why did those stories impact me so much, as a kid? Does Scottie deserve the justice she's asking for? Do I believe in love, now, or not?"

She was quiet. "And?"

"Well, first—you deserve the world, Scottie. Whatever you want. But secondly, yes, I do believe in love. I discovered that. But more than that, I believe in magic."

She cackled, head rolling back. But then she fell silent when she saw I was serious.

Oh.

"I really do," I continued. "I believe in something intangible. In the ideal, even."

It was true, gavel down. Thanks to Scottie, I knew that now. I believed in the fact that I was changing Caleb's life, in the smallest of ways—but that his one life would touch thousands more. I believed Scottie's shoelace had snapped for a reason. I believed in the feeling of walking down Grand Street at Kingston Court, that the walls of that place contained something supernatural, unpindownable, *magical*.

I believed this whole thing had unfolded as one giant undeserved gift to me. Pauper to prince. Shattered to mended. Foster kid to front-page news. Ho-hum day job to meaningful law career. I believed in it. I had lived it. I was actually whistling—*singing!*—now, every day, while I worked.

I was a walking darn fairy tale.

I believed I had to keep talking, or I'd never stop regretting it.

Because I believed I'd found my queen.

"I don't know where you stand now," I continued. "In your personal convictions about the invisible. In fairy tales. In all of it. But it doesn't matter to me. Because I also believe that sometimes magic brings you something you *can* see. And honestly..." I brushed back a strand of her dark hair, risking it. "I can't stop looking at you."

Her lips curved down in a pout.

She was breathtaking, as always.

And slowly unguarded, now.

Her walls were crumbling down.

"I also ... have one more confession," I said.

She found my hand again, closed more space on the bench between us. "What's that?" she asked softly. She started rubbing her thumb on my palm in small circles.

Now I was staring at *her* lips.

"I've thought about you every single day since I met you," I admitted.

Finally.

Fingers entwined with mine now, she turned her knees toward mine. "Yeah? Like—plaintiff thoughts? Or other kinds of thoughts?"

I grabbed her legs and pulled them languidly onto my lap. "I mean, *both*, you little rascal. You basically overtook my whole life. But—mostly unprofessional thoughts. Like super illegal, technically."

She nuzzled her face into my chest, and I slipped my arm around her waist. I felt her lips on my neck softly, then on my cheek, and I turned to her, lifting her chin to me.

And finally, I breathed her in, and put my mouth onto hers. She tasted like heaven, vanilla, and mint.

Just like my dream.

Like her.

She bit my bottom lip, and I groaned.

"I lied, one more confession..." I said throatily, eyes closed.

"What's that?"

"I've imagined you doing that since the first second I saw you."

"At running club?" She brushed her fingertips on the skin of my mouth where she'd kissed.

I nodded, pulling her neck back toward me. Our lips met again, until I parted hers with my tongue, and found her beautiful teeth.

The kiss grew sweeter, hotter, then faster, both of us growing hungrier. I pulled her onto my lap. She began moving slowly, softly, her jeans on mine, driving me wild.

"Can I tell you something now?" she whispered against my earlobe.

I nodded.

"I think I'm falling for you."

...

Epilogue

SCOTTIE
Eighteen Months Later

I believed in fairy tales again on one gorgeous summer solstice. For the love of all things, I tried not to. You've read the proof here, in my words. You've witnessed my grandest of gestures. You've read my whole unbelievable story with no small detail spared.

I gave the fight of my lifetime into dethroning magic and fantasy. Into saving the poor, unfortunate souls, *the ones who might still be saved*! Into permanently stopping the spells and machinations of Kingston.

Life is too hard. Heartbreak, too real. Disappointment, too painful. People are being set up in droves to believe—and be heartbroken.

Right?

Maybe, at times, I'll admit. We will believe, and not be immune to lying on our bathroom floors, weeping.

The people we love, with all that we've got, possess the power to crush us.

It's all part of the deal.

The act of faith, in hoping for anything, is to make ourselves open and vulnerable to the possibility of disenchantment.

But what do we have if not belief in the impossible, in what may or may not be real?

Isn't the magic, the question, in fact, the point?

Isn't it why we're here?

No, I'm sorry to say, I still don't believe that sparkles, gowns, and a pumpkin will change my life.

But I believe they changed Cinderella's.

That Cinderella was kind, and patient, and good to the people who harmed her. She was gracious and strong through adversity.

I believe she went to the ball simply looking for a fun night, a distraction from her pain and loneliness—

And that she happened upon the rest of her life, yes, in the form of a prince. That she danced her way to a brand-new life, to the applause of the world.

And I believe that I was wrong.

Because I *did* have a guardian angel, right there by my side, all along.

I held his arm now, my heart beating evenly, peacefully, inside my chest. My simple cream satin gown flowed like water around me.

Peace, I thought.

I felt peace.

Finally, and at last.

The wedding of my dreams—truly *my* dreams this time—rolled out onto the world-famous Grand Street of Kingston Court. The red brick, white shiplap, and pastel storefronts flanked the intimate audience. The park was cleared, the signs aglow, the green trees fluffy and twinkling. The starless sky was navy ink and would soon burst with fireworks. The familiar smells of waffles and concrete permeated the air. Dozens of candles, white rose petals, and fifty people awaited us.

My eyes were only on Harrison, though, and his were only on me.

No bridesmaids, this time. Just one maid of honor, Peyton, and one ring bearer, Caleb.

I looked to my right, to my grinning dad.

Leaning over, he softly assured me:

He's not going anywhere, Scot.

I smiled. "Let's go?"

My dad was the angel who never left; the one who had given everything to protect me. "Let's go," he agreed.

Step by step, in my crystal heels, I walked toward the kindest, hottest man I'd ever known in my lifetime. We grinned so massively then and all night that our faces would hurt until morning.

Just behind Harrison stood our officiant, Bible flung open between his two white-gloved hands.

Top hat, purple tux, black-patent-leather shoes.

Eyes dancing, sparkling, winking.

The one and only.

Wade Kingston.

His apartment light was off tonight.

No one knew he was here but our guests and the Kingston staff. The park perimeter was lined with presidential-level security. But who better here than him? Abel Iverson made it happen; he sat now in the front row.

Everyone stood then to face me. My throat sealed up, and I tightened my lips. I willed myself not to cry.

My mom was a vision in rose-pink silk, form-fitted to her lean frame. She was sobering, stunning. She smiled—and I flashed back to the nights when she'd brush my hair with her fingers, when I'd just pray she wouldn't leave again.

Don't stop believing, sweetheart.

That smile had kept me going, impossibly, even after it left.

I'd fixed her teeth by myself recently. Damaged by drugs, restored to new. It was a project, my masterpiece. They gleamed now like pearls, revealing her joy, and the love I'd so desperately sought since I could remember. Then a mirage, now a light, pulling me to her, a dream. Almost as bright as the castle beyond us, glowing with sherbet lights from every sharp edge and stone.

I could feel my dad staring at her. Unblinking, and yet, unsure. The first unfurling into the possibility of forgiveness.

We reached the end of the aisle. I touched the shoelace cinching my flowers before passing them to Peyton. She grinned and rolled her eyes happily, nodding to my almost-husband, her former archenemy. Thanks to her widely lauded performance in the case and new business influx to her firm, she'd been the youngest female ever to make partner at Cashion & Baker—and the only one yet to earn the title before thirty. She and Harrison had slowly grown on each other. As if they'd had a choice.

I grabbed Harrison's hands and locked into the eyes that had softened me.

Some dreams, you fought for, with everything. Others hunted you down. I loved him more than I ever knew I was capable. He made me believe again—in love, of course, but in everything. He'd helped others keep the faith, too. I knew we'd have trials, struggles, and tears. Great loss, pain, fears, and grief.

But because of that, I knew how much we both needed *hope* in our lives. I believed now in the power inherent in every wish that we made, the dreams tying us all together with the same string.

From here, to New York, to Shanghai.

To a constellation far, far away.

After everything that I've been through, I've come to think we believe in fairy tales because we see ourselves in their simplicity—and, also, between the lines. The best-known ones simply echo our deepest truths.

Desire and love; longing and magic. Evil and good. Joy. Despair.

In stories and life, there is a King. Goodness and purity, saving. And there is an enemy, always a villain, prowling to devour. Midnight forests, packs of wolves, witches, and poison fruit. We are needy. We are lost. We are broken, and vulnerable.

And we are rescued.

We are redeemed.

Restored, to the fullness of joy.

Crazy enough to believe again.

Child enough to pray.

We can reframe the story, and lift our heads to the sky.

Happily, even after.

...

"I suspect that men have sometimes derived more spiritual sustenance from myths they did not believe than from the religion they professed."
C. S. Lewis

"Now faith is confidence in what we hope for and assurance about what we do not see."
Hebrews 11:1 (NIV)

"When you believe in a thing, believe in it all the way, implicitly and unquestionable."
Walt Disney

Author's Note

When I polled my Instagram followers about their (your) preference (or hate) for Author's Notes, I was expecting a balanced reply, honestly. But no! *No balance, guys!* Nearly all of you want to hear more from us authors, even after The End. Which makes me smile so big and love you even more, because you're like me as a reader.

But also, because we authors pour so much—heart, mind, body, soul, blood sacrifices, ya know—into these books, and the reality is, the story *behind* the story is almost always *at least* as interesting!

Or at least, we'd like to think so.

Since I didn't write an Author's Note for my debut novel, *When We Blinked*, I can't help but wonder what I might have said for that book. One question came up a lot, in conversations, book clubs, and interviews post-release. One that I didn't see coming, but (I promise) feels relevant here.

People wanted to know: "But wait. You LOVE marriage! You LOVE Doug! What made you choose to write a book about a divorced couple?"

I can hear similar versions already for *Suing Cinderella*: "But wait. You LOVE Disney! You're borderline PSYCHO about it! What made you choose to write a book about suing a company like them?"

And for my third book (already outlined, woohoo!), you might ask: "But wait. You LOVE books! You LOVE writing! What made you choose to write a book roasting the book industry?"

I sit with these questions and direct them at myself like Hot Harrison harassing a witness.

Well, why *DO* I like writing about the things I love most, with the harshest, most probing, merciless magnifying glass imaginable held up to their faults and cracks, just waiting for the fire to burn?

I think the answer is both simple and complicated. But if I had to be brief, I'd say this: I'm interested in the shadow. Also, I think fire is beautiful.

My marriage and great love to Douglas, 16 years strong, is one of the most holy entities and great accomplishments of my life. But there have been heartbreaking moments, friends. Our "success" as a genuinely happy married couple is so very hard won. Not all, but yes, much of what you read in *When We Blinked*, we have faced and overcome. But *We Don't Talk About Bruno*, guys! Not as a society—and *definitely* not in our fiction, *especially* if it leans Christian. Nope, all good! *Surface Pressure* only! (Are you catching my *Encanto* references?)

And all this hush-hushing and pearl-clutching serves whom, exactly?

No one.

The answer is no one!

LET'S TALK ABOUT BRUNO, PEOPLE!

Yes, I want to talk about the hard stuff inherent to life's greatest touchstones. I want to make you feel less alone by sharing what I live, feel, and see, however uncomfortable. I want to acknowledge this present darkness (moment for Frank Peretti!) while fighting, *every time,* with hard proof, to show you that the light always wins—and so does the holy fire. The Bible confirms this, repeatedly. "The light shines in the darkness, and the darkness has not overcome it." There. Easy. I could serve up enough verses to fill this whole section, but I want you to read all my future Author's Notes, so I'm not going to risk that (yet).

You'll get to my third book eventually, so let's get back to the one in your hands—and a bit of its origin story.

Oh!

Before that, for legal purposes I must pause and say that the Kingston Company is, in fact, a creation of my imagination inspired by a real company but explicitly not the latter itself. I made the very clear and strategic decision to do this for reasons of creative freedom, artistic expression, and reader enjoyment. Furthermore, the titular fairy tale and all other original fairy tales encompassed within this novel are long out of copyright protection and now part of public domain.

Isn't fiction amazing?!

OK, great.

That's out of the way!

Anyway!

I am admittedly about to focus hardcore on the "inspired" part, but I will reiterate once again that *Kingston is its own thing!*

Ahem.

For those of you who know nothing about me, first, hi, and I'm so ecstatic you're here! Secondly, you should know I'm a mega Disney fan. Disneyland annual pass-holding, Mickey-ear-wearing, Walt Disney World traveling, Disney Cruising, movie watching *superfan*.

Like Scottie, I was raised on the VHS classics. They are practically part of my skin and definitely part of my personality. *The Little Mermaid, Beauty and the Beast,* and *Aladdin* were all released squarely in my most formative childhood years: 1989, 1991, and 1992, respectively. I was born in 1985. I love being 28!

I adored these classics then, and I re-adore them today—but there was a stretch of time in my not-a-girl-not-yet-a-woman (read: teenage) years when I suddenly felt super snarky about them.

Like, what?! Are you kidding?! Ariel gives up her voice, Aladdin's a freaking liar, and don't get me started on *Snow White* and her high-pitched singing.

Around this time, I was also falling in love with writing—like *really* writing, from the sharpest edges of my brain and the biggest parts of my heart. Essays for school, poems at home, incredibly emo journal entries about older boys, whatever. I couldn't write enough!

So, when my favorite English teacher (hey, Mr. Z!) gave us the sophomore year assignment to write a persuasive speech, I didn't even have to think. I was born for this!

Enter my masterpiece:

Why Beauty and the Beast Are the Only Disney Characters

With Hope of a Lasting Relationship.

There. Perfection. Chef's kiss!

That was the verbatim speech title, you guys, which alone made the teacher stifle a massive smile. He *clapped* when I drove home my case, point by point. I thought he might even stand. I knew he was entertained, maybe impressed, possibly even *persuaded!*

At the very least, he approved enough to award the speech an elusive A+—but also enough to insist I join something called Orange County Academic Decathlon (like Mathletes in *Mean Girls,* but nerdier because of the multiple sports, I mean, subjects). At the upcoming OCAD competition, I could deliver this speech for, like, prize money or something.

There was no money.

But there was a medal!

I won!

Yes, an actual panel of real-life judges (no gavels, sadly) adored my angsty teen Disney speech.

I've been proud of it ever since.

Later, when I went to grad school for my master's degree in professional writing at USC, in my early twenties, I realized this Disney idea had never quite left my system. I found myself daydreaming about a novel in the same vein.

Thus, a version of the idea for *Suing Cinderella* solidified like ice-Anna inside my head. What if a girl was *so fuming mad* at Disney that she decided to file a lawsuit? I knew then, fifteen years ago, that this idea was *good,* and that I had to write it someday. I also knew it would require a tremendous amount of legal homework (it did) and general research (even more!)—so I kept putting it off until I couldn't put it off anymore, as we writers both say and do.

Not to mention, over those years, something else happened: I had three daughters. And through my nap-schedule regime, fog of diapers, and the magic of their chubby thighs, I began to see every one of those movies with totally brand-new eyes.

Holy smokes, Ariel was so *brave*. Jasmine, *she took no prisoners!* Belle, you were never the problem; we love you so much! Not to mention the new heroines like Moana and Anna and Merida who had emerged to exemplify courage and kindness and greatness with whole new archetypes.

We memorized *Frozen*. We nailed the Disney family Halloween costumes. We got season passes to Disneyland. Gosh, that magical park truly carried me through some of the hardest years of my life. Postpartum depression, pregnancy loss, identity crises, you name it. But there was Disneyland, always—consistent and sparkly and filled with the scent of churros—with all its magic and healing hope and my closest mom friends, too. I never stopped dreaming, thanks at least in part to that place. God truly met me there.

IMPORTANT SIDE NOTE:

I'm not going to dive into all the controversy surrounding corporate Disney today. Mostly it just makes me sad, all around. Also, it would take up too much space I don't have here. Is it possible, maybe, to just enjoy this piece of art for pure fun? I sure hope so. After spending six months deeply entrenched in research on all things Disney—the business, the brand, the man—I think

Walt would be disheartened by so many things unfolding today with his name attached, *but also* ecstatic for others, and that the good would (still, in 2023, anyway) outweigh the bad.

I mean, have you *ridden* the Avatar ride?!

Tears streamed down my cheeks the whole time. *You can fly, you can fly, you can fly*! I kept thinking, Walt Disney, look what you did. *I'm actually flying*! The innovation, the invention, the magic. One man and his mouse changed the world.

And I felt just barely brave enough to write a book winking at them in pretend court. Plus, it was more interesting now. I loved Disney again! I finally sat down to write this book in the fall of 2021, after six months of research.

Voila!

There you have a summary of the origin story—and now, I'll tell you one more thing that I really want you to know.

Friends, I didn't know how this story would end until I forced myself to sit down and write those final scenes. Really! For a while, I could have gone either way. I didn't know if Scottie should win—or lose—her life-altering suit against Kingston.

What did it mean if she won? That women are powerful and can do absolutely anything and that love is not the only happy ending for us? True, yes, all of it.

But Scottie winning—in my opinion—would mean that I didn't believe in fairy tales, or Disney, or magic, as the author holding the wand. When it came down to it, I simply couldn't write Scottie winning the case without it feeling like a betrayal of what I know and believe about art—which is that we need it like air. Specifically, we need redemption stories, on repeat.

Yes, we need fairy tales! We need love stories. We need romantic comedy. We need hope, above all.

My research for this novel included quite the excavation of our most classic fairy tales in all their original forms—and, yes, across the board, they were *much, much* darker than any Disney film to ever hit screens. This is verifiably accurate. I find it fascinating, but also an artistic choice.

Like mine.

I made the artistic choice to write Scottie losing the case, as my love note to Disney for everything the company has meant to me. And, also, as a nod to women, who are powerful even when (or especially when) we lose, because we are never knocked out (thank you, Kendall Toole, my favorite). Scottie gained everything most meaningful that she did not have at the book's start—and that is the change every noteworthy character needs.

By the way, I always knew she'd end up with Harrison as part of her happily-ever-after. Did I mention I believe in fairy tales and that *this is how they always end*? (Although I *love* that the new *Snow White* reboot coming in 2024 is stirring up so much debate on this topic. Google it!)

In addition to exploring the shadow, I also love asking the age-old question: "What if?"

What if there was a dating app that didn't have any pictures? What if an ex-wife was unwittingly *matched with her estranged husband* and fell in love with him all over again? What if a heartbroken girl sued a fictional company not unlike Disney? Gasp, *what if my fictional company's founder was secretly still alive?*

Not that you asked, but writers, two things: 1.) continue to ask *what if,* forever, and 2.) if given the choice, veil the giant at hand. You will have so much more fun!

Speaking of fun, as I wrap this up, I'm thinking of how much I desperately miss the romcoms of the late 1990s and early 2000s, along with the Disney classics before all the edgier movies and endless remakes. But my hope here is that maybe—just maybe—I have provided you with something that reminds you a little of both.

A little *Legally Blonde;* a little *Cinderella.*

A little of spicy teenage me, beginning to test her ideas; a little of Disney-mom me, with her massive collection of Mickey ears and burgeoning pack of strong daughters.

I'm just so honored to share this book with you—and I think anyone close to me knows I was the one born to write it.

Lastly, I hope you turn the last page of every one of my books with a deep sigh and sense that you were walked through the valleys and shadows, but someone was holding you all along, pointing you to the light. That there was always a fourth in the fire.

I love you.

We did it!

XOXO,

steph

Acknowledgments

Forty-eight hours ago, from this writing, my angel of a last-living grandparent, Milo, slipped from his earthly body into the brightness of heaven. With his absence so fresh, I want to start by thanking him for everything his life and legacy have taught me not only from the day I was born, but this past year specifically, as I've prepared to run the Chicago Marathon for him—and simultaneously fought to publish this book for you all.

It's been a dragon-slaying battle, you know?!

Grandpa, you'd want me to write the book. Chase the dream. Show my daughters that girls can do everything. Hug the stranger. Hold the door. Dance and dance and dance some more. Sing in German. Be honest. Be me. Be vulnerable. Cry alone but also be brave enough to tell people why I'm so sad. Keep going. Exercise. Smile nonstop. Go first but put myself last. Fling open the doors of my home whether it is a box or a mansion. Lift every day up to Jesus before I go live it. Close each night the same way.

That's a good start, anyway.

I miss you forever, Grandpa. Thank you for loving us with all that you had—and then more still, till the end. Please give Grandma a kiss for me.

Secondly, I must loudly thank my Prince Douglas for absolutely everything these past couple years. My goodness, babe.

You've read my drafts and caught my tears and held my whole heart so well—whether I've been bursting with glee over how much I love this story or flexed to throw my laptop over the cruise ship balcony. I love you beyond any words on a page, which is saying a lot for me. You're my happily-even-after forever and into the clouds.

Emmy, Hadley, Reese: you're the icing on top of the fairy tale that I never even knew how to dream. Like I ask you all the time, how did I get so lucky? I am obsessed with you girls.

Next up, thank you to my rock-star legal counsel, whom I am fortunate enough to call family. Brad, David, and Wendy: I walk around knowing you're brilliant, but sitting down for our roundtables to discuss the details of this plot and the law? I am still awestruck by your brains and your generosity. If you felt smarter while reading any part of this book, it is only because of them. It was incredibly important to me that the story could (mostly) hold up in a court of law. The proceedings had to be (fairly) plausible, or I didn't want to do it. And look what we did! Siblings, you also pulled through so big for me when that literary agent got shady. We'll save those details for the memoir I keep on promising, but people, you have been warned. Don't mess with our family!

Thank you to the astoundingly talented team of professionals who helped turn my Word doc into a royal fantasy. Jessica Snell, my magnificent editor, I can't believe we did it again! I'm so wildly appreciative of the way you tightened the plot, strengthened my characters, and added just the right sprinkle of pixie dust. Natalie Johnson, your mastery of beautification leaves me even more speechless than Ariel after signing her voice away. You're my fairy godmother of gorgeous design. Thank you, dear one. Thank you!

Thank you to Devon Daniels, one of the best authors and friends on the planet. Our bond just keeps growing, and I just keep marveling at how lucky I am to call you a friend. You have spoken truth, perspective, and direction into my writing career more times than I could possibly count. You're also exceptionally kind, funny, and pretty—like the characters you write, but IRL. Yep, *she's the real deal*, folks! And like Buddy the Elf, I KNOW HER! Cheers to our new fall books, friend! I cherish, respect, and adore you.

Jill Gunderson, if we had a dollar for every time someone thought we were sisters, we could *definitely* go buy that island. The thing is, though, you are my sister now. I would be lost without you—just walking around aimlessly with too many thoughts in my head and no one to Marco Polo! You've been part of this second book's journey from day number zero. Impossibly supportive, consistent, and true. You're such an exquisite treasure. Also, a major talent! Also, my favorite Canadian. Besides Justin Bieber. JK!

Mom and Dad, every year older I get, the more firmly I stand in awe of you. Life is so hard. It knocks you down. But you remind me that magic exists despite and because of it all. I mean, I still believe in Santa! *So do the lawyers!* Thus, I suppose I can thank you for serving as the ultimate inspiration for this whole book. Thank you for showing me how to believe: in fairy tales, in lasting love, in a carpenter who died on the cross for me. Thank you for shining your light and your love onto me and the whole wide world.

To the rest of my loved ones, early readers, and fellow writers who deserve all my gratitude, whether you have any possible clue how much I needed you: Heather Beylik (Sissy!), Molly Kelley (Bestie Boo!), Allison Sanden, Natalie Pitman, Erin Clark, Beth Morris, Danielle Woo, Shannon Leyko, Ashley Rodriguez, Natasha Burton, Allison Isakson, Casey Pruet, Chelsea Edmonston, Jessica Wrabel, my MCS family of incredible women, and my entire launch team, listed at the end of this section. Grandpa knew best. *Girls can do everything.*

Karen Kingsbury and Becky Nesbitt, thank you for the profound gift of your encouragement and immediate belief in this story. Some of your salient guidance changed its trajectory. I love that we met in a ballroom. Cinderella is smiling. You are both truly magical.

To the legends who walked so I could run with this absolute blast of a tale: Walt Disney, Elle Woods, and most of all, Cinderella. George Bailey, too. You remind me that we need to smile. You remind me that we want happy endings. You remind me that being rejected is the real secret sauce, the good stuff, the possible beginning of everything. Let them look down on you; let them make fun of you; let them dramatically underestimate if not totally disregard you. From there, you will rise, and shine.

To my readers? Yes, you. When I think of you, I start crying. This year I learned deeply that it's not about the industry, the powers at be, or even the actual books. It's about you. Only you. Your hearts. Your thoughts. Your lives. The privilege of reaching you is something I hold with the care of a sacred dove. I love you. I pray for you. I mean that. I can't thank you enough for trusting me with the invaluable currency of your attention. Don't be a stranger, and write to me sometime! It is my life's joy to hear from you.

Finally, to God, my Lord Jesus Christ, the Master Magician, King on the Throne, Author, Finisher, and Savior of Everything. I love you so much, with all that I am. My small brain can't fathom that you trust *me* with these stories. For as long as I breathe, I'll obey you. And for now, that means *write more books*.

I'm here. I'm listening. Let's go.

Like Mariah Carey, I still believe.

...

LAUNCH TEAM

Alana Andrews
Heather Beylik
Rhonda Beylik
Wendy Beylik
Kaley Brandon
Natasha Burton
Ashlyn Carter
Katelyn Cheo
Erin Clark
Julie Dunbar
Katie Eastman
Chelsea Edmonston
Sue Fielder
Hope Flatt
Lindye Galloway
Lindsay Gipe
Blaire Going
Nic Gaudet
Jill Gunderson
Allie Harris
Karen Hobbs

Allison Isakson
Kerry John Pickering
Molly Kelley
Marci Kimura
Kimberly Kirkhuff
Baraka May
Jenn McBride
Jen McNeely
Haley Miller
Linda Mudawar
Brittany Peterson
Natalie Pitman
Casey Pruet
Ashley Rodriguez
Allison Sanden
Celena Shwam
Leslie Straubel
Susanna Szkalak
Kristen Whitmore
Jessica Wrabel
Alyssa Wuestefeld

Printed in Great Britain
by Amazon